The Contingency Man

by Trudy Fong

To Debbie,
Hope this covers a few
contingencies!
— Trudy F.

Dedicated to Greg
The Contingency Man©
First printing, March 2008
Copyright Trudy Fong, 2007. #250211331 originally copyrighted under the name, The Underdog.

This is a work of fiction. Names, characters, places and incidents are the products of the author's imagination. While Frozen Dead Guy Days is a real festival, it has been used herein fictitiously. Any resemblance to people living or dead is purely coincidental.

All rights reserved. Without limiting the rights under copyright reserved above, no part of this publication may be reproduced, stored in or introduced into a retrieval system or transmitted in any form, or by any means (electronic, mechanical, photocopying, recording, or otherwise), without the prior written permission of both the author and the publisher.

The scanning, uploading, and distribution of this book via the Internet or via any other means without the permission of the author or publisher, Lulu.com, is illegal and punishable by law. Please purchase only authorized electronic editions, and do not support or participate in the electronic piracy of copyrighted materials. Requests for permission should be made in writing by contacting: trudyfong@ns.sympatico.ca

Library of Congress Control Number: 2008903567

ISBN: 978-1-4357-0941-6

ONE

YOU'VE BEEN GOOGLED

Vanity surfing, v.t. to search for mentions of oneself over the internet; to determine the relative significance of oneself by conducting an inventory of citations over same; To gauge one's worth by how often one is Googled: to have one's identity searched via the web: as in, "Google ergo sum", I Google therefore I am.

Madeline has been unable to arrive at an accurate diagnosis, despite decades as a member of her family. Life used to be so much simpler before she started reading everything she could get her hands on from the American Psychiatric Association. But now that she has taken that plunge, she feels compelled to come up with a snappy, astute, two word definition derived from a Latin root. It would at least sound more elegant than just saying, "My family is crazy" and leaving it at that.

After all, who doesn't make the claim that they have the craziest family around? Certainly Roger, Madeline's husband did, the first time they met. He hastily withdrew that boast hours after he married Madeline. She had tried unsuccessfully to keep her relatives well hidden away until after the big day. She had seriously considered the idea of hiring a crew of drama students to pose as family members. But when her plans fell threw and her family learned about the wedding, the jig was up.

Luckily, Roger did not make a mad dash out of the church. By then, he was in too deep.

The closest thing that Madeline could come up with was 'toxic narcissism'. Certainly her brother Walter's pattern of grandiosity, desperate need for admiration, and sense of entitlement was straight out of a textbook. But how could that explain the voices in his head? The delusions? The megalomania?

Then there was her sister Jillian, the failed Prima Donna. She was a classic case, with her constant demand for attention, praise and admiration worthy of an Oscar-winning actress. This is despite any noteworthy achievements. Her biggest acting role has been playing a near-dead crash victim whose corpse was later found in the emergency room hallway, untreated. It was a triumph, of sorts, since Jillian got to die on Prime Time, albeit with an oxygen mask hiding her features. The perpetual ingénue has been waiting to be discovered now for fifteen years, and is unwilling to face that her moment is past. In Roger's words: Jillian is a woman crippled by high self esteem. But this overlaps with other troubling symptoms involving impulse control, (particularly involving Daddy's credit cards), and histrionics, the unique combination of which has thrown a wrench into Madeline's attempts at easy categorization.

Yesterday, Roger decided to disturb the tranquility of Madeline's cocoon with a little proxy 'vanity surfing'. The news that references to her antiques expertise were all over the Internet was not greeted with glee.

"You have fans!" Roger had gushed, perplexed that Madeline did not share his excitement. In the dusty world of antiques, being a known quantity was more than a few notches below rock stardom. Still, someone out there is watching, and this gives her pause. In fact, it gives her chills. Maddy, (as she is generally known to her friends), has made an art of being invisible, of being more noted for her table settings than her dress. Unlike her two siblings, Walter and Jillian, she has learned to coast, to float through big events like some kind of nondescript floor lamp that fills up a neglected corner of the venue, so that its absence is not noted as a gaping hole. But once filled, that previously gaping hole does not incur any notice.

Maddy has too much self-loathing to be a narcissist. In fact, as the big-four-oh approaches, she has developed a terror of the camera. This is highly uncharacteristic of her family.

No handy two word diagnosis can come close to the reality of dear brother Walter. At one time, he was merely quietly crazy, enjoying his presumed paranoid schizophrenia the way one would indulge a spoiled but powerless child. Imagine you're Napoleon Bonaparte? Affect a French accent. Think you're hearing voices? Point to the many instances in a Steven King novel where the voices turned out to be real. But no more. Walter has discovered the Internet and a whole new potential for making waves.

Maddy has walked around in a haze dreading his next incursion into the public consciousness, tidal waves stirred up in that vast ocean of people. And happily for Walter, some of them believe anything they read on the web.

Conspiracy theories abound on the net and Walter is firmly behind most of them, provided they supply him with a forum for voicing his patently insane opinions, which can then be confirmed by other, equally unbalanced individuals. Following her husband's revelation of her own presence on the net, Maddy has made a nerve-wracked exploration of the latest citations on her brother. The experience has left her shaken and stirred. The end really is near, (end of Walter's non-hospitalization days). Or at least Walter's absence from an evening news special report. The most remarkable thing, she notes, is how whole groups share the same crazy manias, how there are entire radio networks and a subculture dedicated to every possible fringe of thought and unsubstantiated rumor. Currently, Walter's drift from run of the mill 'end is near' proclamations has lead him right into a stew of conspiracy theories.

Why, oh why hadn't he kept up with the medication?

Thank God I changed my name when I got married, thinks Maddy. When first told of this decision Roger was flattered. He considered that it was because his fiancée was a traditionalist, a WASP through and through, right down to a Silver Jubilee tea set and vintage King George serving platter. Only later did he realize her real motivation to become Mrs. Roger Graydon. One day, in the not too distant future, she'll be watching the national news when her brother's goofy mustachioed head will pop onto the screen. Beneath his carrot-topped cranium an ongoing stream of captions will describe the by-now famous nutcase's affront to national something or other, which precipitated the storming of his compound à la David Koresh.

Name change or not, she still suspects that some ace reporter, some crack, fresh journalism school graduate will ferret out the connection. She just can't shake the fear that one morning it will happen. There she will be: emerging in all innocence onto her front porch to retrieve the paper, shrouded in one of her sister's cast-off Kimonos complete with baby spit, hair uncombed and last night's mascara forming little lace patterns in her crow's feet. And a hoard of crazed cameramen and television tabloid journalists will pounce on her like a school of sharks in a feeding frenzy. Shoving a microphone into her face before she's even had a chance to brush her teeth. Asking her if she had ever seen any signs of serious megalomania in her brother when she was growing up. Funny how nobody ever asked that question when she actually was growing up. Nooooo. It's only when it's too late that they call for the men in white jackets.

And thirty-eight years of dedicated skulking and hiding under rocks and hoping she won't get noticed will all be for naught. She knows she's not the only one in her family who feels this way. Her father echoes her concerns. Walter Senior sincerely regrets naming his first born after himself. He has taken advantage of his grandfather status and his enormous height and hearty build to employ instead the sobriquet of 'Big Daddy'. Safely ensconced in a Florida RV park for the winter, he still fears the day when a connection will be made between father and son.

* * *

He called her just the other day.

"I woke up this morning with this numb tingling in my foot," Big Daddy said. "I thought, Jesus, is this it? Is this a stroke?"

"But it wasn't..." Maddy had unfortunately been cast in the role of free psychiatrist to the family, or at least 'sane person at large'. At least in Big Daddy's case, the calls were not collect.

"Of course not. Would I be talking to you now?" he snapped. "I just slept funny, that's all. But you never know... People here are dropping off like flies. The county morgue gives frequent flier miles. The day before yesterday I got a letter from your brother and that just about gave me a heart attack on the spot...So you never know."

"Please. I don't want to know what he said," Maddy interrupted. She felt it was best. She had followed his career from a run of the mill spiritual seeker to a doomsday prophet, (pre-millennium), and then, following the disappointing lack of Armageddon at the change of the calendar, he had made a turn in the road.

He is no longer waiting for the second coming, he is the second coming. Or at least, that is what they now suspect is the delusion of the hour.

"He has followers," her father allowed.

"Oh Jesus, Mary and Joseph!" she wailed.

"No. I think their names are something like Jane and Clare and Alexis. I can't remember the rest." Secretly Big Daddy blames his dead wife, a failed actress and one-time tone-deaf lounge singer, whose own obsession with capturing the limelight had caused her in later years to plan a funeral that eclipsed both a recently deceased senator's and the local archbishop's. He is still recovering from the excess five years after lung cancer claimed his putative Prima Dona.

He remembers his wife visiting her future grave site, tombstone in place, dragging her intravenous drip and urine bags along on their hospital dolly, still smoking through a hole in her trachea, to see and lovingly stroke her freshly-installed imported pink granite headstone, chiseled to exacting specifications, with a heart-rending epitaph chosen by herself with tremendous care (end date pending). She had ensured that a makeup artist be engaged, since getting around all the tubes running out of her posed some difficulty. A coterie of camera-toting relatives had been press-ganged into attending the unveiling of the monument. Her favorite champagne, *Veuve Clicquot,* was purchased for the occasion. She had insisted that a professional photographer shoot hundreds of pictures of her crouched devotionally in front of her brand new headstone. Even now, when he closes his eyes, he has a vivid picture of her with a bouquet of flowers that would rival any bride's, (Madonna lilies, ivory rose buds and babies' breath spray), smiling, instructing self-same photographer in her throaty, guttural, mechanical half-voice: "Make sure...gurgle, gurgle....you get my good side...gurgle, gurgle...cough, cough."

The most amazing thing was not this little vignette, it was the willingness of her family, cowed by decades of her obsessive self-love, to play along, to hire the photographer, to seek out the professional makeup artist for this phantasmagoric charade, to pre-order the headstone so that she could enjoy beforehand the theatrics of her own demise. It was their zombie-like willingness to point and shoot when bidden.

Afterwards, Aurora lovingly placed the morbid photographs in her very own leather-covered book of remembrance, which she would pull out and press upon unsuspecting visitors, who were dutifully coming to check on the patient. It was only the casual acquaintances who greeted the festive headstone shots with alarm and awkward silences, as Aurora forged on with her picture showing unaware of their eyes darting around the room, seeking escape.

* * *

But we digress. For now, let's examine the two sane survivors of Aurora's life-long roller coaster ride, shaken and scarred though they may be. Let's return to yesterday's call.

"Please Dad. No more. I'm already dealing with Jillian's craziness."

"She's there?" Now he really was getting out of the loop. So much the better. As long as Big Daddy keeps those checks coming, he hardly ever hears from Jillian. On the one hand, it is just as well. On the other hand, the rate that he has to keep the checks coming is alarmingly fast.

"She was. She drops in on family life whenever she feels her ovaries pinch. She thinks its useful to hear some screaming kids and witness a few fights so that her career will stay on track."

"What career?"

"Don't ask her that question. She's so certain stardom is around the corner, she organizes her own entourage...sort of." Maddy sighed. "She telephoned collect to ask me to pick her up at the airport. There I was wrestling my demonically possessed kids into snow suits and tearing out to the airport, only to discover that she'd called a half dozen other people to meet her flight. You'd think she was returning from a kidnapping ordeal in Afghanistan instead of a couple of months in Toronto. The only thing lacking was banners, not that she wasn't looking around for them. Of course, maybe she needed that many cars to carry her luggage."

"What do you think will bring her down to Planet Earth?" Big Daddy mused. In the background he could hear a low crash followed by the excited, awe-struck voices of Maddy's two fiendish kids. They were either at war with one another, or in cahoots. Thank God he spent the winters away in Florida.

"I know one thing that would bring her down to earth, finding a husband, having two screaming kids, developing cellulite."

"When's that going to happen?"

"The day Jillian wakes up and spots the crows' feet."

"She has them?"

"Oh. Yeah..."

Big Daddy could detect something in Maddy's voice, something that had crept in once in a blue moon when she was a kid and her siblings were making asses of themselves center-stage. Was it triumph?

* * *

All Big Daddy wants these days is to be left alone in peace to enjoy the sunset of his life down here in The Promised Land, surrounded by sexually frustrated recent widows with expensive tints of silver to platinum blond hair and surgically restored, albeit wind-tunnel faces; women who were only too happy to Dutch Treat at the Early Bird Specials, provided they got his temporarily undying love for dessert. After decades that felt like a century married to a high-strung, witless prima donna, he has finally been mercifully set free by the tobacco industry.

Every day he gives thanks to God for the makers of Marlboro for these final, golden years of peace.

That and the fact that women in his demographic outnumber eligible senior men twenty to one. It doesn't matter that he has a gut the size of an overdue twin pregnancy and not a speck of hair on his misshaped, liver-spotted head, apart from the sad, scraggly pony tail that trails down his arthritic back like something belonging to a half-dead dog. He has the one essential attribute for a single man his age: a pulse. Big Daddy is a player, at long last, with a virtual harem of blue-haired, cookie-making, lonely widows who have all come to terms with the fact that they have a greater likelihood of winning the New York State lottery as they do of nailing a new husband. He is a *Geritol* gigolo, a *Viagra*-pumped Valentino. He is one happy rooster in the hen house, tri-focal Ray Bans, yellow lounge suits, white loafers and all.

These are the Golden Years indeed. Now if only his damn children would bug off.

Big Daddy is a man always just slightly behind his time. When he married in the mid- 60s, he was just on the cusp of the free love era. Seduced by Aurora's curiously electrifying effect on people, and her great legs, he had given up his freedom in his early twenties. Shortly thereafter came the Summer of love, Spaghetti Westerns, Acid Rock and most devilishly tempting, the film *Easy Rider*. How he dreamed of being that lone rider, striking out on the freeway like some latter day Man With No Name, living with no fixed address, stealing hearts and breaking bones. He imagined himself to be Peter Fonda, only fatter, and homely.

Instead of the open road, he sold garden tractors for the mowing challenged, while all around him men were shunning the responsibility of home and trading in their first wives on more high-octane pursuits. They were growing long hair even as he was losing his own. Big Daddy could never leave Aurora. The bond was too strong. She would have hunted him down and nagged him to death. He became resigned to a lifetime of appeasement.

So he dreamed every year of owning a Harley, a Hog, a stallion of the highway. And then, finally, when he was seventy he became a free man.

He is now free to do as he chooses, but too incontinent and arthritic to do it. The only way he is going to hit the highway is like a hermit crab, dragging his home with its handy toilet along with him. So he has acquired a floating bungalow, an RV, which his snooty fashionista daughter persists in calling a trailer. It is so much more than that: The Beaver Patriot RV has its own satellite dish, microwave- convection oven and two television sets so he can watch two games at once. And to assuage his guilt over burning more fuel than a small country, it even boasts a few solar panels on the roof. It isn't exactly a Harley, but the first time Big Daddy got into his Beaver, he was sold on its potential to give him back the freedom he had given up so early in life.

Not that his daughters look at it that way. Maddy and her husband are heartsick that once he left town they lost the free babysitting. And Jillian is mortified that he chooses to spend half his life in a trailer, instead of somewhere more accessible and closer to a bank. In the face of such fierce opposition, Walter Senior shoots back that since he is not going to get to be a burden to his children in his old age, the least he could do is be an embarrassment to them.

It is worth examining Big Daddy's character in more depth. But to do so, one is forced to examine the character of his now departed wife,

Aurora, who went to her final reward, courtesy of the tobacco industry. In her childhood, she had been raised by a stage struck , but lamentably homely woman who had enjoyed a brief career playing little ditties on the piano to accompany silent movies in the small town in which she lived. Once the talkies made their appearance, her career evaporated into thin air. What to do? As a woman past her prime, who had spent too many years gradually filling up a piano bench with her burgeoning thighs, her attention turned to little Aurora. The daughter was constantly being thrust in the public's eye. Her mother could not be shaken from the belief that little Aurora was destined to be the next Shirley Temple. As such she was dragged endlessly to photographers to pose for head shots, and encouraged to try out for the lead role, and only the lead role in any and all plays, recitals and promotional opportunities. No supporting role would ever satisfy. If one was offered, the high-strung stage mother would pitch a fit of epic proportions. Little Aurora developed an insatiable thirst for attention as a result. She became a black hole of fragile self-confidence that had to be constantly shored up. In most instances, the charm of her magic wore thin at an alarming rate. But for a few years past her pseudo-Shirley Temple stage, she could 'work a room' with decent proficiency. While it was true that her singing talents were rather limited, she was able to turn her personal life into a veritable opera with all the hyperbole and overblown emotions one would expect of Puccini.

Just as she was reaching end point in her lackluster career, she met the young and promising Walter Yarwood. He was entranced to meet a woman who seemed so breathtakingly confident in the public eye. (His selfless mother had been decidedly mousy. Initially, Aurora seemed a refreshing change of pace.)

Poor Walter Senior. Poor Big Daddy. His own father had been a deeply committed, dry, dour upright man of the cloth, a minister who deliberately chose the path of most resistance, and deemed it holy. His mother was unfortunately a saint. A retiring sort who was always ready to lend a hand to church bake sales, providing her own lovingly made scones and clotted cream. A daughter of the British Empire, a member in fine standing of the Monarchist League, who was always ready to honor, to worship, to serve, to step aside, to curtsey, to bow and to scrape. Her subservience was a lightning rod for her son's adolescent discontent. He wanted to cut loose from moral constraint and couldn't understand why she didn't also.

How different Aurora seemed! How exciting! Whenever she entered a room, she seemed capable of realigning the earth's magnetic pull. For a man as schooled in the minutia and aggravation of 'deep in the marrow' humility as he had been, the sight of Aurora resetting everyone's agenda was wildly stimulating. He fell. And when Walter fell, it wasn't just a passing fancy. He took a nose dive. He went down in flames, like a World War I plane that brought him to the ground a broken mess, and well behind enemy lines. So deep into a hostile frontier that there was no escape.

Mark Twain once wrote that it is 'Better to keep your mouth shut and appear stupid than to open it and remove all doubt.' Aurora never understood that saying. Once she was no longer the fairest one of all, she had nothing to fall back on but her failed post-Vaudevillian bag of attention-grabbing tricks, which she employed at every opportunity, with her completely undeveloped mind. She couldn't pass up the thrill of sounding off on topics about which she was completely uninformed, and taking people's shocked reception of her inopportune statements as proof of her ability to dazzle. And yet. She was able to make everyone dance her tune, to turn toward the camera please, and smile as if they meant it. To perform on cue. It was her great gift. Her every conversation began with the words, "Do you want to do something for me?" And surprisingly, a lot of people did.

Walter learned quickly how to live a parallel existence. How to practice selective deafness. How to fall asleep in the face of a crisis, and leave other people to mop up the mess. The one saving grace in all of this was the fact that Aurora's attentions were eventually taken up by her daughters. First, briefly by Madeline, who proved to be noncompliant, bookish, and rather timid. Second by the more malleable younger sister who got with Aurora's program like a duck to water. Soon a baby boy was born, Walter Senior's namesake, to take along, applaud and covet the limelight.

Once Aurora's focus was elsewhere, Walter and his elder daughter were able to form their own little team, gradually distancing themselves from the endless dance recitals, singing lessons and photo opportunities that swirled about them like a carousel. And Walter Senior was able to retreat, once again, into the quiet, almost monastic existence he had experienced as a child, visiting with his plainer daughter, the same kinds of antique shops and flea markets and church socials that, in his childhood, he had reluctantly visited with his intensely royalist mother. Father and daughter, Walter and Madeline, became like a pair of potted plants at family gatherings, there but not there, visible to the naked eye, but unremarkable. Compliant in body, but not in spirit.

Now all Big Daddy wants can be found in a trailer park overlooking the Gulf of Mexico. *Ponce de León* was right. The fountain of youth can be found in Florida...only in a little blue pill. The only fear

Big Daddy has is that, with his daughter's constant demands and seeming inability to land a big fish, he might spend the rest of his life having to support her in the manner to which she has unfortunately become accustomed.

Unless...no that is too scary to think about. He is haunted by the inelegant and all too frequent warnings of Madeline. "What are you going to do Daddy, if Jillian cleans you out? What are you going to do Daddy, if you go broke before you croak?"

To avoid that sorry fate, Walter Senior would do anything to see some rich sucker hog tied to his little darling. But wouldn't it be impossible to find someone sufficiently flattering to Jillian's ego who is at one and the same time clueless and rich? Could such a person exist?

○₃ TWO ∞

IN WHICH WE MEET TWO PROTAGONISTS

This story really hits high gear, from a dramatic standpoint, with two intimate *tête à têtes*. Let's listen in while one of our protagonists, Matt, shares what by his standards is a shockingly expensive meal with Lana, his girlfriend of three years. (I should mention that they are seated in a French restaurant, locally famous for its sublime selections of duck. Matt has acquiesced to Lana's demand for Christmas Eve dinner in a French restaurant, thinking it was necessary for making his case. It comes complete with a famously snooty *maître d'*.)

By the way, since it's Christmas Eve, according to Lana's carefully considered time frame, it's 'the big night' when all those many long, and somewhat painful months of putting up with Matt's incurable male nature will come to fruition. Lana's anticipation is palpable. She is a greyhound waiting for the gun to go off. A goalie in the last minutes of the Playoff. At last. At long last, she thinks. There is only one small doubt: that she has perhaps spoiled 'the surprise' by making the reservations in anticipation of the event. Where was her 'Guy Decoder' when she needed it? What had that *Cosmo* article said about proposals? Has she jumped the gun? Lana considers this for a moment, and then dismisses this worry from her agitated mind. Why should this evening be any different from their usual dynamic? Matt never did take the initiative. She had always been the one to move the relationship forward, prodding him, as it were, with some kind of psychological sharp stick, until he was corralled into the appropriate holding pen. Like doomed beef cattle at the abattoir. Matt, apart from his pulse, shows about as much momentum as a store mannequin. She thinks, that this is just one of the many things she will have to change about him, once he is fully reeled in.

Lana, has taken great pains to prepare for the evening, including a spa facial, a new dress, a hairdo complete with 'foils', followed by frantic and furious exfoliation of every square inch of skin on her lithe body. Despite her best efforts, the fragrant Lana is almost, but irritatingly never quite as good looking as the professionally made-up, air-brushed, starved and digitally altered barely pubescent gazelle-cum-models depicted in the magazines. A last minute glance in her mirror has left her deflated and insecure. But she soldiers on. She is twenty-six, and as her mother has reminded her time and time again, not getting younger. For two years in a row this frantic parent has given her a subscription to *Brides* for a Christmas present. A new copy has already landed in her mail box, just this morning. Lana already has her eyes on a wedding dress. Now she only has to pick out something unflattering for the bridesmaids.

As usual, Matt is dressed in a shirt he dug out of one of the unwashed laundry piles on the floor, pausing briefly to sniff it before deciding it was adequate. The fact that Matt has a stubble of a beard is not some attempt at fashion. What would he know or care about fashion? Rather, he lost his shaver in the mess yesterday and didn't bother looking for it. (Cleaning up would have cut into his nap time). His curly chestnut hair is unkempt but unmanageable anyway, so he didn't bother combing it. For the occasion, he has at least thought to borrow his best friend Josh's slightly soiled and rumpled blazer. In exchange for this, he would have to dry clean it, since tonight's outing was definitely already pushing its wear to the limit. This business of the dry cleaning galls a little bit. It is a toss up as to who is mooching from whom. In the end, Matt has caved in because paying for dry cleaning is cheaper than buying a new/old dress jacket at a thrift store. Despite his best efforts, he is still breathtakingly handsome, on a par with the cover of *GQ*. This is not lost on their waiter, who is fascinated at the sight of the slovenly Adonis.

Matt, despite his astonishingly good genetics, is not exactly Mr. Right. Lana has concluded that he is a crumpled, messy, amotivational work in progress, a man who will surely become Mr. Right once all avenue of escape has been cut off, and extensive personal renovations launched.

"Honey," Matt begins nervously. "There's something I want to ask you..."

"Wait!" she interjects, her hand signaling a full stop like a highway patrolman. "Oh, I'm so excited." She waves her hands wildly, as if in imitation of a humming bird. She gulps a bit of her wine, then braces herself, placing a hand over her heart. "Shouldn't you get down on one knee?"

"Well I don't know if that's really necessary..." says Matt, confused. Is Lana expecting something- he wonders. Nobody ever expected anything from Matt, so the sensation of having some kind of creeping obligation thrust upon him is entirely foreign and disconcerting. He considers several possibilities, but none seems likely. Then, suddenly catching on, "Did Josh tell you anything?"

Quickly recovering from a slip of the tongue that almost screws up the surprise, Lana silences herself.

"Lana...did any of the guys..."

"No nothing," she answers defensively, and takes a hasty gulp of her Pinot Noir. "Go on Matt. Ask what you were going to ask. I'm listening." She fixes her gaze on him like an off-camera prompter, willing him to remember his lines. Her freshly highlighted curls bounce as she nods her head eagerly, mascara caked eyelashes fluttering frantically, like a hummingbird's wings. She eyes him expectantly, like a parent coaxing a first step out of a toddler.

Matt looks nervously around at the other diners, so safe and warm in the cocoon of their own personal Christmas dramas. "Um. Maybe I should give you this first."

He hands her a small box, expertly wrapped at a mall booth manned by a group of soccer moms disguised as Santa's elves. "Here."

Lana reaches out with shaking hands, wondering, -how big can it be? She looks dreamily into his eyes as she struggles with the ribbon. Matt is still seated, his knees not called into valiant action. Oh well. Modern times. Finally she hits pay dirt. A black velvet jewelry box. She opens it with practiced hand motions, her ring finger twitching slightly in anticipation. It's a locket. "A silver locket?" she snarls, not bothering to conceal her distaste.

"Lana," he blurts out hastily lest the warm glow of his gift giving blow over before he gets to score his point. "I need to ask if you'll watch Finnegan tomorrow. Me and a bunch of the guys managed to get a sweet deal on a ski lodge right next to this hill 'cause its Christmas week and I guess less people will be on the hill tomorrow. But I need you to watch Finnegan..."

At this moment, Lana is sputtering. She is a drowning woman coming up for air between frantic gulps of incredulity. It crosses Matt's mind that this isn't the first time Lana has inexplicably lost patience with him. "A locket? A silver locket? This is what you give me after three years of putting up with your crap?" She is already winding her arm up for a Major League baseball-caliber pitch, black velvet box firmly in hand.

"...You know Lana, I guess I should have bought the gold one. But I needed new ski boots..."

"And now the only question you can think to pop is will I take care of your drooling behemoth on Christmas Day?" A trio of the posh restaurant's snotty waiters are eyeing her nervously as her voice rises to a crescendo. As she pelts the gift box at him full force, Matt ducks with a sportsman's well-practiced grace. She beans their waiter, who has been cowering at the back of the dining room. "What could you be thinking? What? What?"

Matt has still not picked up the vital clues. He starts again. "Finnegan doesn't drool that much Lana. And he's at least ninety percent housetrained..."

"You and that dog! You and that goof ball dog are two of a kind! The question is," Lana shouts as she rises to her exquisite black lace and rhinestone-stiletto clad feet. "Are you housebroken? Apparently not!"

And with that, she storms out of the restaurant, leaving him (Matt supposes), stuck with the distressingly undivided bill, (they always went Dutch Treat), and an as yet unopened second present. (They were milk chocolates from the corner drug store. These were purchased just before the Christmas Eve closing, at a discount, after Matt had suffered a few twinges of insecurity about the inadequacy of the locket.) He sits distractedly eating them as he awaits what has now grown in his head into a cataclysmically high bill. He ponders what to do about Finnegan. If he doesn't find a kennel tonight, on Christmas Eve, his ski trip is off. It is extremely upsetting.

And then it dawns on him. Maybe she isn't just ticked off about his asking her to watch Finnegan. Maybe she doesn't like the locket. Perhaps his gesture has not been sufficient proof of his devotion? In fact, Matt considers it entirely likely that Lana has just dumped him for good. Maybe. Women... Who could figure them out?

* * *

A half hour of puzzling and considering later Matt finds himself at the foot of his apartment building's front steps, when a cab pulls up and disgorges another tenant who lives down the hall from him. First one glamorous foot exits the sedan, then the other, followed by their fur-clad owner, in a perfectly executed charm school dismount. Matt watches with rapt attention as the stunning redhead unloads a backseat full of shopping bags emblazoned with logos from designer boutiques. Matt has previously spotted her opening the door of her flat which along with his, occupies the western end of the second floor of their converted Victorian-era mansion. Toward Matt she directs a stare which is at the same time coquettish and commanding. "Aren't you going to help me with my packages?" She asks this with such authentic astonishment that it leaves Matt flummoxed.

Embarrassed, Matt can think of no reason why he could refuse. Besides, this blue-eyed goddess looks at him with such an expression of conviction, of certainty that she deserves to have her packages schlepped up to her apartment that it would be a violation of the laws of God and nature to ignore any vigorously expressed request that escapes her Christian Dior ruby red lips. The only thing missing is a choke chain. So he begins stacking the packages under his arms, extending his fingers to their maximum stretch so that he could hold the larger bags by the handles. As he follows her into the building, (while bracing one smaller box on top of the other with his chin), he tilts his head slightly and checks out her skin-tight, high-heeled boots and the way they cause her tidy little bottom to twitch visibly under her mink baseball jacket. Humm- the machinery in his brain whirls. Is he single now or not? Maybe she's flirting? With lightning speed, Matt's thoughts jump from skirt-chasing to ski hills.

Single girl on Christmas Eve...his brain cogitates excitedly. Maybe alone tomorrow with no relatives underfoot to cook for. Maybe she would watch Finnegan, Matt thinks hopefully. He looks for an opening, asks, "Been Christmas shopping?"

"I'm sorry?" She appears taken by surprise. "Oh... Christmas shopping... Yes, well... I'm sure there must be *a few things for somebody* in there but I was just picking up a couple of little necessities. You just wouldn't believe the designer bargains you can get on Christmas Eve!"

She pauses in front of her door, key in hand like a small dagger, ready to dispense with him as soon as he deposits his load of shopping bags. Then something about his eager, almost vassal-like willingness to please appeals to her. She casts an appraising eye at the firm muscles of his forearms. She does need to have a few things done around the place, some stove fuses and whatnot. And who knows when the super would get around to it at this time of year? (He was a drunk even when it wasn't the holidays.) "Care for a whisky before I send you back to your apartment?" she asks, now in her best "Good Boy! Here's your doggie biscuit" tone of voice. She flashes her most engaging, camera-ready smile (stretching from capped bicuspid to capped bicuspid) and opens the door to this newly released stray doggie and takes him in out of the cold.

Although hopelessly overwhelmed with feminine accoutrements, Jillian's cluttered apartment, (her *pied à terre*, as she called it), has obviously 'been done'. This is in stark contrast to Matt's thoroughly undone place down the hall which resembles the waiting room at a dog groomer's at the end of a long week. On her longest living room wall is a display of seriously high glamour, professionally illuminated and executed portraits of Jillian herself, (some complete with autograph), a selection of full-body poses of Jillian, and to round off the collection, an assortment of smaller, but elegant three-quarter shots depicting various and ever-shifting moods and more subtle elements of Jillian. It is a complete portfolio of her life in pictures. The largest of these masterpieces are contained in frames that come with their own gallery-style lights on top. She is featured with at least five distinct hair colors.

As Jillian hands him the whiskey, Matt takes note of the large pink stone ring that she is wearing on her right hand.

"Like it?" She looks lovingly at the ring. "It's a pink diamond! My last ex-boyfriend gave it to me."

"Then you'll be giving it get back?"

"Not on your life! As far as I am concerned it's compensation for time wasted. Besides a gift is for keeps, it's *not* a certificate of deposit."

Matt looks around the rest of Jillian's flat. A twinge of embarrassment strikes him, the kind of discomfort he felt once when he accidentally made a wrong turn into a ladies' locker room. Except in this case, he has stumbled into the world's largest walk-in closet. It shows no traces of male-influenced decision making. He guesses that the most recent ex-boyfriend has not only never lived there, he transited the place at breakneck speed, like someone in a relay race. Otherwise, (Matt reasons), there would be the telltale detritus of a recent party, along with a heap of crumpled men's clothes, a gaping bathroom door opening onto a moldy smelling bathroom complete with a visibly upright toilet seat, stacks of old newspapers (really just purchased for the sports sections), a massive television set complete with surround sound, and a sink full of empty beer cans. Like every living space Matt has ever infiltrated.

"And your current boyfriend doesn't mind? He doesn't..."

"You don't understand. My last boyfriend was my boyfriend up until three hours ago." She suddenly affects a tragic expression, and strives to inject more emotion into her voice. "We broke up." Then, adding the obvious, (simply for the sake of emphasis), "On Christmas Eve!"

"Was it hard?" Matt tries to strike a sympathetic but masculine note, caring but not needy. He still isn't sure if he is single again. This woman might not even be a dog lover. But it is worth establishing a rapport, just in case. After all, he already has the new ski boots.

"It was terrible! I almost cried!" she says in her daintiest voice.

"Almost?"

"And then I thought. What the hell? He's too old for me anyway. His wife can keep him. And I went shopping."

> *"Beauty is all very well at first sight: but who ever looks at it when it's been in the house three days?" -George Bernard Shaw.*

☙ THREE ❧

IT'S THE MOST WONDERFUL TIME OF THE YEAR

"Oh... My... God. Madeline. You have to save me," Jillian whines into her ersatz Art Deco phone. "My neighbor's puppy just mistook my designer Christmas tree for a fire hydrant." As she speaks, she surveys the silver white artificial tree through the filter of her creamed, gauze-shrouded, partially manicured hands. "Christmas is supposed to be a day of beauty, grooming and rest. Not this!"

From across the room she can see that several of the chichi hand-crafted wire and silk bird ornaments have been mangled, where the wires with which they had been tethered to the tiny, perfect, artificial tree had prevented them from being successfully retrieved for an imaginary hunter. Or perhaps Finnegan had mistaken them for a toy. Or a teether. Finnegan is sleeping contentedly next to one of Jillian's mangled high heels, over which he has draped one protective and massive paw. A puddle of drool completes the tableau.

"You're doing a favor for a neighbor?" Her sister gasps back. "You? A favor? Did you take your temperature? Have you changed your dosage without medical advice? Since when does Jillian Yarwood do favors for neighbors?"

"I could do without your sarcasm right now. I'm in a very vulnerable place." Instinctively Jillian's free hand reaches dramatically to her forehead, and she affects a tragic pose, under an imaginary spotlight. A lock of spectacular, color-enhanced red hair falls across her face. Jillian wonders fleetingly if she resembles Rita Hayworth in this pose. "One of my boyfriends just left me for his wife. On Christmas Eve."

"You're in a vulnerable place? I've got to produce a *cordon bleu* Christmas dinner for the in-laws while two overwrought children insist that I help them assemble Lego toys containing a gazillion pieces each. Did you know that some Lego blocks will pass easily through the digestive tract of a four-year-old boy?"

"I'm not even going to ask how you found that out."

"Look, single girl. You have no idea what trouble is. That bitch

Martha Stewart has raised the bar for all of us. If I don't wear myself completely out today, I'll look like a complete failure as a wife and mother in the eyes of someone who never brought home one paycheck in her entire life. Any minute she'll be showing up with her white gloves to check for dust under the DVD player."

Jillian remains silent on the other end of the line, checking her eyebrows in one of her concave tabletop mirrors.

Madeline continues impatiently, "Just how much work can one little puppy be after all? How old is he?"

"Four months," Jillian pouts, "If I weren't watching my figure I'd eat a gallon of chocolate ice cream right now. Rollo flavored. With chocolate sauce. My face would explode. I'm so upset. He's already eaten one of my Jimmy Choo shoes. They cost Daddy eight hundred bucks. It's a good thing they were last season's."

"The dog is four months old? Four months? And you're acting like a martyr over a tiny little, four-month old dog?"

"He's a Bernese Mountain Dog."

"And this means in English?"

"That he could haul an ox cart for a living. I'm pretty sure he weighs more than I did when I was Prom Queen."

"So does the average ten-year-old. Why did you take on such a behemoth? What could you have been thinking?"

"He's cute."

"The mutt? Since when have you become a dog lover?"

"The guy. He's totally cute but a little self involved, maybe. Needs to be kept on a tight leash."

"Figures. You're always getting your panties in a knot over some hot but totally wrong guy. When are you going to grow up and settle down? When are you going to wake up and smell the damn coffee? Find someone half decent for a change."

"Because old married lady, anything worth getting has already been got. Almost. By the time you reach ...er...twenty-nine, practically the only guys left on the market are pathetic losers. You can almost bet on the fact that if they are still single and gorgeous they come complete with a fatal flaw. So I have to keep my options open."

Madeline is silent on the other end of the line, considering, counting to ten. Then, "If that were true, then it begs the question: if only losers are single at your age, then what does that make you? Can't it be possible that there are some good ones left out there?"

"Spouse shopping these days is like arriving at a cocktail party at five minutes to midnight. Have you ever had a good look at the hors d'oeuvres tray after eleven o'clock?"

"What if a new tray gets brought out from the kitchen?"

"That's just my point. The only hope are men who're re-entering the dating scene. *Hors d'oeuvres* fresh from the kitchen, as it were."

"Yes, but you're into snatching them while they're still in someone else's kitchen."

"The early bird gets the crab cake." Jillian commences filing her nails as she eyes the stirring Finnegan suspiciously. "There is something to be said about married men. They're already housebroken."

"Yes, but if you manage to get one of these housebroken men for a husband, how can you trust him knowing that's he's already strayed?"

"Because my dear, I have strategy on my side."

"Strategy?"

"Absolutely. I'm committed to squandering every red cent Mr. Right makes. That way he'll never be able to afford a divorce. He'll be so busy scrambling to keep up with my spending habits, he'll become a big success! He won't even have time for a roving eye. In any case, he'll never be able to manage the alimony."

"Cute. Very cute." Over the line, Jillian can hear Madeline's children erupting into a fierce fight over a cookie, despite the existence of several dozen more in the near-by jar. "Look, I have to go. But think about what I said. You're getting a little too old to play the ingénue. You're only two years younger than me, you know. That would make you thirty-six."

"Would not."

"Yes it would. I've only got two years to go before I'm forty. That means you've only got four years before the big four-oh."

"You must be wrong! Let me get my calculator..."

"Oh for God's sake, Jillian. It's simple math. You've turned twenty-nine eight times already. How long can you keep it up?"

The other end of the line is dramatically silent. Jillian rummages in her purse, with the phone receiver crammed between her cheek and upturned shoulder. No luck.

"Jillian? Are you in there?"

"I'm thinking. O.K. Under duress, I might admit to thirty or so, but still, who's to know?"

Madeline is losing patience, "How much longer are you going to keep life on hold while you're waiting to be discovered? If it was going to happen, it would have happened ten or fifteen years ago."

"It could happen any day."

"Could not."

"Could too. I'm reading for several interesting projects right now. A play...a commercial and even a made for television movie...It could still happen."

"You're expecting to get a part as the ingénue? The innocent young girl? Really? Pushing thirty-seven..."

"Christ! Don't add years! I'm still just thirty-six. God! Did I say that? Not to worry. I encase my face in plaster every night before I go to sleep. I've already compiled a list of noteworthy plastic surgeons. I no longer go to tanning salons. I have a fake tan sprayed on in some kind of ultra-futuristic gas chamber. I regularly get poked, prodded and laser zapped to the point that even I don't know how old I am anymore. And, if that doesn't keep me in the running for a starring role, I've got a part-time job as a private investigator."

"A what?"

"A private eye. Mostly I've been hired to catch cheating hubbies in the act, or at least catch them on the prowl."

"You can't be serious." Madeline is torn, between wanting to intervene in the living room wrestling match, and gathering more information on her younger, and definitely crazier sister.

"Dead serious. Seems I'm cut out for the job, according to the agency. Isn't that a hoot?"

The children's screams by now are reaching a crescendo.

"I've gotta go." Click.

* * *

Meanwhile, on an almost-abandoned chairlift near the top of a wind-swept ski hill, Matt is unburdening himself to Josh, another single pal who has managed to escape the whole bother of Christmas, in favor of more worthwhile amusements. "I don't know Josh. I think the Lana thing is definitely on shaky ground, if not Kaput, over, finito."

"Yeah. Probably. But you gotta ask yourself. If she won't watch your dog on Christmas Day, especially when lift tickets are half price and nobody else is on the hill, what kind of relationship did you have? It's a question of priorities, after all. As Dr. Phil would say, how's that working out for you?"

"Good point. She has a nice body, though." Matt fiddles with his visor, readies himself to dismount from the chairlift.

"Yeah. She does have that."

"But at least this way I won't have to tell her about taking a year off from school."

"Boy! She would have bit your head off about that one. You're lucky there, Matt. You really dodged a bullet! Especially where your parents cut you off. How you going to get by, buddy?"

"A little of this, a little of that. Dog walking, house painting. Minor repair. Covering those little contingencies for people. Things like that. There must be tons of ways I can be useful to people."

"You're going to go door to door?" Josh squirms forward a little on the chair lift.

"Not exactly. But I can post my skills on the net. Picture this: an ad for an odds job guy, I'll call myself: The Contingency Man."

Josh glances sideways at his friend, as he moves the ski lift's safety bar up and readies to dismount. "It could work," he says, encouragingly. He points his ski tips upward, adjusts his goggles.

"Oh, man. I know it could work. You wouldn't believe how useful I've been to my neighbor already. Fixed a couple things for her last night!"

"What neighbor is that?"

"The one watching Finnegan. Sexy high maintenance type. A redhead."

"Sexy huh? Likes dogs?"

"Apparently. And Finnegan made himself right at home. I think we could have a special bond."

The pair land with a thud, then turn toward an expert trail, to their immediate right. A vast shimmering expanse of white powder stretches before them, as yet unmarked by skis. Behind them, one empty chair after another follows its passage around the ramp and back down the silent hill. An Arctic wind is blowing across the open expanse at the top.

Christmas doesn't get any better than this.

FOUR

THE TOP BITCH IN HER CLASS

"Cleopatra likes her walk immediately after her eight forty-five kibble. She doesn't abide waiting. She wants her coat if it's raining. She'll even want her coat if it threatens to rain. You mustn't bring her home immediately after she's done her business. In fact, after she goes you'll have to walk her for at least ten minutes longer so she won't start to think that she's putting an end to a good thing by doing her doo doo."

"She's told you this?" Matt inquires of Cleopatra's mistress, a brittle, stiffly-coiffed and lacquered executive secretarial type who has managed to parlay 300 cc implants into a starring role as the second wife of the CEO, her former boss. Matt is trying desperately to look sincerely interested in Cleopatra's routine, because, apart from repairing several broken items in his neighbor's flat, he's been completely out of work. And he is still waiting to get paid for that. He has a nagging suspicion that payment from Jillian might take an infinitely long time arriving.

"Her behaviorist told us. He's a genius. A real genius. A regular Doctor Doolittle. He's even been on cable television! Whatever he says goes." She hands him the elegant leather leash of the hyper and eager Cavalier King Charles Spaniel and shows Matt to the door. Her hand reaches for the knob, then suddenly stops. Her heavily made-up face suddenly becomes animated, causing an earthquake of fine cracks to appear. "One other thing..." she turns and looks at him full on. "You are not to take her to that park you saw just two blocks east. Under no circumstances, do you hear?"

"There's something wrong with the dog park?"

"Oh! The people who go there. You just can't imagine! They ought not to be allowed to even have a dog. That place is full of mixed breeds! I even heard a rumor that some of them were from the shelter."

"You don't say?" replies Matt, who feigns shock, for the sake of business.

"As if the off-leash, un-neutered mutts weren't bad enough, their owners are the worst sort of layabouts. Worthless creatures."

"Worthless creatures?"

"The sort they invented day time talk shows for..."

"Talk shows? Are we talking about dogs, here?"

"The owners, you dolt! The owners. They'll let their dogs hump anything! We can't have my prize Spaniel mixing with the likes of that, can we?"

"Mixing? You mean..."

"Exactly. If any one of those brutes wants to canoodle with my little Cleopatra , he's going to have to pay through the nose for it. She certainly doesn't have to give it away!" On this note her tone becomes indignant, as if she has already had to fend off a few uncouth and unfunded canine Lotharios in search of top notch bitch. "Besides. Who knows what kind of attitude she'll take on, what sort of bad habits. You never know how it could affect her chances of winning..."

"So she's won a lot of..." Matt attempts to ask.

She points to the trophy wall with a sweeping gesture. "They're all hers. By now you must realize that she's the top bitch in her class. She can't be associating with just any mutt..."

"I suppose not," Matt reassures her, somewhat insincerely, since he has been planning to take the dog immediately to the neighboring dog park and let her run loose with his very own slobbering Finnegan. He is at this very moment stashed in Matt's friend Josh's mother's car, parked just outside the building, drooling and chewing.

"And I should warn you about the half-Pomeranian mongrel in the neighborhood..."

"The Pomeranian? He's vicious?"

"Not the mutt. But the owner is horrid. Just a completely unworthy human being. A lout. A fool. And he lurks around this neighborhood all the time. I don't want my precious baby having anything to do with that beastly mongrel or his owner."

"What if there's more than one Pomeranian-type dog around? How will I know which one to avoid?"

"Simple. The mutt to avoid responds to the name: Bartender."

"Unusual name. Clever."

"Not really. It's probably the first name that came to his owner's mind when he got him. In fact I'm certain it was."

"Why's that?"

"He's my ex-husband."

With that, she hands him the leash, and shoves Matt and his four-legged charge out the door.

***

"I hope you're not planning to take HIM along every time," says the elderly gentleman who covers his face with a hankie as he accusingly points a finger at the eager, slobbering Finnegan. In his other hand he is restraining a border collie who is determinedly sniffing around Finnegan's hind quarters, looking for a thrill.

"Well," Matt says defensively, "He is my dog..."

"I was hoping that he'd have some one on one time...I didn't know he would have to 'share' you..."

"He's just going for a walk..."

"Yes, but Casey doesn't like other dogs...He might be allergic," the man says defensively, as he yanks forcefully on the leash, pulling Casey away from Finnegan's backside.

"I can't exactly abandon my own dog."

"You can't?" He seems a bit surprised by this response. "Oh well. I suppose it was worth asking...just to clarify."

***

The door is answered by a young woman sporting an extravagant head of strawberry blonde hair. She is dressed in a satin kimono with kitten mules sporting puffy marabou toes. Sizing up Matt, and his three furry charges, she intuits, (after a pregnant pause of thirty seconds), "Oh you're the dog walker?"

"That's right. I'm here for Diva?"

From somewhere behind her kimono comes the persistent yap yap of a small Bichon Frizé dog, a ball of white fuzz, the top knot of which is dyed pink. "Oh don't mind her. She's just a chatterbox. Aren't you Baby? Aren't you Baby?" she asks as she scoops the dog up into her arms. As if on cue, the dog shuts up. "Diva can sing. Can't you baby?" she asks, with some persistence, as the woman spontaneously breaks into a tuneless version of *New York, New York*. No sooner has she started into, "Start spreading the news..." does the little Bichon break into frantic wolf-pack caliber howling. Across the hall, Matt can hear a tenant yelling, followed by forceful pounding, as Diva's owner continues nonplused with "I'm leaving' today!"

Awoo! -Continues the little dog, as Finnegan and Casey, (looking pained), hang their heads low. "You're telling me you're leaving today...I wish!" comes a voice from somewhere behind the neighbor's door.

Diva's owner continues unrattled, "I wanna be a part of it! New York, New York!"

Diva wails even louder, this time with her head skyward. The neighbor's door gives a loud thud and shakes, as if a shoe has been thrown at it.

"I wanna wake up in a city, that doesn't sleep!" By now, Casey and Finnegan have joined in the howling.

"We don't sleep either..." comes the voice behind the door.

By this time, Diva's owner is becoming flustered. She has stopped singing, but the little dog continues for another minute of obedient howling before slowing to a feeble whimper. "Oh don't mind him! He's such a spoilsport since he was put on night shift. Isn't he Diva, honey? Come on, come on..." she continues, picking up the tune with the next verse, "These little town blues, are melting away!"

"Jesus!" comes a voice from across the hall...soon to be drowned out by Diva's howling.

* * *

Meanwhile in a hotel restaurant across town, Jillian is hard at work spying on an aging lecher and his youthful protegé. This is a job she had fallen into while she was between acting roles. Since this state of affairs happens more often than not, this and her allowance from Big Daddy provide the great bulk of her income. Acting provides mere crumbs on her table, but gives substance to her dreams. When asked what she does for a living, she would never in a million years say, "I put the touch on Daddy's wallet," or add, "When I'm not working over old farts for their spare cash, or spying on other dirty old men whose wives have grown tired enough of their philandering to prefer a fat divorce settlement to their wayward husbands."

Instead, she is able to say, not without some pride, that she had played a small but significant part in a recent film, which due to the unfortunate reception instigated by some know-nothing critics, had gone straight to video. She would omit any mention of how much her part had been edited down. That would hardly have helped her cause of becoming the next big thing.

Meanwhile, kitted out in her vast array of wigs and a stylish Burberry trench coat, (paid for by the company dime), she works her tiny video camera, her parabolic microphone, her ability to disregard all rules of the road when on the chase, and even to bribe hotel employees when no other means is available to catch her prey in the act. If it weren't for the fact that she feared being caught herself by some other private detective, it would be the perfect job. As it is, she sometimes gets pointers while eavesdropping on her victims' conversations. Today is a case in point.

"Sweetie, I don't think I'm going to be able to see you tomorrow," purrs the protégé demurely.

"Why's that sugar?"

"I've got to pick up a couple extra shifts. The bills are just getting way out of hand." She pauses to let the news sink in, examining her manicure for flaws so that she can maintain facial control. She finishes off with an expert hair flip, then remains silent...waiting as her lover squirms his sizeable bulk in his chair. Waiting. Waiting.

"Isn't there any way I can help?" he finally interjects.

"Oh! I wouldn't want to put you to any more trouble. You're already so good to me. No. I'll just have to pick up some more work at the call centre and that's all there is to it. I'll be able to see you in a couple of weeks."

"A couple of weeks! When I think of you out there wearing your poor vocal chords to the bone. My heart just about breaks!" the sugar daddy replies on cue.

"But what can I do? I just have to get a career started and my boss assured me that six more months of manning the phones and I'll get promoted to junior sub-supervisor or something. I know it doesn't sound all that impressive, but I just have to find some way to pay for my singing lessons and put food on the table." (Jillian has a passing - and let's face it, bitchy- thought of the futility of this last action, since the tart is skinnier than Kate Moss, apart from her implausible breasts).

"Isn't there any way I could help?"

"Now that you mention it..." the young ingénue purrs, just as a waiter passes in front of Jillian's parabolic microphone and begins laying silverware on a table situated between the two of them. From a far corner a waitress drops a tray of glasses. -Crap, Jillian thinks - there's always something.- By the time the chaos is settled and the view is unobstructed the conversation has reverted to paying the bill and her marks putting on their coats.

* * *

> "I'm tired of all this nonsense about beauty being only skin deep. That's deep enough. What do you want, an adorable pancreas?"
>
> -Jean Kerr

⊰ FIVE ⊱

CATTLE CALL

In 1435 AD Galileo was excommunicated for his contention that the sun did not revolve around the earth. Poor Galileo spent the rest if his life under house arrest for his audacity. And for all that, he was wrong. The sun did not revolve around the earth. It revolved around Aurora and by extension her daughter. If only other people would realize that. Then Jillian would not have been having such a terrible day at the end of a terrible week. Come to think of it, it was a terrible month. There had seemed like only one thing to do.

Go shopping. But even that would not fix the mess she finds herself in. Her packages are scattered around her dressing table legs as she slumps forward onto the beveled glass top.

Her much anticipated part has not come through. Worse yet, the director had suggested that she try out for the role of the mother. Her platinum card bills are sky high from Christmas, (especially the post Christmas sales), and now this! What's wrong with the world when a woman only a teensy little bit over twenty-nine, well, thirty something, is getting cast in the wizened *hausfrau* role?

She stares anxiously at her intensely illuminated face which glowers at her accusingly from the circle of her magnifying mirror. She tugs at the outer edges of her brows with her pinkies, urging them upward and checking for laugh lines. Is that what the director detected? Under the makeup the creep of time is slowly working its hateful karma? She is overwhelmed with shallow and troublesome thoughts. Is there life after crow's feet? Would she end up being hounded by her favorite design boutiques for unpaid bills? Is Daddy hinting at cutting her off?

Jillian's mind flashes to Daddy's 'Live Free or Die' tattoo, acquired mere days after he bought his Beaver Patriot and hit the road. Could it have been some kind of coded message? Could it have something to do with her?

Any discussion of Jillian's spending habits would lead one to conclude that the girl has no wits about her at all. That is absolutely untrue! Every purchase is the result of a finely honed strategy of acquisition. Jillian examines every fashion publication the way a military tactician studies *Jane's Defence Weekly* for its analysis of current weaponry, for example. In particular, she struggles with the advance guard: poring over French and Italian Vogue, with the aid of a small multi-lingual dictionary.

With a strict seasonally-dictated turnover, she maintains scrupulous order in a clipping file of proposed 'looks', with a view to being ever at the forefront. Frequent purges of soon-to be popular and therefore outmoded styles are the key to an *avant garde* wardrobe. She wisely throws out her shoes as soon as they pass from favor in Europe. This spares her no end of embarrassment. For example: she foresaw disaster long before mere mortals had concluded that excessively pointy-toed shoes looked patently ridiculous, particularly when after the minimum of use these same toes begin to curl back into apostrophes at the end of the wearer's hideously elongated feet. She is never caught having hammer toes, or pointy toes or peek-a-boo toes when these have become common enough to make their way into major department stores, let alone the sales.

It is a bit safer to buy lingerie. After all, men are generally too distracted to check the labels before diving in, as it were. But there is always the risk that the item in question would look less than optimum if worn for more than one dirty weekend. For this reason, Jillian permits herself the sin of buying designer lingerie at a discounted price provided it is made of something like silk charmeuse, is of the highest quality, and its use is not repeated with the same man twice. After all, she has her standards.

In short, Jillian's purchasing strategy is the sum and substance of who she is, her philosophical underpinning, her *acquiro ergo sum*, (I buy, therefore I am), as it were.

Furthermore, Jillian is generous with her shopping expertise. Whenever she sees Madeline on the verge of some horrendous sartorial *faux pas*, she tries, (as gently as she is able under the trying circumstances), to let her know something is amiss. These interchanges are many and varied. A sampling of Jillian's admonishments follows:

"Is that what you're wearing?" complete with upper lip curl and snide, disparaging tone.

"Please tell me this is not what you are wearing!" delivered sometimes with a tone of mockery. At other times, Jillian feigns surprise, horror or incredulity. (In truth, Jillian is never shocked by

Madeline's criminal lack of fashion sense. She fully expects her to be as dowdy as a vicar's wife in a BBC drama, or a young Margaret Thatcher. Jillian just enjoys chastising Madeline, every chance she gets.)

"Can you tell me why you are wearing that?" with a scolding, parental tone. (When one considers that Jillian is the younger of the sisters, and yet she has stepped effectively into her mother's shoes, one can well imagine why Maddy finds her so galling.)

And the most direct: "You are not seriously going to wear that!" This is said with a tone of outright shock. The intent is the same, each time. Maddy must be reigned in, if not for her own sake, than to spare the world the offence of seeing her looking ridiculous. Jillian always feels gratified whenever she is able to affect positive change in her chastened sister.

Jillian's love life is another story! Here is where Madeline does get to play the role of older, wiser and therefore critical sibling to Jillian's perpetual party girl image. It doesn't help that, on top of her credit troubles, Jillian's romantic prospects lately have been really circling the drain. One by one the men have dropped out of her life, like mosquitoes after the first frost. She can't figure out what it is. She hasn't noticed any real slippage as per her figure or general appearance. The single guys she could understand: they are all so gun shy these days that going any longer than three dates is a signal to do a ceremonial 'duck dive', a 'now you see him now you don't' bailout to ensure that they wouldn't be hog tied to any one woman. Even so, she hasn't been too unreasonably demanding...certainly she hasn't pushed for commitment. Quite the contrary, she's been happy to just play the married guys at least with no strings attached. Maybe it's their wives. You can always expect a spoilsport in that quarter. It's not as if Jillian really plays that game very far: she usually just waves the possibility of good times to come like a toreador's red cape so that she won't have to eat alone or pick up the tab. Usually.

Jillian tries to remember when romance died for her. It was sometime after she had dated her second commitment-shy guy who claimed that his divorce wasn't finalized yet. That was an understatement. Neither one of these divorces had been finalized because the errant men were still cohabiting with their blissfully unaware wives and families.

Here are some of the dead, (but ignored), give-aways: they called only on cell phones, they gave only work addresses, they never introduced her to their friends, and most tellingly, they were never available on weekends. Now, Jillian is constantly on the lookout for these 'modus operandi', from her newly jaded perspective. Not that she has given up on men whose divorces haven't come through yet. But if they are going to play her, she is going to play them.

Shortly after these not-quite-free of the old ball and chain revelations, (Both times involving harassing late-night phone calls from irate spouses), she took her job in private investigation, sussing out cheaters. Her on and off day job. The bread and butter that keeps her dreams of stardom alive. It has been several years since the stiletto has been professionally on the other foot. Ironically both her acting and her private investigation careers involve disbelief, and the suspension thereof.

She has been known to confess: "My only regret is that I have never been assigned to store detective work, and given my very own handcuffs. What fun to slap the cuffs on a perp, just like somebody in *Law and Order* or *CSI*!" Jillian consoles herself with the notion that she just can't fade into the crowd well enough for that sub-specialty. What may be more to the point, the detective agency isn't certain that she won't just lose sight of the job she is doing and spend all her time shopping.

But we must return to Jillian's problem at hand: if she isn't discovered soon, the idea of playing the ingénue is off. And then what kind of career prospects does this leave her? What talents? What special abilities? Professional shopper? What, if anything would keep her in clover once Big Daddy stops sending his check? What other big daddies are out there?

Would she just have to pack her tent, -so to speak- in the middle of the night, and skulk off to Pearson Airport for parts unknown? Should she show up at Big Daddy's door in God's Waiting Room and throw herself at his mercy? Would she have to stoop to a forty-hour work week? She has considered becoming a buyer for one of the big department store chains, but then again, where is the fun in buying stuff for somebody else? If you pick something you like, you'd live to experience the horror of seeing a whole lot of other, (less worthy women), wearing the same thing.

In the midst of this reverie and self-recrimination, brought about by the 10X magnifying mirror on Jillian's dressing table, the phone rings. It is a breathless Madeline.

"Jillian! I've been Googling."

Jillian giggles. "That can be a lot of fun."

"I don't think so!"

"What do you mean, I Google all the time. I find it very

reassuring."

"You do!"

"Yes. I read all these reviews of me and count the number of hits an article mentioning my name gets and how many times I appear on the web. It lets me know I'm really somebody."

"That's not what I'm talking about. I Googled Walter."

"Oh...My...God...Never, never ever Google Walter. What did I tell you Madeline? What you don't know can't hurt you. Are you nuts? What could you have been thinking of?"

"So you do know?"

A sigh. Another sigh. "Well. Yes. He calls me from time to time, remember. Whenever he visits this planet."

"He upsets Daddy quite a lot," allows Madeline. "Maybe that's why he ran away to Florida."

"He's old Madeline, lots of people run away to Florida. They're escaping the weather."

"Maybe it's more than the weather. Maybe they're escaping their kids."

Jillian's mind flashes to her latest visit with Madeline, Roger and their two demon offspring. –'These are the golden years', Roger kept pointing out. Could he honestly say it wasn't getting any better? Jillian shudders, wonders if her father had complained about her spending habits to Madeline. "I was speaking to Daddy recently, too."

"Were you?" asks Maddy.

"He's having those psycho...what do you call them...psycho...somnambulist chest pains again..."

"He's always having those." Madeline does not bother to correct her sister's vocabulary, knowing by now that Jillian is un-teachable.

"Do you suppose he'd get upset if I ask him to help me out with my cards again? It's a little soon after the last time, but I've had some unforeseen expenses."

"What could those be, Jillian?" Madeline sighs audibly.

But Jillian doesn't feel at liberty to say. How can she make someone as dowdy as Madeline understand that the January sales were not to be passed up? Especially when they featured couture items that had at least two good months' worth of use before they were past their season? She swiftly sidesteps that item of conversation. "How are Roger and the kids?"

Madeline sighs. "I'm glad I took that First Aid course, if you get what I mean. They're constantly doing something self-destructive."

"And Roger?"

"Oh Roger! No problems there. A good husband should be like a house cat. Present, but self-contained. We're going to just carry on forever the way we're going. At least," Madeline allows, "Until they invent a vibrator that takes out the garbage and changes my tires."

"A greater love the world has never known."

> *"All bachelors love dogs, and we would love children just as much if they could be taught to retrieve." -P.J. O'Rourke*

ෲ SIX ෲ

HAVING A FIELD DAY

Matt finds himself fighting the urge to doze off as his collection of dogs romp around the park. Over the past month or so, he has managed to collect quite a pack of dogs whose owners don't want to face the nasty winter weather long enough to give them their outing. Matt ponders whether this would hold up with Spring just around the corner, (if you could call it that in Toronto, in March)? He certainly hopes so. It isn't like the Fortune 500 are beating a path to his door.

He hasn't really been able to get much else going...Not that he hasn't tried. He is proud of the fair to middling job he has done of the following trades: he has changed a light fixture, replaced washers on several taps, hung a set of curtains and painted an apartment in his building. Unfortunately he had not disconnected the fuse while changing the light. The resulting minor shock caused him to crack a little plaster when he jabbed the wall with his screwdriver. Was it his fault the rug in the apartment below had been soaked during his amateur plumbing gig, that the drop sheet had not caught all the errant paint, that the taps still leaked a little? He had tried damn it!

And several of those jobs were on good skiing days. He has managed to get two letters to the editor published, (of course they were free, what did he expect?), and has tried out for a job as a singing waiter, which unfortunately involved waiting on tables and not just singing. How could someone in the prime of life, someone this good looking, for God's sake, be so unemployable? Why does he have to earn a living when his father is rolling in dough, after all? Unfortunately his father now refuses to support his struggle to find himself. A dilettante he called him. A dabbler. Little Abner he called him, after that old-time comic book character whose sole job was as a mattress tester. That is so unfair. Most of those jobs just didn't suit. All of them actually. Matt scratches his belly and turns his sleepy gaze back to Casey, Finnegan and Diva. But where is Cleo? Ah! There she is with another group of dogs. Having a little harmless fun...Good girl letting Matt sit and take a break like that.

-Whooo boy some of them are really going to need to be hosed down-he thinks as the prize Cavalier King Charles Spaniel rolls around in the melting snow and mud with a pack of a half-dozen other dogs of all kinds. Cleopatra is at times fully immersed in the mud, leaves and God-knows what-all-else that have gathered into a murky trough at the bottom of a hill. She must have found something exciting, because all the other dogs in the park have suddenly clustered around her.

"Bartender!" shouts a man of indeterminate years and questionable sobriety who is seated next to Matt. As his mouth opens, and spittle sprays out, Matt catches a whiff of hard liquor. "Get away from there!" The man rises unsteadily from the bench and stumbles towards a feisty black dog that has now mounted the exuberant little pooch.

Too late. She is mixing with the great canine unwashed. Cleo is not only doing what comes naturally to dogs, but, Matt's most lucrative dog sitting gig is now seriously on the line. If her owner finds out that her little bitch is giving it away for free, and lets his other clients know, Matt could be thrown at the mercy of his father's financial whim. No good. That path leads straight to Dad's firm's windowless mail room.

Matt and Bartender's owner approach the pair who are locked in illicit congress with what can only be called 'fierce determination'. "I wouldn't go in there if I were you," calls out another owner who is rapidly attaching a leash to his own agitated animal. Matt considers his options. The sharp teeth and frustrated libido win out over the fear that he will lose his job. -What are the odds, after all- Matt thinks as he retreats from the scene to a better vantage point. After all, she isn't even in heat.

The next day Cleo's ecstatic owner calls to cancel her outing. "I'm sending her off to mate with an absolutely superb specimen. She's in heat!" she squeals. "You don't know how I've dreamt of this day. You can't imagine what the stud fees cost, but it will be worth it! The puppies will be worth a fortune."

-Two months. Matt knows from his brief and largely forgettable foray into pre-veterinary studies that he has roughly sixty days before little Cleo gives birth. -If the puppies aren't purebred little Spaniels that owner just might neuter me- Matt shudders. At the very least the world's softest gig will come to an end. And dog walking is such a great job. -You don't have to do anything but let the dog take a crap. Damn it, he thinks dejectedly. It almost is like Little Abner's mattress testing. Before this disaster, Matt had been seriously considering committing to dog walking as his life's work. After all, he'd have to do something -if he ever plans to retire.

Matt spends the afternoon reading the classifieds in the *Globe and Mail*, then the *Post*, and finally the *Star*. Finding nothing, he considers searching the notice boards at the grocer's, thinks better of it and begins composing a letter of contrition to his father. If he is suitably apologetic and promises a return to his studies, it might break through the old man's reserve.

Generally his dour father only cracks a smile when he is foreclosing on some business or other. Hostile takeovers are the only thing that truly warms this curmudgeon's heart. But if Matt eats enough crow, you never can tell. With shaky hand Matt commences trying to set the right tone with a sprinkling of "You were so rights..." and "How I wish I had listened to you in the first places..."

As he is wadding up the fourth failed attempt, the phone rings.

"Are you the Contingency Man?"

"The who?"

"You know. The Contingency Man. That's what it says on your website. Odd jobs performed, crises averted. All contingencies considered by Jack Of All Trades?"

"Oh yeah. Yeah. Right. What did you have in mind?" In the back of his mind, Matt is worrying about references. Of course, his experience so far has been that people who hired an odd jobs man over the internet usually didn't bother to check references.

"I need my gallery painted in preparation for a show. Pronto. Can you start tonight?"

"Tonight?"

"Please! I'm desperate. I just found out I'm getting profiled in two designer magazines and one spins off into a television show. This place has to look camera ready by tomorrow afternoon. Please! I'll pay top dollar!"

Matt tosses his fourth wadded-up letter to Dad in the waste paper basket. "Give me the address. I'll be there in an hour."

* * *

The gallery is one of those converted factory spaces that has become all the rage in Toronto's tony downtown Queen Street neighborhood: stripped down to its bare rafters and exterior brick, the space has only two very large interior walls and a few dividers that need painting. The gallery owner, Damian, has removed all the paintings from the area to be worked on and stored them in his back office. He has also, quite considerately placed a massive, canvas drop sheet in front of the wall and held it in place by bricks at all four corners. As Matt and Finnegan enter the space, Damian gives a start and points mutely at the panting and eager Finnegan, who by now has attained a good ninety pounds, much of it hair.

"Oh don't worry. He's housebroken."

"I should hope so. But he doesn't ...shed...does he?"

"Not deliberately..."

This seems to satisfy the gallery owner, who Matt knows is in a jam and not likely to back out of hiring him. "Well. I suppose since it's after hours anyway. Nice doggie. Nice doggie," he says gingerly as he proffers a trembling hand for Finnegan to lick. Finnegan looks on with boredom, thinking, no doubt - Where's the treat?

With a sweeping gesture Damian indicates the walls: "I want this main wall crimson," he says with precise articulation on the word crimson. "This divider I want in aqua. And this wall must be puce."

"Puce?" Matt blurts out.

Damian looks back at Matt pedantically, making a little sideways jerking motion with his head that makes it look almost detached from his upper body. "I was sure I said that clearly. Puce. P..u..c..e.."

Matt still looks at him with a glazed expression.

"Oh all right...if you will aubergine. But it's not really. And this divider should be mustard. Now I'm going out to a function and I won't be back until the morning. Make whatever progress you can. Here are all the painting rollers and thingies."

"Thingies?"

"Paint trays and rollers and whatnot. I'm sure you know the drill. Now do try to be neat. I'll tidy up tomorrow before the press gets here. Here's the key. Good luck."

* * *

Matt is determined to do a proper job this time. Who knows where this could lead? After all, the guy is getting interviewed and photographed for local design features. Maybe he might get some more painting gigs? Matt warms to this idea. Maybe painting is the way to go. He could work his way into a supervisory position, eventually, where he wouldn't even have to lift a brush, and still get paid. That could be good. Of course there is still the problem of getting this all done tonight, and passing muster with this Damian character. Granted the guy is a little high strung, but he is under pressure. Maybe in the normal run of things Damian will be able to cool his jets, to chill out.

Matt sets to work with what he feels is admirably firm resolve while Finnegan settles into a warm spot in the loft for a good nap. This is a great relief to Matt, who has discovered that Finnegan has developed separation anxiety of late. He just can't handle solitude after spending whole days romping with Matt's four legged charges in his dog walking business. Now that Finnegan is out of the solitary habit, he is prone to running in circles for hour after hour of tail chasing and barking at the top of his lungs whenever he is left alone. He'd usually finish off his tantrum by taking a dump in one of Matt's running shoes, if left alone long enough. Matt has considered giving his apartment key to his next door neighbor, since she and Finnegan seemed to have really bonded over his Christmas ski trip.

Also, she has expressed a great deal of anxiety about the fact that whenever Matt is out Finnegan barks all night long. It's nice that she is so concerned about his dog's well being- it just goes to show that just because she has what seems to be a glamorous lifestyle, it doesn't mean that she isn't capable of thinking about others.

Just the other night she was so concerned about Finnegan that she was just about ready to wallop Matt for leaving him all alone until two in the morning. There she was, in her fancy designer robe, ready to pounce as soon as she heard him put the key in the lock.

"Where the hell have you been all night?" she had bellowed.

"Hockey game."

"Do you realize that Finnegan barked and cried non-stop for six hours while you were gone? What the hell do you think you're doing?"

She certainly seemed to be pretty worried about Finnegan.

"Finnegan just has some adjustment to do."

"Adjustment? I'd say he needs more than adjustment...Maybe even a volume control button."

Yup. It might be a really good idea to get her to dog sit Finnegan sometime. Of course, Matt thinks, as he is busily applying the last color to the final portion of the walls, Finnegan is pretty quiet tonight. -He's such a good boy. I should stop by the health food store and get him a nice tartar bone to chew on. Good old Finnegan. My best buddy. The best dog in the world! Ever!

It's a rule of dog ownership, as well as parenting that when everything is really quiet and the person in charge is feeling completely relaxed and unsuspecting that at that very moment disaster will strike. At that very moment, as Matt is thinking these kind and benevolent thoughts Finnegan has stirred from his reveries and is exploring the trays full of crimson, aqua and p-u-c-e paint that have carelessly been left laying around while Matt has gone off to paint the mustard wall, (without the drop sheet). Lucky for Matt. What are a few drips here and there compared to what Finnegan has in mind?

Because by now Finnegan's furry front paws and legs and a good bit of his undercarriage are well coated in color which he is now frantically trying to remove by scrambling round and around on the massive drop sheet.

Tonight is a real turn in the road for Matt. He works diligently, without any flaking off. And just before midnight, he puts the finishing touches on the last room divider. As he is wiping a bit of errant paint from his hands, he pokes his head around the panel to check on the sleeping Finnegan.

"Oh my God!" Matt screams as soon as he sees what Finnegan has been up to. "Bad dog. Bad!"

Finnegan recognizes that tone. He is in trouble! And whenever he is in trouble, he has learned that the very last thing he wants to do is face the music. He starts to bounce, dodging from side to side, avoiding Matt's grasp. "Come here Finnegan, please!"

Bounce, lunge, bounce, lunge.

"Bad Finnegan! Bad!" Matt shouts, unwisely. This has the effect of making Finnegan duck for cover, knocking one paint tray on its side where it drips the remainder of its aqua contents in a large, explosive splash which he subsequently spreads across the drop sheet during his retreat.

"Damn it." Matt rethinks his strategy. "Come get a treat Finnegan! Oh come get a treat!" Matt holds his hands together as if he is hiding something in them. Finnegan edges closer, his moist nose twitching. He sniffs again, confused no doubt by the paint odor which wafts up from his paws.

"Finnegan," his owner calls out in a sing song voice. Finnegan looks closely at his master's hands. Sniff. "Come on Finnegan. Come on..."

Finnegan edges closer to get a better smell. Closer. Closer.

Matt grabs him. "Gotcha!" Finnegan looks at him with sad eyes. He is deeply hurt, in particular because there is no cookie in Matt's hand. "Come on boy, let's get you cleaned up."

While Matt rinses acrylic paint off Finnegan's Technicolor paws, he surveys the scene. Thankfully Finnegan has left almost all of the mess on the drop sheet. Matt rinses down Finnegan as best he can in the tiny gallery washroom, wipes up some spills off the floor surrounding the drop sheet, while still grasping Finnegan by the collar. He then ties the overwrought dog outside, to a banister. He has every plan to return to the scene of the crime, but the door has locked behind him before he realizes that he has left the key to the gallery on a work table. He walks home in a deep, bottomless funk. Another fine mess. A chastened Finnegan drags himself up the stairs after him and exiles himself to a spot by the window instead of his usual place at the foot of Matt's bed.

Thankfully the fridge is full of beer, most of it left over from his most recent BYOB. These 'Bring Your Own Booze' parties have taken on the quality of a fund raiser, so Matt holds them every week and subsequently lives off the surplus beer and potato chips. Matt helps himself to a half dozen lagers originating from various obscure Eastern European breweries that specialize in respectable suds at rock bottom prices. He passes out on the coach with the Sports Network still blasting out the day's scores.

The next morning he awakens to the insistent sound of the telephone ringing from under a mountain of sweaty clothes and dog hair. "Yes?" he mumbles into the phone.

"Matt!" gushes an eerily familiar voice.

"Mummmh?" Matt stretches and scratches his belly.

"It's Damian." Every hair on Matt's head stands on end.

"Oh jeez. I can explain..." Matt has a flashback to the chaos of the previous night: Finnegan howling amid the overturned paint trays, the spilled brushes, the wads of green tape that still lay on the floor of the gallery.

"My God, I had no idea!"

"No idea?"

"None at all."

"None?"

"To think I hired you to paint walls! Isn't it a crime to have to compromise yourself that way?"

This latest comment leaves Matt a little confused. It is true that over the past decade he had abandoned his pre-med, pre-veterinary and then his pre-law studies, (following an ill-fated stint in commerce and one term in philosophy, during which he had been detached, nihilistic and existentialist, depending on the readings he was avoiding at the time). But, how could Damian have known that he is even a screw-up in dog walking? "Oh yeah, well...times have been a little rough since I lost direction..."

"A creative impasse, yes!" Damian squeals. "I can understand that. The public can understand that. You have suffered a soul-destroying blockage and come out the other side, damn it! This is just explosive."

Matt isn't sure what would make Damian consider the mess in which he'd left the gallery the night before the result of a creative impasse. And the word 'explosive' didn't bode well either. His father would just write it off as just another proof of his son's bone idle, aimless nature. If Damian is willing to be so forgiving, who is Matt to contradict him? "So you're still going to pay me for the painting? You're not worried about the mess?"

"Worried about the mess?" Damian shrieks. "It's genius. You're a genius. I want to put it on the walls for tomorrow's opening. Who represents you? What other galleries? Do you have any other pieces you're willing to let me look at?"

"Are we talking about the same thing here?"

"I'm sure we are. That drop sheet you felt compelled to work on is quite honestly the best piece of abstract art I've seen this year. You must have had a major breakthrough. The layering. The use of color. The emotion. The sophistication!..." Damian pauses, then gushes, "The tension! You must let me show it. How much will you sell it for?"

The next ten minutes of conversation happen in a blur. If Damian is willing to forget about Finnegan's antics and even willing to put the messy drop sheet on the wall, who is he to argue with him? He just wants to rush down there fast and get his check for the night's painting before the public finds out what a phony he is. And if they don't, he might make a few extra bucks.

-What the hell.

SEVEN
DROWNING IN LABELS

The gallery doors are locked in preparation for the new show's opening the next night, but a roughly scrawled sign has been taped to the front, glass door:

The sky is falling, but if you must persist, knock and we may let you in.

Matt taps on the door. Nothing. He knocks harder. Nothing. Finally he pounds on the door. Still nothing. Finally he sees someone, not Damian, approaching the door tentatively and then turning the lock. A perfectly coiffed and goateed head pops out, "We're not open right now. Damian is having a heart attack. He's up and down like a toilet seat."

The man's eyes roll as in the distance a new round of ranting begins: "I can't work in these conditions! It's insupportable! I can't and I won't. I'm not ready!"

"I'm Matt...."

The man gives him a puzzled look.

"...The Contingency man," says Matt. "Damian had me paint the gallery last night. I just wanted to...."

"Wait here." The man turns quickly on his heels, leaving Matt just inside the door to listen to Damian's meltdown.

"I knew I needed a stylist. I knew it. I'm so mad I could just spit. The photographer will be here any minute and just look at me! Look at me!" he shrieks.

"Who are you wearing?" his companion asks gently from behind the divider.

"Lauren, Boss, Piaget, Prada....Gucci. God it's just too much. Look at me! I'm drowning in labels. I should have known better. It's better to just sprinkle them. But oh no! I'm a fashion travesty, a pastiche. I'm hideous! I'm a laughing stock. You never mix Lauren and Gucci. What could I have been thinking?"

"Stop it. Stop it." From behind the divider Matt hears the loud crack of skin being slapped. Then silence. Finally sniffling. "Wake up and smell the Chardonnay. You've got to get a grip this instant," Damian's friend is saying in a decidedly parental tone of voice. "I'm sorry I slapped you but you needed to calm down. Do you want bloodshot eyes for the cameras?"

Damian continues sniffling. "They're all going to be here..."

"Pull yourself together, man. Nobody will know who you're wearing. Really. You haven't got one prominent logo. I mean it's not like you've got freaking Tommy written in gigantic frigging letters across your chest. You haven't sunk *that* low. The great unwashed are not going to take a magnifying glass and examine your picture just to see if you're wearing Gucci shoes or not."

"You're sure?" Damian asks weakly. "They won't think I'm guilty of label overkill?"

"Of course not." His friend's voice is maternal. "Oh, there's someone here. A Contingency man, I think he said." His voice is quizzical.

Damian has a complete personality change, and once again returns to his commanding id, "Quick, bring him here. That man is a genius. A pure genius. Now where are those contracts?"

When Matt arrives before Damian's desk, he has a stack of papers thrust before him before he can even take in the expression on Damian's reddened, tear-stained face. "We're going to make you famous. Now sign here, here and here. Wait till you see how your stretched canvases turned out."

"Canvases?"

"I hope you don't mind. The drop sheet had a seam running up the middle so I cut your painting into two separate canvases."

"They're already done?"

"First thing this morning. Look!," he says, indicating the red wall.

There before Matt is what now appears to be two abstract paintings. Undoubtedly they are the drop sheet which his dog had produced in a frenzy the previous night. One was predominantly the product of the spilled blue paint. The other showed clearly where Finnegan had rolled around frantically trying to shed the p-u-c-e paint.

Matt knows nothing about art, and it is just as well. He can't tell junk from genius, but if Damian can't either, what difference does it make? As long as Matt is paid for the previous night's paint job and gets away unscathed before he is exposed as a fraud.

"I'm willing to guess I'll get four grand for the wider piece. Three for the smaller. Of course you realize my fee is forty percent. Sign here and here..."

Matt's head is still spinning with the mention of four grand, when Damian leans forward, and adds. "Of course, if you happen to have anything else lying around from an earlier period, before your blockage, preferably on a stretched and primed canvas, I might have room for two more in this show."

"Two more?"

"Two more. About the size of the three grand job over there..." Damian points to a massive multi-hued splash of red on a three foot by five foot canvas. To break up the red the painter had splattered some other, indeterminate dark blob, which appears to have been overlaid by tire tracks.

Hummm, Matt cogitates. "Let me check around my ...ah...studio. I have one or two that didn't...ah...move before I reached my...um...creative, my creative...my..."

"Creative slump. That's fine. See if you can bring them by later on today. I won't have time to preview any slides of them. The show starts tomorrow night. That's all..." Damian waves him off as if Matt were a servant and Damian, a Maharaja. The rest of the afternoon is spent tearing over to an artist's supply store, where Matt skims some books on technique. These allow him to cram just enough knowledge of acrylic painting to qualify as a dilettante. He purchases two large, pre-stretched, pre-primed canvases and a beginner painter's gift set of acrylics, before racing back to his apartment and his four-legged Picasso.

Jillian bumps into him as he is struggling with the front door and his oversized packages from the art supply warehouse.

"What have we here?" she queries in her friendliest voice. (She isn't sure what tasks remain to be performed in the apartment, but she is sure she can think of something.)

"Oh, just some art supplies. Paint, some canvases. That sort of thing..."

"Canvases?" Jillian pauses. Then a moment of dawning knowledge. "You paint? Something other than walls I mean."

Matt clears his throat nervously. "Oh yes," he says somewhat guiltily. "I have two canvases hanging right now in a gallery show opening tomorrow." Curiously, he likes the sound of that.

"Oh you're a professional!" Her head is spinning, like tumblers in an unlocking safe. She has been dismissing him as a somewhat cute, moderately useful handyman with unfortunately no real prospects. Now she is forced to reevaluate. He is somebody, possibly. Not a big somebody you could recognize because you saw his picture a lot in the papers or on some important television show like *Entertainment Tonight*. But, somebody that somebody else who is a somebody would recognize. That is some kind of somebody, isn't it?

Funny how she never noticed before just how astonishingly good looking he is.

* * *

As soon as Matt arrives in his apartment, he starts spreading newspapers and old sheets on the floor. He feels it is important to minimize the mess, if only because he doesn't want Jillian to see the tell tale signs of Finnegan's painting technique. What if she tells someone? He might be exposed! Damian wouldn't even pay him for painting his walls, let alone his drop sheet. Finnegan, who had been moaning dejectedly by the door until he came in, is placated with a large bone his master has brought from the butcher's. He chews contentedly while Matt works quietly to prepare the work surface.

Finally he places one of the canvases dead center in the room, on top of a piece of insulating foam, so that his hulking dog won't just tear through the canvas when he steps on it. Matt opens three tubes of paint, squeezes their contents into separate Styrofoam dinner plates and stirs water into them to create a more liquid mix. (Matt's kitchen is stocked with hundreds of Styrofoam plates and bowls, so he'll never have to wash up.) He places them strategically around the canvases, spilling a little as he reaches across. Then he tip toes over to Finnegan and removes the tartar bone the dog has been gnawing at contentedly and throws it half way across the room, onto the other side of the canvas. "WWWWrooof!" Finnegan half growls, half barks. Confused, he pads over the newspapers and drop sheets, looking for his bone. It doesn't take long for him to discover that the potential for making a mess has just been placed before him. He tentatively sniffs at the colors, then puts a furry paw onto the edge of one of the Styrofoam plates. It springs back, spraying his chest fur with orange paint. "Arrwoof" barks Finnegan, now starting to get intrigued.

"Here Finnegan. Here Finnegan. Come get the bone. Come fetch..."

Finnegan gallops across the canvas, spilling another plate of paint, this time black, onto another section. Just as Finnegan approaches the left side of the canvas Matt throws the bone across to the right upper corner. Finnegan bounds back, tramping across the red paint, and clawing at it, making rhythmic but haywire markings this way and that.

Matt checks his kitchen clock. No time to waste. For another quarter hour, Matt plays fetch with Finnegan's tartar bone across the increasingly filled canvas. Then it is a quick wipe down for Finnegan and on to the next canvas, which Finnegan paints in record time because Matt deliberately dips the dog's left front paw in a pan of green, and the right paw in a pan of purple. Then he places a large glass marble in the middle of the canvas and taps it at one end so that it slowly makes its way across the canvas. Finnegan pounces on it in full predatory mode, scrambling unsuccessfully to grasp it as it rolls around on the white background and in so doing blends the two colors. The overlap makes a strong grey-black color, which Finnegan's claws score with tight scrawls that resemble pen scratchings.

Matt decides the painting is done, and drags the reluctant and howling Finnegan into the bathroom to give him a thorough cleaning.

From several apartments away the daytime occupants can hear Finnegan's resentful howls as the water strips the artist of his medium.

At nightfall, while most of Toronto is hurrying home through the traffic, Matt is racing against the current as he makes his way back downtown to the gallery with the two paintings, checking left and right as he makes his way down the apartment building's hall and out the door. The fewer people he has to explain anything to, the better.

* * *

Madeline decides to call Jillian to find out if Daddy did, in fact, cover her sister's latest credit card disaster. She has grudgingly accepted that, despite her having children and many more expenses, Jillian is entitled to perpetual care, like someone invalided by the shopping channel. Jillian answers her vibrating cell phone in a whisper.

"Madeline, I can't talk right now, I'm working."

"What, filming?"

"No, silly. My regular day job. I'm currently seated at an out-of-the-way table behind a large fern in one of the city's poshest downtown restaurants, wearing a black wig and a Burberry trench coat, courtesy of my employer. It's fabulous. I might get reincarnated as a brunette. They even bought me this fantastic new phone with a built in camera. It's great, I can take tons of pictures of myself and download them straight onto the net."

Madeline has an instantaneous vision of her PC's mailbox being crammed to capacity with thousands of pointless jpegs of Jillian's nostril, Jillian's ear, and other grotesque, digitized, out-of-focus treats, produced at arm's length by none other than Jillian herself in a frenzy of misguided self-worship. "I need to talk to you about Daddy."

"Well I can't right now," she whispers. "Oh gosh. Here she is."

"Who?"

"The woman I've been paid to spy on. Damn. I don't even think this camera-phone is powerful enough from this distance. I'm going to have to dig through my purse and get my camera with a telephoto. Shit.

I can never find anything in there. Damn phone."

Madeline is treated to the sound of a loud crash as the cell phone is dropped on the table, then some heavy breathing as Jillian continues to forage in her bag. (Jillian is a sophisticated bag lady, who carts around all personal necessities in case of earthquake, doomed love affair or government collapse.) Jillian adjusts the lens on her tiny camera, then retrieves the phone.

"Oh my God, Madeline. I only just broke up with the man she's with. He ditched me for a tart in a cheesy off-the rack shirtdress. How could he do that? Wait a minute. He's giving her a present." Jillian zooms in on the package. "That bastard. That's a much nicer present than the one he gave me a month ago. The cheap lying scheming bastard. The cheapskate."

"Jillian get a grip. Quiet down! You're supposed to be working." In her own home, the children are working themselves into a cyclone of fighting. Madeline grips the phone tightly and prepares for hysteria in stereo.

"I'm so mad I could burst into flames. I could Madeline, really burst into flames! I'm so furious. Who does she think she is? And him! I have a good mind to call his wife!"

"Jillian, what did you expect from a cheat? For that matter you were going out with a married man. What did you expect?"

"What are you saying Madeline? What are you trying to imply? I have standards. I have a moral code. After all. I'm single. I'm not the one cheating."

"Oh for God's sake, Jillian. Stop acting like he was your late great knight in shining Armani. He was a cheat. He is a cheat."

"You're telling me he was cheap! Look. I can't talk right now," she says sullenly. "You're going to have to rake me over the coals later. I have to work." And with that, she shuts the clamshell phone and tosses it into her massive purse. The nerve of that Madeline. The nerve of that man! So cheap.

> *"One should never make one's debut with a scandal. One should reserve that to give an interest to one's old age."* -Oscar Wilde

EIGHT

IN FLORIDA'S PROMISED LAND

Big Daddy lies in bed thinking, assessing as he listens to the sounds of the RV park waking up: the troops of senior ladies taking their early morning gossip/walks, which revives the constitution and replenishes depleted stores of venom. He can hear the cough and wheeze of late model Oldsmobiles being readied for shopping expeditions. And he can almost set his clock by the sound of his next-door neighbors' first argument of the day. Amid the shouts of, "I tell you that son of yours is a bum!" and "Don't you call Charlie a bum. He's just had a run of bad luck," Big Daddy is checking the state of his general health.

Toes still wiggle pretty good. Legs can still bend up a stretch. No numbness there. Fingers, he thinks. He fiddles them a little. Still not too sore, not numb. Right shoulder still attached, but just barely. Back aching. Butt sore. Head pounding. God. What had made him do it? He had met up with a bunch of wild and crazy senior women from Omaha and been convinced by the youngest of them to go para-sailing.

His giddiness could not have been helped. He had been taking a late afternoon stroll near the shoreline but close enough to the wintertime residences and condos and small hotels that he was able to spy on new arrivals and occasionally make the acquaintance of same. The group was sitting under an awning, their needlework projects laying across their generally ample thighs as they chattered gaily about their departed mate's bad habits and the current lack of men and their demands. They might have looked like something out of a Norman Rockwell painting if it weren't for the garish, brightly colored touristy muumuus and oversized straw hats that did a substandard job of protecting their pale mid-western faces from the brutal Florida sun.

Enter Iris, a platinum blonde sixty-two-year-old who didn't look a day over fifty-nine. She had gone straight through her second childhood and was working on her second adolescence. Hence the para-sailing. She had seemed impressed by his daring-do until he had been yanked crudely off the dock with his right arm still casually draped over the pull rope. Big Daddy had been too busy waving and puffing out his chest feathers to notice the boat's engine was revving up for take-off.

He has followed this assault on his system with happy hour at the ladies' beach-side hotel. Hence the whisky shooters hangover. Maybe he was getting too old for the singles scene.

Brring. Brring. Big Daddy fumbles for the portable phone, which is nestled in its caddy on the bedside table. Brring. Brring. He fumbles with the phone's tiny buttons in the twilight of his Beaver's bedroom.

"Mummph?... Hello..."

"Daddy."

Big Daddy feels a shudder of dread. It is Jillian. "Daddy!" she squeals. "How are you?"

Now he is really nervous. Jillian only asks how he is when she is seriously in need of cash. That or she is experiencing another wild fluctuation in her romantic wave patterns. He doesn't know which he dreads more. The money grab or the play by play of her amorous roller coaster rides, which always end badly. Big Daddy braces himself, resisting the urge to bark out, crudely: what do you want, and asks instead, gingerly: "What's up? I'm not really in the mood to talk now. I'm still in bed."

"Now Daddy. You're not sick are you?" Her tone is curt but solicitous.

"Not really....I'm just..."

"Good," she interrupts. "I have news. I'm getting two auditions this week."

"That's wonderful sugar. Awww. And you thought to tell me. How nice." He wonders if she got the sarcasm. Probably not.

"I'm going to need to go shopping."

"Why on earth? You're not auditioning for the shopping channel are you?"

"Of course not Daddy, what made you think that? No. I just need something really *au courant* to wear when I try out for the part. I don't have anything appropriate. I was watching *What Not to Wear* and *Ten Years Younger* and I realized that my clothes are just not young enough for me to get the young lead."

"Your clothes aren't young enough? Are you sure that's the issue? Maybe you should be trying out for something more in keeping with your real age. I was talking with Madeline the other day and she said...."

"Maddy? What the hell does she know? She's ancient. Why she's a specialist in antiques, for God's sake."

Big Daddy continues, forging out of the fox hole and into No Man's Land, "And she said you ought to think about finding the right guy and getting on with your life. That's what you should be thinking about instead of trying to pass yourself off as an eighteen-year-old."

On the other end of the line Jillian is sputtering. The truth is she has already been shopping and needs the money to pay for it all or else she'll have to take most of it back before it bumps her credit card bill seriously over its limit. Quickly, she considers a lateral maneuver. "It just so happens I have met someone. Someone important. A real somebody."

"Not another playboy," he whines in irritation. Damn it. Why didn't he get that vasectomy after Maddy was born?

"No. Not another playboy. He's an artist. His show is opening tonight, in fact. He'll probably make lots of money. If I'm going to go to the opening, I'll need to wear something really special so I'll stand out."

Big Daddy sighs. His head is pounding. "God Jillian, I can't think about this right now. I'll send you a check for a grand and that better cover it. Now let me go back to sleep. I spent all of last night doing shooters with a bunch of retired hookers from Omaha." And with that he rolls over in the bed, shuts off his portable phone, returns it to its caddy and presses the -hold- button so no calls could interrupt his hangover.

On the other end of the line, Jillian sits facing the frosty window in her still darkened room, (the winter sun rises much later in the morning in this northern clime). As she holds the telephone receiver in her shaky left hand, (in precisely the same way she had for her nearly successful *Dial M for Murder* stage play audition), she considers this latest piece of news. Her father has probably not properly grieved her mother's passing. Why at times he has seemed positively gleeful to be single again! No less than a week after the funeral he had traded in the tastefully appointed family home for a trailer and made plans to decamp to an RV park in Florida. The humiliation of her father living in, as he put it, his Beaver. And now this!

It is time to stage an intervention.

* * *

"Maddy... Maddy, have you talked to Daddy lately?"

"Just a few days ago. Why do you ask?"

"I think he's gone off the deep end. I was talking to him this morning and he told me he's been shooting up with hookers. This is what comes of being holed up in the Pearly Gates RV Park living in some tin can with nothing but the Early Bird Special and a new set of elastic stockings to look forward to."

"Daddy? He said that? You must have heard him wrong."

"I swear to you. He's blowing our inheritance on some old hookers from Omaha. And God knows what else. Those trailer parks are the waiting rooms for Purgatory. Who knows what kind of deviltry they'll get up to when old men think the grim reaper is lurking!"

"Well. I don't believe it. I'm sure he's just trying to get your goat. He's very concerned about you, you know."

"That's right, Maddy. Make this all about my issues. That's just like you..."

"I'm serious. He's worried that you're letting life pass you by while you chase after a shooting star."

"Well I'm not. Everything is unfolding according to plan, actually."

"Whose plan would that be, Jillian?" Madeline is starting to cast an eye around the kitchen for her children, Charles and Diana, who have now scattered, leaving a trail of chocolate chip cookie crumbs in their wake. The counter has several damp, buttery imprints where the purloined cookies had been. The house is suspiciously free of noise. "You kids get back in here! Sorry Jillian, where were we?"

"Daddy living in his stainless steel suppository and chasing after lewd old gold diggers."

"Oh that. Well. My feeling is, after the many years he spent attending to Mom and her tremendous craziness, he has every right to chase around with whomsoever he wants to chase."

"But Madeline."

"Jillian. Dad can handle his own retirement. You're the one we all need to be concerned about. There you are in your thirties..." Madeline could now hear a gasp on the other end of the line, "You're not getting any younger."

"No!"

"You live in an apartment Daddy rents for you. You have no full-time job and no job training. And you still haven't got a steady boyfriend."

"Well you're wrong!" Jillian says defensively. Glancing out her window she spots the super loading some garbage in the building's dumpster. "It just so happens that I am seeing someone right now!"

"Seriously?"

"Would I lie?"

Madeline considers this possibility. Truth be told, Maddy is never able to say with certainty whether anything that Jillian says is true or not. Any kind of answer to a problematic question is prone to trigger some creative truth telling, with the embroidery of the story sometimes bordering on the absurd. (This is particularly true of her financial dealings). In contrast, her sister has always been too forthcoming with the details of her love life. So much so that family members now try to change the subject whenever she starts to recount the blow by blow of yet another breakup, or the startling-to-her revelation that yet another man has turned out to be flawed. Is Jillian actually 'seeing' someone, as in dating? Or has she just said she is 'seeing' someone when really all she has meant is that the poor sucker is in her cross-hairs? It is anybody's guess.

From the other end of the kitchen a chair topples, complete with two year old Diana, who immediately breaks into loud, convulsive wails. Charles is standing over her menacingly, holding the last cookie high over his head. Madeline shouts into the phone as she hangs up, "Jillian, I have to go. Those two are fighting again. I'll catch up with you later."

Once again Jillian is left on the wrong end of a dead phone line. What is she going to do? She takes a calming breath. She counts to ten, and trying to remember the advice in that *Cosmo* article she skimmed, she summons her angels. She looks out the window at yet another snow squall whipping up. She examines her perfectly manicured nails. She fluffs her recent coiffure and examines her highlights in one of her mirrors. Truthfully, she has never been able to figure out which is her best side. They are both spectacular, she concludes. Jillian can hear the distinct sound of barking, the steady drone of something vibrating inside the building.

It is all very simple. She pushes her feet into a pair of kitten heeled mules, reapplies her Chanel lipstick and exits her apartment door. All down the hall, she can hear the sound of Matt and his dog bouncing around inside their own apartment. Are they playing catch in there? Inside the building? Is that a rubber ball she can hear bouncing off the walls? Or the dog? Jillian shakes her head and knocks on the door. A disheveled Matt opens the door, looking flushed from some kind of activity. He is dressed in a shirt that would have been more suitable for making Molotov cocktails some time ago. She suspects he has been creating a masterpiece. The process of creation seems to be a noisy one. He glistens with sweat. He is gorgeous. She fixes her mesmerizing gaze on Matt, and for an instant, says nothing as her captivating stare works its well-practiced magic. There is one thing about Jillian that is absolutely authentic. She has the most remarkable pair of turquoise eyes, a trait which she shares with both Walters, father and son. So intense is their blue, so iridescent are they, that people feel compelled to wonder if they are real. "Are they yours?" people would sometimes blurt out.

"Who the hell else's could they be?" she'd snap back.

But why not ask that question? Much of Jillian's beauty is the result of intense and purposeful grooming, medical intervention and overworked credit. Not that she ever admits to any of it. She would daintily answer any aesthetics-related questions with a qualified, sporting response along the lines of: "Not that I've ever had anything done myself, but I wouldn't deny any woman the right to self-improvement, if she felt she needed it."

And women 'in the know', women who had themselves stealthily crept off to the plastic surgeon's for a little boost here, a little nip there, and then subsequently denied all intervention, would nod significantly. As if they believed her avowals as assuredly as they hoped others would believe their own. They knew the truth. Twenty, thirty years before, there had been two kinds of girls in their school: the girls who did and the girls who didn't. Now, decades later, women of a certain age can still be divided into two different camps: the women who did, and the women who didn't. The only difference is that we are talking about two completely different things being done.

And so, ironically, the one thing of beauty that is authentically, legitimately hers, is the one trait which people are absolutely certain is the result of cleverly tinted contact lenses.

Matt stands at his door, held captive by Jillian's gaze, looking like the crumpled, flustered mess that he is. "Sorry about the noise. I'm trying to tire Finnegan out a bit. I have to go out to the gallery's show and I wanted him to sleep."

She ignores the comment and scrutinizes his profile. He really is quite striking to look at, she thinks. Except for his clothes, which appear to have been retrieved from a hamper, and smelled faintly of damp dog hair. Once he is whipped into shape, they'll look good together.

"...so he wouldn't bark and disturb you." Matt prompts, smiling.

"That's not necessary." she responds coyly, quietly, with her sweetest well-practiced smile. She'll have to make a project of him. She'll have to take him shopping. This is essential, in her books, if they are ever going to make a fantastic gorgeous power couple.

"It isn't? But I thought you were worried about Finnegan's

barking..."

"I won't hear it," she replies, looking him square in the eye.

"Why not?"

"Because I'm coming with you," Jillian says with the certainty born of expensive, perfectly aligned teeth and a statuesque, surgically-enhanced figure spray painted to a healthy glow.

"You are?"

"I am. You don't have a date, do you?"

"Well, no...actually...I"

"You do now."

∽ NINE ∾

FORTUNE SMILES UPON US

Matt can't believe his luck. He realizes as soon as he crosses the threshold of the gallery that Jillian is the perfect, impressive arm piece that completes the illusion he is trying to create of a worldly, up and coming artiste. It is as if she has trained for this role her whole life. There is something mysteriously electrifying about her, thinks Matt. She almost causes an atmospheric change wherever she goes- like a gale whipping up force off the coast, or a burst of positively charged ions just before a lightening strike, or a whirlwind that would soon suck up everything in its path and turn it into a tornado. From Matt's point of view, and limited life experience, this is all to the good.

Let us examine our hero for a moment as he comes to grips with the turn his fortunes have taken. Only a few nights ago he was a bum bouncing from one badly performed odd job to another, with a bit of intermittent poop scooping on the side. Now he is on a date with an actress, no less, a woman who is if nothing else a legend in her own mind, and decked out in a wardrobe that surely she could not afford if she isn't making top dollar in some television drama or other. With her by his side, and his insouciant air (resulting from his natural sloth, and combined lack of wardrobe sense, color coordination and a proper hair cut), he gives off a decidedly Bohemian, artistic aura. He is a man on the move. His friend Josh's jacket has once again been pressed into service. It is a handy choice since Matt has not yet taken it to the dry cleaner's. (His life has been a whirlwind since Lana dumped him.) As a finishing touch, Jillian has insisted he wear a silk scarf a former lover had abandoned in her apartment, (during a rather frenzied exit). The scarf makes Matt feel decidedly silly and he toys with its loose over/under knot nervously, but Jillian has reassured him that artists wear scarves whenever she sees one profiled in *Vogue*. He doesn't feel qualified to argue with that.

He is met with enthusiastic handshakes and congratulations from people who, for the most part, are too busy posing themselves to bother checking out his artistic credentials. His original intention in going is to satisfy his curiosity. That and to partake of the free champagne and munchies. (Matt's highest culinary achievement is Kraft Dinner). Would any of Damian's clients believe that his paintings are anything other than drop cloth accidents? That Finnegan's frantic claw marks are artistically valuable? Or would none of them want to be put in the embarrassing position of pointing out that the emperor is wearing no clothes? Matt looks at two people standing in front of one of Finnegan's canvases from the day before. One is rubbing his scraggly 'soul patch' which resembles a worn shoe brush glued onto his chin. He is saying repeatedly, "The tension, the tension." The other stands there with crossed arms, remarking:

"...astute...profound...crisp...original..."

To which the other replies, "But how will it look behind the coach?"

Matt suppresses a laugh and goes in search of another hors d'oeuvres tray. (He has been slipping the less gooey items into Josh's jacket pockets, for later consumption at home.)

Jillian meanwhile has discovered that the design show television crew from the previous day has returned for the party. They are her new best friends. She has determined this after working the room with all the precision and determination of a heat seeking missile. As she strikes an elegant pose next to the producer of this refurbishing orientated program, (sponsored by three major retailers of household products), she takes note of the fact that her date's paintings have attracted quite a buzz. The gallery owner is standing in front of one applying a red dot to the side of it. Has it sold already?

Could it be? Could this rumpled, albeit handsome handyman really be the next new fad? Could she have stumbled upon a winner despite herself? How has he kept this from her? How has she missed the vital clues that would have tweaked her radar? It is certainly puzzling. Previously he had struck her as a layabout who was determined to fail at life in as many ways as humanly possible.

Matt isn't sure what he feels about Jillian. But one thing is certain. His blood pressure raises thirty points in her presence. Could this racing pulse be the famous chemistry his friends have always told him he could one day find with a woman? Could she be the one? To be truthful, Matt has never been much of a romantic. Women simply decide that he is worthy of their attention, and then decide (rather quickly for the most part) that he is not. Gentle reader, Matt's three year personal endurance record with Lana can most likely be put down to Lana's mother's proxy matrimonial panic, which served to turn off Lana's powers of discernment well past Matt's usual 'Best Before Date'. Romance for him is a lot like being a fish in a stocked pond with a well-established catch and release program. Periodically he finds himself being hooked, reeled in, and then doing a half-assed job of following along the relationship dictates until he is deemed to be not a keeper. What does he know of being swept up in a grand passion?

He just counts himself lucky to occasionally make it into the net.

* * *

Jillian is thrilled. She has finally met a man who is both single, good enough looking to satisfy her ego, and apparently successful. These are the magical three requirements for admitting that she has bagged a potential mate the next time she speaks with her older, (read: judgmental, punitive and superior) sister. Maddy is always critical of Jillian's constant fretting about a man's looks. What does she know? She can't wait until Maddy realizes how wrong she has been about her sister. Three days after the gallery's Wednesday opening, Matt is to have a mention in the Saturday *Globe's* 'Arts and Entertainment' section, tucked into a story about the show. This is the first, and usually only part of the weekend paper she ever reads. To see the name of a man she has singled out for special attention suddenly appear in the *Globe & Mail* that very week, seems to her to be the stamp of approval for her choice. He is apparently not only an artist to be reckoned with, she has snagged him before the pesky competition catches wind of his availability.

And, even better, two of his works were sold on opening night by the gallery, and they have asked him for at least a half dozen more paintings. At several grand a painting, that makes for a very profitable week. She is already dreaming of the nights on the town to celebrate, and the presents he will buy her.

What she will have to change about him however is his astonishing cheapness, sloth and general lack of initiative. The night after the gallery show, when he had already received word that another of his paintings might be sold, he could only be coaxed out to dinner when it became apparent that Jillian couldn't cook and he had run out of cheap Eastern European beer and no-name potato chips and therefore had nothing to eat at home. They went to a local sports bar, where, in the absence of an NHL game, the room took on the atmosphere of a funeral parlor anteroom. Not that she had expected it to fulfill any romantic fantasies. But in the absence of beefy guys yelling: "shoot, shoot," or alternately, "hit him!", it did have a certain unexpected intimacy. Jillian could hardly concentrate on her rib steak and fries as she tried to conjure up an accurate memory of the last *Cosmo* survey designed to determine if a man was 'the one' or not. She decided, that if she couldn't find that back issue on the floor of her spare room's closet, she'd just have to play it safe and act coy. She didn't even grimace when he paid only his half of the check.

After the sports bar, when he returned to the apartment building with her, she said goodbye when they reached their floor, with a near-virginal kiss and an explanation that she needed to get to bed early because the next morning she had an important audition, followed by a photo shoot. Matt played the moment as coolly as she did, leaving her feeling a little nervous and needy. Should she have turned up the wattage a little on that goodbye kiss? No, not yet. It is always hard to know how to play these situations. Jillian always wants to be in control, and she is smart enough to realize the utility of acting coy, and seasoning these interactions with a little frustration. The next day she tore over to the library and scanned biographies of famous artists, to get an idea of the kind of tributes that their mistresses received once the geniuses achieved success. It was quite intriguing. Some were quite generous, but there were a few cases where being an artist's muse backfired. Rodin's mistress ended up in a nut house, she learned. And as for posing nude so that her beauty would be immortalized, she wasn't so sure. What if she ended up looking like Picasso's mistress, all bent out of shape and sideways. Boy, she thought, that mistress must have been some pissed off at Picasso after that. Unless, perhaps the mistress had pissed off Picasso before he even did the painting. Yes, that must have been it. She'd have to be careful not to drive Matt up the wall before she posed for him, if she didn't want the wrong things immortalized.

* * *

The next evening the phone rings while Jillian is busy examining her pores after a stressful day of posing and smiling. This is harder than it sounds: to hold an animated look perfectly still for an agonizing several minutes at a time, to fake an emotion in mid-expression and then repeat that exact same expression with minute modifications for hour after hour until you felt that your face would break, is far from being natural. It always soothed her to get into a really hot tub, so hot that lobsters could meet their doom in the water, and then afterwards settle into a little exfoliation and squeezing. So rigorous has been her program of purging her face of any flaws, that there are hardly any pores left on the surface of her skin. But still, she attacks the project with all the vigilance of a SWAT team.

She slowly emerges from the vanity table and drifts over to the phone. At this hour of the night, it is hardly going to be an agent. And anyone else knows enough to let it ring until Jillian feels damn good and ready to answer.

"Jillian it's Walter!" Jillian casts a quick glance at the phone's caller ID, trying to ascertain where he is from the area code. One never knows. Walter is like the Jack in the Box that she had received as a small child from a clueless uncle. She had obediently set it on her lap and turned the crank, as directed. Suddenly a horrifying clown popped out of the box, with a hideous maniacal laugh, its head poised on a spring and bobbing back and forth drunkenly. She had disliked clowns before the box incident. Afterwards, she was terrified of them. How like a Jack in the Box is Walter. All it takes is a slight turn of some mysterious crank and out he'd pop, unexpectedly, acting like a clown and scaring the crap out of her.

"Walter! Where are you?" She tries to sound pleased and unafraid.

"I don't know if I want to say. Can you be certain that this phone line is safe?"

"Safe from what, Walter?"

"I'd rather not say." Walter hums distractedly on the line, then sighs. "O.K. I'm headed to Moscow. I'm meeting some...scientists there."

"Then what did you call to ask me?"

"What do you think of time-shares?"

"You call me in the middle of the night to discuss holiday properties in the Urals?"

"Not that kind of time-shares. What do you think of Dewars?"

"It's yummy. I love Dewar's, especially when I have a cold. It's Daddy's favorite whisky, you know. You should buy some in the duty-free on your way back."

"Not Dewar's. For heaven's sake, Jillian, don't you know anything? A Dewar flask. Named after the first guy to liquefy hydrogen. It's a kind of chilled vacuum container. I can get a deal on a set from this guy in Russia that uses them to cryogenically freeze brains. For fifteen hundred I can store ten brains on a group plan. Then when the time is right, they can be thawed and their personalities uploaded into a really good computer."

"Oh God, Walter. I'm not in any big rush to freeze my brain."

"Don't you want the possibility of living forever?"

"After all the money I spent on this body? If I can't take it all into the freezer with me, I'm not going. And I'm certainly not sharing space with anybody else. Sharing a jar with Madeline and the kids would be just too gauche."

"I'm hurt. I had really thought you would be the forward thinking one, Jillian." Leave it to her to let vanity get in the way of a good thing. After that, the conversation goes downhill, except for one small piece of news.

"Daddy's off his rocker," says Jillian. "We're going to have to go down there and talk some sense into him."

"Why will he listen to me?" asks Walter. He already has some difficulties getting the family patriarch to take his side.

"He's taken up with a geriatric gold digger from the mid-west. You better get down there soon, if you know what's good for you."

"Will he want some Dewars for the both of them?"

"If you're talking about booze, maybe. If you're out to sell him a fridge for his brain sometime in the future, I suspect not. She'll probably have his bank account cleared out by then."

"Good heavens! Something has to be done! As soon as I return from my...ah...speaking engagement, I'll have to get down there."

Walter hangs up while still worked into a lather. Jillian is satisfied. She is no fool. Of course Walter is not going to be able to talk sense into Daddy. But with any luck, that retired hooker from Omaha would get one look at Walter and take off. If the gold digger knows what is good for her. Only someone barking mad would take on a family like Jillian's. She is certain that she, Jillian, is the only sane one in the bunch.

* * *

"Madeline! He's rich!"

"Who?"

"The guy I was telling you about. The painter."

"The guy *you say* you're going out with?"

"You say that as if you don't *believe* me," says Jillian defensively. It is her ability to strike this defensive tone that always effectively deflects criticism from her. It is one of her most effective survival strategies. "In any case," she continues. "He's mentioned in the *Globe!* His paintings caused a real stir. Several in the show have already sold! Can you believe it? And the others all have people interested."

"What does he paint?"

"Hummm. I don't really know exactly. Damian, that's the gallery owner, called him an abstractionist, post-expressionist whatcha-macal-lit. You wouldn't believe that writer in the *Globe!* She seems completely taken with his genius. I can't figure out what she's saying!" At this very moment Jillian is clutching the story in her hot little hands, hyperventilating.

"So you don't really know what he painted? You were looking right at it!"

"He's like some kind of Picasso, or something. The first one that sold was called, 'Fetching.' Cute, huh?"

"I see."

"You're just too old fashioned, Maddy. You think that if you can't recognize real things in a painting, that's it's not art."

Maddy's head is spinning. She is discussing the definition of art with Jillian. With Jillian, for God's sake. It doesn't get more absurd than that. "Jillian, what is art?"

"For one thing. Art is something that matches your curtains and goes well in your living room. At least that's what's selling. Isn't that what matters?"

A groan comes over the phone line.

Jillian then quickly changes the subject. "I spoke with Walter."

On the other end of the line Madeline launches into a coughing fit. She chokes out, "Voluntarily?"

"Of course voluntarily. Nobody made me do it."

"Where on earth is Walter?" Her voice lowers, as if she doesn't want Roger hearing her.

"Who knows? I tried to figure out from the area code, but I didn't even recognize it. He said something about heading to Moscow. I told him about Dad," says Jillian. "You may not be concerned, but I'm really worried."

"You have a lot more to worry about than I do."

"What do you mean by that?" Jillian lashes back.

"Dad does send you money, doesn't he? If he took up with, as you put it, some old hooker from Omaha, the financial apron strings might be cut."

Jillian responds with a moment of dead silence, then a consumptive sputter. "Madeline! I'm shocked. Gobsmacked. Hurt. How can you make this sound like something that *only* concerns money? I'm talking about honoring the memory of our dear Mother. How are you going to feel if Big Daddy installs some seedy interloper in her place? This is about a lot *more* than *a little bit* of filthy lucre."

"You're right. It's about the entire bankroll."

"Now you're talking. That old hooker could be out at this very moment spending our hard earned inheritance."

Madeline snorts on the other end of the line, "Hard earned?"

Jillian forges on, nonplused. "Madeline, it was Mom's money too."

Madeline considers this gem of wisdom. It is true that it was also

Aurora's money. In that case, it is a hard earned inheritance indeed. Why her progeny's psychiatrists' bills alone are monumental. Staggering.

It has been Madeline's good fortune to be the less pretty of the two sisters, and therefore passed over for much of Aurora's narcissistic mania. Madeline had, in early infancy, one short-lived episode of being the centerpiece, the bouquet as it were, in the midst of Aurora's many madcap photo sessions which masqueraded as family life. But with the birth of her younger, more promising sister, Madeline's brief career as a focal point came (happily) to an end.

Is this why Madeline has managed to retain her sanity while all about her the rest of the family has been trained to behave like a dog and pony show whenever a camera is pointed at them? Madeline has a flashback to her mother's deathbed scene. It was a short time before her demise, when the cancer had rendered speech impossible. Aurora had pointed weakly to a notepad and pen that lay on the bedside table next to the wadded up Kleenex and the dog-eared copy of *People* magazine. Madeline handed it to her, thinking her mother wanted desperately to express some last wish, and watched as she scrawled out feebly, her dying words- *how do I look?*

How can Madeline expect anything less of the daughter that is virtually Aurora's clone?

Jillian now launches into her boldest plan. "So. As I was saying, I was talking to Walter. He said he was headed out of the country for some big deal convention or something, and when he gets back, he'll help us plan something."

"Oh Good Lord. Not Walter!"

But before Madeline can outline the many reasons why Walter should not be called to action in this battle, Jillian is gone. And Madeline is left standing there, holding a dead phone line. Gentle readers, you need to know that by now Maddy has discovered Walter's personal weblog, where his illusions of grandeur are given free reign. It is called the *Sanctum Fact-orium*. In it, Walter is able to broadcast all sorts of news and views from his electronic pulpit, to replicate his lunatic theories with alarming ease. It is like adding sugar to a bucket of ever-expanding yeast. With each passing day, his site receives more hits from potential lunatic followers, feeding his malignant self-love. Salient tidbits are as follows:

- An apology for his earlier foray into survivalism and Armageddon prophecy which consisted of selling substandard canned goods from a warehouse in central Texas in anticipation of a millennium holocaust. (His site failed to mention that since the canned goods had already reached their expiry date before they were re-labeled with gimcrack religious symbolism, Walter bought them on the cheap.) This should have yielded enormous profits but, sadly, because the world didn't end, it instead triggered a U.S. federal audit, for which he was heartily sorry.

- A description of an inter-galactic flight with the Angel Gabriel to check out missile silos from Colorado to Titan.
- Paranoid rambling about men in white coats, the C.I.A., the F.B.I., CBS and the President.
- A smattering of testimonials by people who are currently financing his efforts to clone beloved family pets and other experiments to freeze relatives for future thawing.
- A brief outline of his exulted lineage that proved he is a direct descendant of Moses, and therefore as good a candidate as any for the second coming.
- A call for female devotees, (between ages twenty-four and thirty-six, hopefully with large breasts, good cooking and people skills.)
- A searing rebuttal of his federal audit, and a threat to fight on, if apprehended.

He has come so far. At one time, he had merely been a follower, in what Madeline used to call the 'Church of the Month Club.' Now, thanks to the power of the internet to indulge his grandiose fantasies, his malignant self-love, he has his own club. The web provides a vast hall of mirrors which can infinitely reflect Walter's inflated persona. A witless coterie of minions who can feed his fascination with himself. There are even books written by former, now-estranged devotees, exposing him as a false prophet. For the low price of seventeen ninety-five, plus shipping and handling, Madeline could read exactly why Walter was not a god.

There are no prying neighbors who could point out, as in the past, that the boy down the street was off his rocker. Long gone are the days when people had to parade their craziness in such a way that they would be promptly apprehended. It takes so much more than that to call public attention to his delusions. And in the meantime, there are ever more deluded people, just shy of the requisite megalomania to become leaders themselves, who are willing to follow.

* * *

It's important to understand where exactly Madeline is coming from. Growing up in a family where appearances are everything, she has tried to focus on detecting the real from the fake, finding the antiquated silk purses in a sea of old sow's ears. She had spent her early childhood years fantasizing about days of old when men were gentlemen and women were ladies, and really good gentlemen were knighted.

Madeline was the only little girl in her high school with a subscription to both the British *House & Garden* and *Majesty* magazines. She has an impressive set of commemorative Royal tea service cups and saucers. The highlights of her collection are her cups from the Royal Wedding of the Prince and Princess of Wales, (some of which had been discounted off at second hand stores following the infamous royal split). But Madeline is a true believer. She keeps the faith, she holds the course. It is undeniably true that this fairy tale romance was a mere chimera, only smoke and mirrors fed to a hungry press. Sadly, she thinks, the press also fed off its collapse. But she has not turned away from her Royalist fervor, even though the marriage had not worked and its tragic bride was chased to her death by crazed photographers eager for a buck. She tells herself, if it weren't for the gossip mongering, rapacious press, it could have recovered. It should have. So she keeps on collecting. And subscribing to the Royalty obsessed press, which paid the paparazzi's outrageous fees. When she gave birth to her first child, it seemed only natural to name him after her original Prince Charming. And when his birth was followed by that of his sister two years later, Maddy didn't think twice about naming her baby Diana.

It is however unfortunate that sibling rivalry has spoiled the idyll so that Charles and Diana are constantly at each other's throats. Friends have mockingly suggested that if she ever does, (God forbid), give birth to a third child, she should call her Camilla. Madeline's husband, Roger, threatens regularly to get a vasectomy. In the meantime, he has taken up golf all summer long in a club that barely tolerates adolescents, let alone children. During hunting season he has the perfect excuse to retreat to a shack in the deep woods in search of wild game and solace, with a pack of similarly encumbered friends who spend more time stalking the wild single malt than firing a hunting rifle. As long as one of them bags a deer or a moose or something, their collective escape route remains open. In the winter he plays gentlemen's hockey, (that's hockey without the potential for assault charges), three times a week. The rest of the time he sequesters himself in his study, refurbishing model boats and practicing the obscure sailor's art of scrimshaw. While all around him the chaos of his home goes on unabated, Roger is painstakingly carving intricate designs on bits of old walrus bone, passed down to him by his grandfather. That gentleman managed to have thirteen kids, and could barely remember their names.

Roger has a vivid memory of Madeline's sainted mother, as Jillian likes to portray her. He has only to glance at his wedding photographs to be transported back to the event where the grand reveal had taken place: the entire family having conspired to keep her a secret until the very last minute, lest he decide to run for the hills. There in the dead center of every wedding shot Aurora stood, bridal couple board-checked forcefully over to the far corner, camera pointed directly at his new mother-in-law, by royal decree. Aurora was a maelstrom around whom everyone writhed and turned. How had they managed to keep her hidden away like some deeply buried trinket in the bottom of the *Cracker Jack* box? His head spun every time he recalled her storming into his house, both barrels firing, as her husband Big Daddy tried to wheedle some solace out of his stroke-inducing bargain. With no success. And then, as if by some miracle, she was gone, leaving in her wake a huge messy gap, like low tide after a storm surge. And suddenly, after decades of holding so many people's peace of mind at ransom, she has been recast as a saint. Someone who is sorely missed.

Because, frankly, the truth would be just too embarrassing. The truth would make the truth teller look bad.

And it is all about how it looks.

"If at first you don't succeed, failure may be your style." - Quentin Crisp

❦ TEN ❧

AN OVERNIGHT SENSATION

Matt stretches out on the park bench watching his dogs romp. He is half awake, silently counting out the number of spectacular failures of which his life is composed. There is no accounting for at least some of it. One thing has always been certain. He has a special gift for screwing up. Improbably, and through no effort of his own, his long run of crash dives may have come to an end. Can he help feeling nostalgic?

He sighs. Life has been good, nonetheless. He owes much to his personal charm and his good looks. And he admits to himself, it helps that his mother has been able until recently to blackmail his father into continued 'child' support as he stumbles sluggishly through his university studies in fits and starts. Actually accomplishing anything of note has always loomed as an alarming and not altogether welcome possibility. Why, anything could happen if he actually managed to succeed at something. Expectations would arise. People would begin demanding things. He shudders to think what life will be like if he has to start shouldering burdens. As it is, he can scarcely remember to keep Finnegan's feed bowl full, and cold beer in the fridge.

And now, ironically, his dog has made him a success of sorts. Written up in the *Globe*, no less. Actually the dog is the success. With several paintings now sold, Matt has to accept it is more than a fluke. In fact, he soon might have to rely on Finnegan's paintings to pay the bills.

When he considers it, even dog walking comes with its own set of worries. Here it is mid-February and he is now worried about the wayward habits of one of his prize pooches. Cleopatra is now obviously pregnant. The humping incident was just after Christmas. If Matt guesses correctly, she has two weeks to go before it all comes out, for better or worse. Her swollen abdomen hangs low, and her stubby little legs can barely keep her burden from dragging on the slushy ground. Her owner is almost frantic with notions of future champions dancing in her head. If Cleo has not been knocked up by the purebred date her owner had lined up for her, and is instead carrying the illicit mongrel progeny of the scruffy and ill-mannered Bartender, all hell will break loose among his snooty clientele. Can he sink lower than being black-listed as a dog walker?

Matt casts a furtive glance at Bartender's owner, who is shuffling along on the other side of the park, advancing unsteadily toward him with a small brown paper bag. How had he become such a broken man, he wonders? Had he always been such a basket case? How then had he ever attracted his ex-wife, the tightly wired and perfectly coiffed owner of Cleo? Maybe he had once been a shining king of industry. Maybe the owner of a sports team, or an investment banker, or a real estate developer. Maybe it was the loss of the brittle ex-wife with the withering stare that had laid him low. Maybe it was success itself, with all its attendant terrors, that had done him in. Then again, it may have been the contents of the little brown bag.

He is standing in front of him now, proffering his bag. "Pretty cold out today," he says, by way of striking up a conversation.

"Yup," Matt answers lazily, cautiously.

"Care to take a drink out of my paper bag? Warm you up!" the man says encouragingly.

"Nah. I try to limit drinking from a paper bag to late afternoons and evenings."

"Nothing wrong with it!" Bartender's owner says defensively.

Matt is now nervous about where this is heading. "Oh no. That's not it. Just watching the calories, you know. The calories..."

"You're one of those Atkins people."

"Yeah. Atkins, right."

"Oh well that's all right then." Bartender's owner seems satisfied. He sits down next to him, surrounding him in an aura of stale cigarette smoke, whisky, and damp wool. "Randal Sommersby the Third," he says out of the blue. He thrusts a stubby, gloved hand at him. "I know you... Didn't my dog hump your dog just before New Year's?"

Matt looks at him cautiously. "Funny you should mention that."

* * *

Big Daddy stares out of the porthole over his Beaver Patriot RV's kitchen sink. Had he really done what he thinks he did last night? He takes another sip of instant coffee and looks at the calendar duct taped to the side of his Beaver's tiny kitchen cupboard. It's the fifteenth all right. Making yesterday Valentines Day. Oh good God. It was no dream. He has proposed to Iris.

How has it come to this? Was it the magic of the warm Florida evening, made even more enchanting by the certain knowledge that everyone back home was freezing their butts off? Was it the nostalgic music at the local Senior's Center? The paper cut out Cupids? The hot pink and red decorations, which matched the red icing of the dietetic cake? Could it have been the manly, confident thrill of leading his partner around the dance floor? Of doing the *cha cha* with the lovely and eager widow from Omaha, who unlike his other women did not shuffle around on swollen blue-veined ankles, but rather actually stepped lively in time to the music? Perhaps it was the sense that he had the potential to sweep her off her nimble feet that had emboldened him? Either that or the six *Cuba Libres* that he had imbibed while showing off to her circle of friends.

Now he remembers. Most of them were headed back soon. They gave many hints about the significance of Valentines Day and cast him in the flattering light of 'young suitor' for their delightful companion. They prodded him with reminders of their tour bus's imminent departure. As the rum and coke started to slow down his trips to the dance floor, and increase his trips to the bathroom, he began to grow morose. Then there were the unflattering florescent lights of the center's bathroom. As he slowly washed his hands at the sink he caught a horrifying vision of himself, and realized that he was no more attractive than Rodney Dangerfield just before he kicked the bucket. How much longer, he asked himself sadly, before another new widower came to the RV park to take his place among the hopeful and the desperate old ladies who were trying to beat the odds in the geriatric remarriage game? When were the cookies and bridge invitations going to run out, he asked himself in a rum-induced panic? He moved closer to the mirror. His bulbous nose was covered in burst corpuscles. His puffy eyelids had more folds than a ruffled tuxedo shirt. His tan was really just a mass of liver spots that had melded together. How much longer could his good looks last?

If he could find someone to love him, someone to wash his socks and tolerate his snoring and something-died-up-there flatulence, someone who wasn't wheelchair bound, crabby or incontinent, he had better latch onto her fast before that bus pulled out of town. Big Daddy concluded he was in love, checked that his fly wasn't open and forged out of the men's washroom into the subtle pink twilight of the Senior's Center.

Now, a full twelve hours later, he is getting cold feet. At this point in his life, romance takes on a grim, Mexican Standoff kind of quality. What if she has the health crisis first? Then, instead of him being taken care of, he'd be stuck shuttling her around from one specialist to the next, from medical appointment to therapist, and so on. He wanted first dibs on that wheelchair, Goddammit. If someone is going to have his drool mopped up, it damn well better be him.

After all, he has already paid his dues. He had been married for forty-two years to Aurora, and had only occasionally considered murder. As he weighs his options, he feels the need for sanity, for cooler heads to prevail. He reaches for his phone and dials his elder daughter.

* * *

Two hours later, Madeline is able finally to reach Jillian. She had been out getting prodded, waxed, buffed, polished, pedicured and spray painted. The whole half-day process had left her breathless but ready for her five minute organic all-natural oven cleaner infomercial. "I have news," Madeline begins. "You'd better sit down."

"It's Daddy isn't it?" Jillian asks dramatically as she rummages for a Kleenex in her brand new, perfectly darling Prada bag that only cost Daddy five hundred bucks. "Oh my God!"

"Yes. It's Daddy."

Jillian composes herself and gets ready for a good dramatic cry. "O.K. I'm ready. Tell me." She places her hand over her heart, expectantly.

"He's engaged."

"WHAT?" Jillian wails back into the phone. The shock is too much for her. She has been expecting something straightforward, like a heart attack, or a stroke. Maybe even a little touch of prostate cancer. Not this! "What are we going to do?"

Madeline is resigned. "You know. I'm of two minds. On the one hand, I can't imagine why a woman as reportedly youthful and attractive as Iris supposedly is, would want to marry someone like Dad..."

"Iris...her name is Iris? Did he mention the hooking again? Is she the one he was carrying on with last week?"

"He's not clear. He said something about wheelchairs and chocolate chip cookies and bridge club invitations and bed pans. He seemed a little confused..."

"That's it! We'll have him declared incompetent!" Jillian can feel a rush of relief at this thought.

"As I was saying, Jillian, on the other hand if he can find someone to make him happy, who are we to interfere?" Maddy doesn't even want to respond to Jillian's suggestion. Who wanted to open that can of worms? Big Daddy may have been nuts to want to remarry after forty-two years with her mother, but she couldn't exactly think of him as mentally incompetent. Just fatally amnesiac.

"I can't imagine what he could be thinking of. How could he do this to Mother?"

"Mother is dead, Jillian."

"Funny, you sound just like my therapist when you say that."

"Well, she is. You're expecting maybe that Dad should wear her mummified foot around his neck until he's dead?"

A pause. Then a sigh. "I wouldn't go that far. But I think he shouldn't be thinking about remarriage. There's something so...so...complicated about it. Do you really think he can be trusted to make this decision alone?" Jillian titters nervously, as if she has a very slight suspicion that she is exposing too much of her own interest in the matter.

"He's a grown man, Jillian. Why shouldn't he decide who he's going to marry? He made up his own mind about our mother after all."

"My point exactly."

* * *

"Madeline," A breathless Jillian bursts out into the phone during another, late night, frenzied call. "How much cash do you suppose Big Daddy has?"

"I couldn't hazard a guess. The house must have been worth a lot before he sold it. And then there was the garden tractor business, the snow blower division, the investments..."

"But look at what he's living in now!" Jillian counters. Already she is fishing around in her purse for her calculator and a small note pad, as she listens to Madeline enumerate the crucial details.

"Those trailers can cost a quarter mil' sweetie. The house was worth at least three times that, maybe four times..."

"Seriously?" Jillian gasps, amazed. "For a stainless steel suppository? A tin can? That hulk? Why on earth would he choose to live in one of those instead of a house?"

"Daddy may just want to keep things simple. Feel like he's on holiday. Make sure his money lasts as long as he does."

"How long do you suppose he'll last?" Jillian gives a nervous little laugh, and quickly tries to gloss over her *faux pas*. "I mean, it will last? I mean, do you suppose he has enough to last him? Until he no longer is lasting...I mean."

It is a distinguishing feature of Jillian that she has learned to skate backwards with one foot planted firmly in her own mouth. And even if she doesn't manage to pull off a perfect pirouette, she is able to convince, (at least herself), that her diversion and sidestepping tactics make her actions less than transparent. Embarrassing disclosures of self-interest, narcissism or greed therefore can be dismissed from memory almost as soon as they slip unguarded out of her mouth. Madeline calls it 'embarrassment amnesia'. Aurora had been the past master of this conversational maneuver.

Aurora taught Jillian everything she knew.

⊗ ELEVEN ⊗

THESE LITTLE TOWN BLUES

Matt is feeling particularly low today, as he approaches Diva's door. So many things are weighing on his mind that an outside observer would assume he is the head of a large corporation, under federal investigation. Here is a sampling of what is on his (hungover) mind:

Casey's owner has accused Matt of giving his dog a cold. To quote: "Unless of course, you've been exposing him to cats! You don't have a cat, do you? I won't have anything to do with cat people!"- Casey's owner had hissed in as hostile a tone as an asthmatic could muster. He proffered him the leash with a gloved hand.

Finnegan seems at the moment to have lost interest in messing around with Matt's paints. Is it creative pressure? Could a dog feel creative pressure? Does he need to start plying him with alcohol à la Hemingway? Is it the exhaustion of having to make a dozen canvases in six nights? How long would this dry spell last? Finnegan isn't telling, and Matt, never having had a creative streak, doesn't know. Not that Matt hasn't tried to get to the bottom of Finnegan's creative slump. He had spent an entire evening encouragingly dipping one of Finnegan's front paws in a dish of paint and coaxing, "Hey boy...can you think of anything you want to do with this? Huh, boy?"

To no avail. Finnegan looked at him lazily, sniffed at his paw, and then slumped down on the drop sheet and fell asleep, his paw still dripping blue green paint. Matt had finally cleaned the acrylic paint off his pet's paw, before it dried. Since the paint was already mixed, he tried a few tentative brush strokes with one of his house painting brushes.

But, in the words of someone like Damian, the results didn't grab him. He 'didn't know what to say'. His 'artistic vocabulary' isn't 'fully realized'. He is struggling with his medium. He didn't have the faintest clue. Matt is panicked. -This is what comes, he said to himself, of reading a few newspaper critics. This is the result of starting to take their praise seriously, of starting to crave their approval. Finally, he becomes too aggravated by the sleeping dog's loud, self-satisfied snore and he leaves the room, grumbling, "That damned dog never *has* to read a review." Matt cracks open a beer and proceeds to polish off several more cans before passing out on the coach watching the sports network.

That night he has a nightmare of himself walking aimlessly around Danforth Avenue in search of the perfect Souvlaki, while off in the distance packs of dogs howl in unison to the tune of *New York, New York*. These days he can't get that song out of his head.

To top things off, less than a week after a very promising beginning, Jillian seems to be unusually preoccupied with some kind of crisis that her father is undergoing in Florida. He can't make out if her dad is getting married, committed or freeze dried. Perhaps it's just a clever excuse. Perhaps Matt is headed for a very premature dump from her, breaking previous records by several weeks.

And there is still the problem of Cleo and her upcoming delivery. If his dog doesn't paint any more, Matt has nothing to fall back on but the dog walking business. If he is known to get pedigree pooches pregnant by just any mutt, even that is headed for failure. How much lower can he sink, now that his father isn't going to bail him out?

Isn't there some other college he could get into? Isn't there another chance to get back into his father's good graces? Usually, when he makes a mess of his life he just grabs a university calendar and takes the path of least resistance. But who will let him in now that his reputation has preceded him from one department to the next? He just doesn't know any more.

He knocks on Diva's door with outright dread.

"Oh look Diva! It's Matt!" Diva takes one look at the approaching leash and runs to hide under the kitchen table. "Look sweetie!" Diva's mistress looks back at the awkward Matt, still standing at the door. "She missed you the other day," she says reassuringly as she chases after the dog and pulls her out by her stubby knob of a tail.

Grasping the animal in her hands while four fuzzy little legs kick reluctantly to get away, her mistress continues: "She just doesn't like going out much when it's cold. Don't ya baby? Don't ya? Come on honey, sing for Matt!" she commands, as she breaks into *New York, New York* again. Matt squirms uncomfortably and tries to extricate the wailing dog from her grasp.

Even as he makes his way down the elevator, with the still howling Diva, he can hear the off-key echo in the elevator shaft of "These little town blues, are melting away..."

* * *

While Matt sprawls out on the park bench, he does a rough count of the days since Cleo's little misadventure. It is nearing the end of the third week in February now, and Cleo and Bartender had their fling in late December. That means Matt has less than two weeks to go before all hell could break loose, if the puppies turn out to be the wrong sort. Matt suspects, that since the high-priced third generation champion stud was likely from an extremely limited gene pool, his sperm might contain the lack-luster dribblings of inbred stock. If she had been with both dogs, what kind of sporting chance did the pedigree dog's sperm have? Was it merely a question of timing? Or would the rival sperm have duked it out somewhere in Cleo's reproductive tract?

Matt suspects that some kind of subtle hormonal signal that Cleo is 'up the stump', as Matt puts it, is now being sent telepathically between his collection of canines. Casey and Finnegan in particular are compulsively digging deep pits in the half-frozen muck and snow every time that Matt's attention is diverted elsewhere.

On this day, Matt is also minding a Neapolitan Mastiff named Ralph, the much beloved pet of a noted plastic surgeon. Ralph figures prominently in the family portrait in the surgeon's downtown office foyer: all of them have faces pulled so tight they look like they are in the draft of a jet engine. In stunning contrast is Ralph's massive, baggy face, which seems to serve as a stern warning about the perils of atrophying facial muscles and their attendant slack jowls. Ralph seems to be completely unaware of the size difference between himself and Cleo, even though his drool-saturated face hangs around the little barking mutt like pleated drapery fresh out of a soapy wash. He too has commenced digging with a vengeance in response to Matt's general disinterest in amusing them.

Are these pits supposed to house Cleo's illicit progeny? Do these other dogs imagine that they have done the dreaded deed, and in a great rush of paternal emotion feel compelled to burrow to China? (There are times when all anyone can see of the dogs are the top halves of their heads, as their eyes peer out from their fortifications. In Ralph's case, as his head bobs up and down, his jowls perform a little flapping motion which sends slobber flying far and wide, like mops in an automated car wash.) Matt finds himself constantly having to redirect their energies elsewhere, and has taken a Frisbee to the park by means of distraction. It puts a pall on his day's outings, however, since instead of his usual quasi nap, he keeps having to shake off his Seasonal Affective Disorder to chase them away from their digging. Sometimes, he just gives up and leaves them to it. The dog park is beginning to look like an exploded minefield.

It is a beautiful late winter day. Although the wind-chill is making it biting cold, with the cloudless sky, and no snow in the day's forecast, people are grateful and many dogs were out in the park. In Toronto, in mid-February, one can't expect much better perhaps.

"Cold enough to freeze the brass balls off a Christmas tree, eh?" The sun is so bright it is almost blinding. It takes a moment for Matt to realize that the man standing before him is Randal Sommersby the Third. He holds his whisky out before Matt like a kind of sacred offering.

"You said it." This time, Matt takes a sip from the ever-present paper bag, then hands it back as Sommersby takes up his post next to him on the park bench.

"Tough way to make a living?" Sommersby says sarcastically, indicating the pack of burrowing dogs with one hand as he grasps his disguised bottle with the other. Another glug goes down the hatch to banish the chill before he returns the bag to Matt. Bartender bounds over to greet the other dogs, tail waving energetically.

"Beats the stock market," Matt replies, taking another sip. "Course, there can be problems."

"Tell me about it." Sommersby exhales sadly and tilts his head back, pouring the whisky down full force. "Up the long ladder and down the short rope!" he says, before suppressing a belch.

In defiance of all good common sense, Matt has decided to confide (some of) his woes to the perpetually quasi-drunk owner of Bartender. It only takes a minute to confirm what Sommersby has suspected all along.

"Cleo?"

"That's right."

"Elizabeth's Cleo?" Sommersby asks excitedly.

"That's right."

"And you're sure she was in heat?"

"I'm afraid so."

Sommersby slaps his hand on Matt's knee, and lets out a loud hoot. "That's fantastic! I finally got the bitch! Never underestimate the redemptive value of revenge. Hah! This calls for celebration. Let's get out of the cold. I know of a bar near St. George's where they'll let you take your dogs."

"No kidding?"

"Seriously. It's my place."

Sommersby's condo is in a surprisingly decent building, which for some reason allows his mutt entry by the front door. The condo association only made the request that he use the service elevator to take Bartender in and out, away from the view of the other residents. This time, he and Matt have to smuggle in a few canines extra, but everyone appears to be either away at work, or hunkered down for the winter, somewhere south of the forty-ninth parallel. His furniture and in particular his dining room sideboard/bar is particularly impressive for a worthless drunk. The only peculiar piece of decor is a dartboard sporting a digitized wedding picture of Sommersby and Cleo's mistress.

* * *

Big Daddy has had about enough of women. Somehow he has been hornswoggled into letting Iris move into his RV when the rest of her crowd left town. As a fiancée, she is turning out to be less fun-loving than he had hoped. After all the partying, drinking, and all manner of hilarity in the run-up to their engagement, Iris has suddenly turned staid, upright and uptight. It is as if she has gone through a process of mystical revirgination.

He has found himself having to give his nice comfy bed to his fiancée, who suddenly reverted to being an old fashioned girl who insisted that she wouldn't share a bed with a man until she is 'good and married in the eyes of the Good Lord'. He has a sore back from sleeping on the cramped coach in the RV dinette. Not even married- he thinks- and already I'm in the dog house. The only good thing about it is that Iris performed a sweet little ritual every night, tucking him in with a bowl of ice cream. Then she pads down to the other end of the RV and shuts the door.

He spends the nights tossing and turning, and imaging the comely and petite Iris in her nightie on the other side of the thin door dividing the sleeping quarters from the rest of his mobile former love palace.

He doesn't know whether to be impressed by her moral rectitude or bugged. (After all, he has argued, "It's not as if you could get pregnant!" Iris resented the suggestion, and Big Daddy, falling back on old husbandly habits, shut up and went along with her plans). In the Beaver Patriot's bedroom Iris has already installed her huge make-up case, a suitcase full of shoes and a hand made rug she had brought all the way from Nebraska. It features a four-sectioned parody on Andy Warhol-style pop art, this time with four high-chroma images of her deceased cat.

Both his daughters had called this morning to harass him over the upcoming nuptials. Apparently it has already become the occasion for some sibling tug of war. Worse yet, Jillian, kept asking him annoying questions about his general state of health and sanity.

Madeline's husband, who fancies himself an amateur Spielberg, wanted to know if they would all get to converge on his Beaver, (including the demon children, Charles and Diana), ostensibly so that Roger could film the grand event. Then Roger wanted to know if he *could leave* the demon children there in the RV park with their arthritic and hypertensive grandfather while he and Madeline took a brief winter holiday! That suggestion left him with throbbing veins in his temples. He quickly took an extra blood pressure pill, (washed down with rum and coke) just to be on the safe side. (Funny how Aurora had never had high blood pressure, mused Big Daddy. She must have just been a carrier).

Madeline, (who seemed resigned), was more subdued during the call. Her chief concern was his personal happiness, countered by the potential for Walter and Jillian to make a scene. She proposed that Big Daddy and his beloved skulk off to Vegas to tie the knot.

"I'm not going to dress up like Elvis to get married, Goddamnit!"

"I'm not saying that, Daddy. I'm just saying that lots of people decide that it's the best way to just get remarried with the least amount of fuss."

"So you're ashamed of me is that it?" he had shot back defensively. Madeline had backed off just as Big Daddy realized that he didn't really want any kind of fuss made at all. But now, if he didn't make a fuss, it would seem as if she had won. Big Daddy hated losing. He had done it way too often.

Jillian's call followed. She seemed torn. On the one hand, she acted like he had gone senile or was committing post-mortem adultery. At first, she spoke to him alternately like a health professional dealing with a child, or a proxy for a wronged spouse. On the other hand, in the face of her father's apparent determination, Jillian was entranced by the occasions that the wedding created to go shopping in a really big way. After all, she wanted immediately to know how much "all this holy acrimony" would cost and how big a budget he had. And how much of it she could help him spend.

Walter, thankfully, is still AWOL. Otherwise, Big Daddy thinks, he might have threatened to officiate the wedding as a minister with the Church of the Gone Off to Some Other Planet With the Other Intergalactic Nut Bars.

Maybe he is cryogenically frozen somewhere and Big Daddy will be left in peace to run barefoot through Iris's artfully tinted head of platinum blonde hair.

✧ TWELVE ✧

A DAMSEL IN DISTRESS

Matt sits munching on a bowl of granola and staring with a glazed expression at the Weather Network, considering the unfairness of life. Josh's mother's car is on the fritz, possibly for a week, (more if Josh's mother expects Josh to shell out some money to help pay for the repairs). And here is meteorologist Chris St.Clair smiling and explaining in his gentle, pedantic way about Lake Effect Snow and Weather Bombs and dropping millibars and predicting the best damn blizzard of the year. And he can't get out to the ski hill. What is the point of snow if you can't ski on it?

On top of this, when it snows this heavily, his dog clients start feeling too sorry for their canines to send them out for those lucrative walks. Truth be told, the city will only be good for dog sledding, so he can see their point. There is no hockey on TV. And Finnegan is still in a creative slump. He hasn't painted for almost a week, even though Damian is demanding more and more. So Matt has absolutely nothing to propel him out of his apartment except cabin fever, and the need to restock his fridge with cheap Bulgarian beer.

But just down the hall is Jillian, waiting to pepper him with questions about famous artists and the women who inspired them. Matt knows this because when his dog had started whining and scratching at the door to be taken out for a pee at seven in the morning, she had pounded on their adjoining wall. As aggravating as she is, it's sweet how she worries about Finnegan so. Even though their own auspicious beginning was threatening to sputter out. Is it over before it even begins? Did Jillian just use him to get to the gallery opening? Is there no room in her busy glamorous universe for a man like Matt? He decides to find out. Sneaking past the sleeping Finnegan, Matt slips out the door and pads down the hall to Jillian's place.

"Hey," he says when she opens the door. "Big storm coming."

"I heard," she replies looking at him coolly and deciding that his outfit is all wrong. Will she be needing to have her balcony cleared if she isn't going to be in town for the storm- she wonders as she glances at his arm muscles. Matt just stands there while she mulls over what to say. He watches as her eyes roll once, as if she is following a bouncing ball. She thinks- who can think of a good response to some line as lame as 'hey it's snowing in Toronto in February, go figure eh?' -and another thought -can I be *seen* with this man dressed like this? But despite her perfectly-executed eye rolls and silence Matt is still standing there in his threadbare sock feet and baggy jeans looking at handy convenient Jillian. He doesn't even have to spend cab fare to see her. This is more to the good, and takes away much of his reluctance to get off his coach and go see her. Is something this perfect doomed to fail? She finally opens her door wider. "Want a coffee?"

Matt enters to find her apartment in a state of wild confusion, with several large suitcases open on the floor and shoes strewn everywhere. "Going somewhere?"

"Florida, actually. Tonight. Hope we'll get off the ground before the blizzard hits."

"Didn't know you were planning a holiday."

"It's not really. My father is *thinking of* getting married." Suddenly she has a thought. It isn't a very big thought, or a very deep one. But it is a thought. And when Jillian has a thought that isn't about fashion or grooming or jewelry, it is marked by its rarity. It forces itself into her conscious brain, sometimes causing momentary lightheadedness as if too much blood has just traveled to an unfamiliar territory inside her cranium. What if she were to bring a supposedly steady, unmarried and therefore eligible, boyfriend down to Florida? Maybe her father would be so distracted by this unheard of occurrence, by the possibility of at long last unloading her and her spending habits on some other man, some other bank account, that she'd have a chance to think of some way to get that wedding called off. At least until she could convince Big Daddy to get that old hooker Iris to sign a pre-nuptial agreement.

As she stares at Matt lovingly over her Nescafé, she sizes him up. How easy would it be to get him to play along, she wonders? She wouldn't want to have to spell it out in blunt terms. Just coming out and saying, "Hey, want to come to Florida to help me foil my dad's wedding plans?" is an impossible thing to say without coming across as a scheming manipulative cow. Besides, there is something so very wrong about being so direct with a man when being indirect is equally, if not more effective. Instead, she considers strategy, as she rolls her eyes some more. Finally, she exhales seductively and says in a soft voice, "The weather here is going to be a real drag for the next few days."

"That's what Chris St. Clair says." Matt eyes her brightly, hoping to be invited to her bed to cheer her up. After all, it's been known to get the Eskimos through a bad winter.

"So," she clears her voice. "If you don't have anything much to do, why not grab a stand-by seat on my flight and come down to Florida with me? Somebody in Daddy's RV park should be able to find us a place to stay. And the weather there is terrific. You could just putter around the beach, meet my Dad. Maybe even play a little golf with the old man. After all it's just going to snow and snow and snow here."

"So Chris St. Clair says."

All Matt has to do now is convince Josh to take on Finnegan for a few days and hop on a plane headed south. It's not like Josh would be doing much other than digging out his driveway. And then Matt could take off as free as a bird. And he wouldn't have a care in the world.

* * *

"Well. That settles it," Madeline mumbles as she replaces her telephone's receiver.

"Huh?" says Roger, who has one eye on the television while he is making himself a club sandwich. For a few brief moments the children are napping, shoring up their energy for their next assault on their parents' sanity.

"Jillian is going down there to throw the kibosh into Daddy's love life."

"To Florida?" Roger can scarcely hide the envy in his voice. "She's going to Florida? Now?"

On the television Chris St. Clair is carefully explaining how the jet stream works and how Roger and Madeline's fate is all tied up in the mess that is currently bearing down on Toronto. It will reach them a day or so later. Secretly Roger has already been searching the net for the cheapest fares possible to Florida, driven not only by a desire to escape the cruelest week of the cruelest month, but also a desire to stand shoulder to shoulder with the man whose fate has also been tied up with the family's crazies. From the day he had met Aurora, Roger couldn't help but feel Big Daddy's pain. Madeline may have been sane, but she has expended an inordinate amount of what should have been marital energy dealing with the lunatics in her family. He considers his father-in-law's decision to remarry as fool hardiness akin to Russian Roulette. A perverse impulse urges him to witness this ritual sacrifice up close.

"Oh Honey, we should go. I mean. It's your dad."

"But they haven't even set a date yet, let alone decided *how* they are going to get married. And I hear that Iris is already living in Daddy's RV. Maybe they've decided to be modern and forego the formalities. Besides, who would they invite to a big wedding anyway?

Most of the potential guest list is probably already six feet under."

"Good point. Still. Even if your father has decided to live in unwedded bliss," (at this last comment Roger sniggers a little, imagining the old man draped in chunky gold neck chains and soaking in a Playboy Bunny-saturated hot tub), "I think we should go meet your new step mother and make a show of support, what with Jillian going down there and all. And if Walter shows up..."

"I think he's off at some genetics forum or other..." she shudders. The last time she saw him, he was talking about cloning people from the scrapings on the inside of mouths.

"He just might surface. Especially if Jillian's worked him up into a lather."

Madeline glances from Roger's eager face to the television, which is now showing a clip of snow plows and houses buried up to the second floor of a family home. Children are exiting the bathroom window and sliding to the ground on their bellies. From Roger to Chris St. Clair and back again to the sliding children. It's funny how she feels her fate is never in her own hands.

"What are the odds of us finding a baby sitter for the kids for a week?"

"Zero. Our last sitter switched to an unlisted number."

"So we'll have to take them."

"I'm afraid so."

"Hmmmm." Madeline casts her memory back to Jillian's last traumatic visit, the pretense she made of loving the kids. "Of course, with Jillian down there we can always pressure her into playing auntie. That should give us an afternoon off at least, before she and Dad start planning an exorcism for the kids."

"At least. An afternoon off."

"Let's do it."

* * *

Walter is quite pleased that his sister had told him about the family meeting in Florida. He has lately been rethinking his business plan to build stainless steel capsules that he could shoot into space with its deep-frozen human pre-remains. It might be a good idea to check out the space center and look into eventually renting space, kind of the way less developed nations shoot up space satellites as pay-per-payload passengers on NASA rockets.

-It is possible, thinks Walter. -Why not? Lately his cryogenics proposals are gaining interested people. It just seems like a much more attractive package. It has more copy appeal. Let's face it, Walter tells himself, people are much more likely to sign up if they think that when they have themselves stuffed into one of these steel torpedoes that they would be flying, passenger style, to the Pleiades Star Cluster or the Hale-Bopp Comet, or where ever the hell else it is that they are supposed to go to in order to get superior medical care to that offered in Beverly Hills or the Mayo Clinic, for example.

But we digress. Walter tells himself these plans, ruminates on them, dreams about them. And then, in some deep recess of his cerebellum, he starts to believe in them. Once he voices these ideas to an underling, and there are more each month, it takes on the luster of reality. The more he discusses these ideas with followers who parrot them back, the more credible they become. Let's recap one of these encounters:

"Reverend, I may be so bold?"

"Please feel free," replies Walter as he struggles to remember this new member's name, "Ask whatever you wish."

"How are we going to pay for the cartage on our capsules?"

"We'll have a raffle." This idea having come to him just seconds before.

"A raffle?"

"Well yes. There are plans already afoot to set up auctions to let people take a trip in space. Why not a raffle?"

"For the pre-dead?"

"Sure. I'm sure that they'll be easier passengers to handle. No in-flight meals, no complaints about the movies. No lost luggage. that kind of thing."

"But these people just get to orbit the earth and whatnot." The minion shook a little. It was imperceptible to Walter but enough that the minion became even more worried. That perhaps his lack of faith would reflect badly, would influence the great leader, the reverend to shun him and seek out another member to answer telephones, lick stamps and dodge phone calls from federal agents.

"What was that?"

"It's just that...I'm not sure there is a planet close enough for NASA to get to...where terminal people will be able to get the medical cures they need."

"I'm not talking about now, Harold. I'm talking about the future! My plan is to eliminate death in the future! That's it! That's what we have to explain to people. That instead of dying, they'll get to wait around until the next time that the stars and planets are in the right alignment, and their lottery ticket comes up and then we'll just park them on a pay-per-trip flight up there to the best damn hospital in outer space. They can wait, fifty, a hundred, two hundred years if that's what it takes, Harold."

"But they'll have paid for a guarantee."

"And that's what they'll get. A guarantee that they'll get a shot at life everlasting as soon as medical science on Mars or whatever catches up. And the beauty is that when they've deposited their life savings with us, we'll make a tidy little fee all the while."

"That does sound logical, Reverend."

"I knew you'd see things my way. My church is the first to directly combine banking and death as a profit center."

"Yes, you're right, reverend. A tidy little fee. Like interest at the banks."

"That's right. Interest for fifty years can really add up Harold."

"Yes, it can Reverend."

"But won't these people's heirs complain? Make a fuss...take you to court?"

"What was that? What heirs are we talking about? This is the beauty part, Harold. People won't really die. They'll be in suspended animation, and all the while, the potential that they could be thawed will mean that their assets can't get handed over to anyone else."

"That's brilliant. You're a genius, Reverend."

"I think so too."

"But won't there be long drawn out court fights?"

"That's true," allowed Walter. "But here's the beauty part. All the while the lawyers get to charge a big fat fee. And our contract says that the lawyers for our clients are paid for by our clients. The lawyers for the other side are paid for by the so-called heirs who are trying to get at the cash but haven't yet. Sooner or later, the heirs will get tapped out."

"How do you know that?" asked Harold, who struck Walter as being kindly but dim.

"Simple. These sorts of things can get tied up in courts for decades. It is an unwritten law of the universe that lawsuits never ever get resolved until the cash runs out. And of course, our lawyers will have a much bigger pool of cash to draw from. The opposing side will have to drop out long before our clients' lawyers' fees eat up all their money."

"That is beautiful."

"Make a note to myself, Harold. See if we can't start a legal center ourselves. The one hole in my plans is that so far, I've been unable to attract any lawyer types. Critical thinkers don't seem to go for cryogenics Harold. We've got to make life everlasting come with a guarantee that they won't end up just going to hell. If we want to attract lawyers, I mean."

* * *

Madeline spends the afternoon in a frenzy digging out summer clothes from the deepest recesses of her basement. She also has found two disturbingly tight bathing suits which she had purchased after giving birth to Charles and before she became pregnant with Diana. They both make her look like a package of Pillsbury cookie dough that has contents oozing out of both ends. She used to be as skinny as Jillian, but after the pregnancies, she discovered that unlike Jillian, she could not on a daily basis stuff her fingers down her throat to purge supper and thereby regain her shape. This has served to enhance Jillian's tendency to be critical of Madeline's appearance. Roger is nonplussed. (In truth he didn't mind the fact that there was more flesh to grab.) Over the years, Madeline has become resigned.

"Did you know," she tells Roger, who is busily scanning Florida brochures in the bedroom while Madeline stands amid a heap of discarded clothes, "That the great sixteenth-century painter Peter Paul Rubens actually used male models to make those Rubenesque nudes? He'd pad them up to look like women, more or less, and away he'd paint. Otherwise, the church would have pounced upon him."

"And your point is?"

"Just that, when someone says a woman is Rubenesque what he's really saying is that she looks like a chunky guy with falsies."

"I didn't need to know that."

"It's comforting in a way."

"Why?"

"Well. I still look like a woman. As opposed to a chunky guy with falsies."

"Is that why you became an antiques expert? For these little tidbits of history?"

"Perhaps so."

Later that same night, Madeline reveals to Roger that her sister has supposedly bagged a new man, who she is bringing to Florida.

"Another man about to undergo an extreme renovation?"

"She said something about him being absolutely perfect and a genius." Madeline stares at her bedroom ceiling, recalling former 'Mr. Jillians'. "Do you suppose she's actually discovered there's more to a relationship than how they look together in the pictures? Do you think this guy might have some actual character?"

"Can't be." Roger observes, "In Jillian's book 'character' is another word for homely. Besides, when she falls for someone, there's always something terribly wrong about him, that she feels driven to fix. Or, else he is a replacement Daddy who she'll drop once she's depleted his funds. Generally speaking, if a decent man actually falls for Jillian, she is driven immediately to question the soundness of his judgment. On that basis alone she usually throws him out."

"Maybe she's come to her senses," allows Madeline. "After all, her biological alarm clock sounded a couple of years back..."

"And you think Charles and Diana played a part in that?" Roger asks, incredulous.

She pauses. Attempting not to consider this last comment too seriously, she speaks softly. "I'm just so relieved."

"Why?"

"To be married. To have kids. To not have to agonize ever again about whether or not I should have them, or when I should have them. Or whether or not I'll meet a guy. Or whether he's the right guy. I'm just so glad to be married and saddled with the little buggers. So I'll never have to give men or kids another thought again."

"Glad I could be of service," says Roger, as he rolls over and turns out the light.

* * *

The next morning Roger feeds his father-in-law's parameters into a web site featuring a survey conducted by the University of Chicago in 1992. It is entitled, *"No Sex, Please"* and claims to determine just how frequently people do the nasty, based on their gender, age, politics, income, education, number of small children and marital status. Initially he is comforted to learn that he was 'over his quota' of 1.49 shags a week. That is until he fed in Big Daddy's potential parameters as a geriatric newlywed. He'd be getting more than twice Roger's weekly allotment.

THIRTEEN

GOING FOR BROKE

Damian is irritated, even though he should be thrilled. He has a naive and eager new artist to promote, and paintings to sell at a whopping forty per cent commission. But it is so unfair. The *Globe* article hadn't mentioned a thing about Damian's outfit, and the reporter had generally given the gallery's refurbishment short shrift. And yet, the reporter, an impressionable young female journalism graduate, had waxed euphoric over Matt's work.

She practically had to be exfoliated from that slob Matt after she had finished interviewing him. Damian is driven to ask why life has been so unfair. Matt is just another in a long list of people who have been unfairly favored by that bitch Mother Nature. Through no merit of his own, that human version of a stray dog looks like an unkempt Greek God. He doesn't care if his shirt is unironed and has pulled out of his waistband. He doesn't bother with hats or sun block or moisturizers and yet, the fine traces of lines actually add to his allure. His hair is no doubt cut in a cheap walk-in Barber Shop, for God's sakes. But it curls rakishly, and without the aid of 'product' while Damian pays ten times as much to the most chichi salon in Yorkville to get his hair done and it still turns out wrong.

All the work that went in to being a Metrosexual! The scrambling and cash that it took and is still taking In order to one day land on a 'Best Dressed' list. And then some fool of a designer undoes it all with another grungy distressing kick complete with 'bed head' hair, that makes slobs like Matt look like they are *avant garde*. Designers are just jerking us around, he thinks.

His only solace is that he is making a bundle off the guy, who seems to have no business acumen whatsoever. He not only doesn't know what his art is worth, he has no inclination to even try to find out, either.

Now, just when things are starting to take off, his new artist is leaving the country. Damian knows something has to be up. The only reason that he could think of is the shrewd female barracuda he had come to the show with. She had spent the entire opening networking. What else could it have been about? Is she taking him to Florida to meet some hotshot Palm Beach art dealer? Damian has no idea how to get to the bottom of it.

Maybe he'd have to give him a better percentage.

Life is so unfair.

*　*　*

Jillian is out of sorts. This entire trip to Florida had got off on the wrong foot. The first thing was the crisis about buying the plane ticket. This was entirely the fault of the January sales, which had recently maxed out her credit cards to the point that the last infusion of cash from Daddy was only the merest drop in a very deep bucket. She found herself unable to pay for the flight until she had rifled through her closet for impulse buys which still sported the price tags. Then she had to scurry off to the shops where she had purchased said items and try to wheedle a refund out of the staff when they were far past the date when a refund was normally permissible. It's a good thing that she was on close, intimate terms with the staff in all these stores.

One bright financial note was her decision prior to Valentine's Day to cancel her standing order for a massive bouquet of roses. Always thinking ahead, Jillian customarily sent herself three dozen red roses with a coy card which claimed they were from a secret admirer. This year, because she had been between boyfriends and therefore had nobody to make jealous, she decided to spend the money instead on an extra spa treatment. Surprisingly, when the day came and went and no flowers arrived, she felt a small pang of remorse. She always did enjoy the whole business of getting flowers from an unknown suitor, even if her secret admirer was none other than herself. (She consoled herself with a box of Godiva Chocolates and a bottle of *Veuve Clicquot* champagne.)

She doesn't have much time to think about regrets now. She has arrived at the airport with barely enough time to switch into her chic warm weather clothes and out of her sub-arctic snow squall survival suit, (a mink jacket, Calvin Klein jeans, and Gucci boots), before the airline calls out her flight number. Will her latest gambit work? As she stands in the departure lounge, she has been struck by the absurdity of her situation: here she is flying down to Florida with a new man who she barely knows. Her family however will immediately lurch into panic mode. How well she remembered her last beau's encounter with her father.

"Mr. Yarwood, you have a very beautiful daughter," said the elegant well-heeled beau as he shook her father's proffered hand.

"Marry her," Big Daddy had grunted in reply, 'I'm tired of paying off her credit card."

Well, that started off a really dreary weekend and effectively drove the first nail in that relationship's coffin. Jillian remembered being particularly distressed by this whole chain of events because, quite honestly, that particular beau was perfect for her. It was true he was famously commitment shy. But, he had been stinking rich and probably would have paid off her credit card balance if she only had had a chance to ask him nicely. She had packed a Versace nightgown for just such an occasion.

Here she is at the air service desk, standing next to Matt and she needs to think of something to put him at his ease, something that would have the effect of neutralizing any pressure that her family might apply. She straightens her crisp Prada shift dress, and casts an approving glance at her emergency pedicure. (The esthetician crammed her in at the last minute because Jillian told her it was a matter of life and death. She couldn't be expected to go to Florida with grotty toes, for God's sake.) As she considers her plan of action, she notices a disturbing trend among the other passengers.

Shouldn't they all be in school?-she thinks. What the hell is going on here? They are sporting tacky rubber thong sandals, threadbare collegiate sweatshirts and garish to the point of hideous board shorts that they have apparently worn right to the airport in sub-zero temperatures. They are giddy, breezy and worse yet, precisely the age which Jillian has been trying to pass off as her own. As she stands amongst them looking coy and trying to fit in, a chilling realization strikes. They look, for all intents and purposes, like they are from another dimension. She becomes light headed. She grasps Matt's arm with a pincer grip.

"Oh good God!" she sputters. "It's Spring Break."

"Don't worry. I've been on a dozen Spring Breaks. I'll know how to handle it." Matt turns a languid gaze toward her, soothes her with his dulcet-toned voice. Is that natural calm in his voice, or does he merely lack the energy to get excited? She doesn't know. She does know, however that she doesn't want any of the grungy university crowd's backpacks touching her own elegant luggage. Why Daddy had positively choked when he found out how much he had paid for them! The least she could do was keep them perfect. Who knows what kind of offence could spoil her Louis Vuitton cases, if they were tossed willy nilly onto the ramp with a mass of sweat-stained *U of T* gear bags? She tries to inch along the line, edging her bag a little away from its closest neighbor: a greasy 'repurposed' hockey gear bag with multiple protrusions, held together with duct tape. Its pimply owner smiles at her, perceiving the difficulty she is having with moving her case's bulk, and picks it up. "Want some help 'Ma'am?'"

Jillian sucks air in audibly. It has happened. She has been 'Ma'amed. She represses the urge to say: Step away from the bag! She grabs the weekender's shoulder strap and looks him square in the un-laugh-lined eye. "It's Miss. I'm a Miss. Not a 'Ma'am.'"

"Sorry, eh? 'Ma'am.'"

"It's Miss." She yanks the bag away from him.

"Right, O.K. sorry...eh?...Miss."

For the next hour, as they board the plane, as they shoe-horn themselves into their economy class seats, as they eat their foil wrapped, pseudo-lethal peanuts and drink their tiny cups of mediocre coffee with artificial creamer, she works it over in her mind. She has been 'Ma'amed. She had been blind to this possibility. But now it has happened. Out of the blue. What could this mean? Had she really looked so different to them? So unlike them? Is it that obvious? Quickly she forages in her clutch purse for her compact and holds it to the side of her head, close to her eyes, next to the stark, unforgiving sunlight at 35,000 feet. She is aghast at what she sees. Despite all her strenuous efforts, and no small amount of the finest skin cream known to womankind, she can see tiny webs of lines emerging not just on the outside of her eyes, but around her mouth as well! She hasn't even adjusted to being nominally twenty-nine just yet, how the hell can she live with thirty-six? Anger sweeps across her face but she quickly suppresses the expression. Who knows what kind of damage that could do to her already ravaged looks?

Next to her, Matt is catching some shut eye. With that satellite dish in his apartment he had been able to catch English football in the wee hours of the night. Manchester United's exploits always leave him a little dazed the next day, but he is always able to catch a few *Zzzs* here and there. Up and down the aisles, the frenetic university students are becoming more and more boisterous. Their joy only heightens Jillian's sense of impending doom.

She had been 'Ma'amed. Is it time? What next? Is her sister right? Should she face facts and move on? It is obvious, in the face of authentic early twenty-year-olds, that she is not cut of the same cloth. What next? Has her prolonged adolescence come crashing to an end? How could that bitch Madeline be right? She needs a fall-back position. A contingency plan. She looks over at the rumpled and guileless Adonis sleeping next to her, with his long, muscular legs sprawled out into the aisle. His unkempt, obviously unwashed and uncombed hair is a mass of chestnut curls. Even his stubble looks sexy. The unfairness of it all. That he should be so effortlessly, so undeservedly handsome, so blissfully unaffected by the passage of time, seems nothing short of criminal. She wants to hit him. And yet, thinks Jillian. To think she has been living down the hall from a successful, unattached artist all this time. And she hasn't even had him on her radar. He really is handsome, she thinks warmly, as she looks at the snoring, sprawled mass of wrinkled clothes and dirty hair. Is he more manageable than his dog? Or just like him? Could he be the one? Could she fall in love with Matt? Could he be trained? I mean, she thinks, how hard can it be?

* * *

Big Daddy remembers hearing about the *Vagina Monologues*, and the fuss people made about them back home. Now he is living through the Virgin-reborn Monologues. Since Iris has moved in, and her friends have left town, his are the only pair of ears available for her endless stream of consciousness. He has been subjected to a steady drone of chirping, twittering and other kinds of running commentary, to which he has grown unaccustomed during his brief stint of widowerhood. It is always, "My poor husband, Jack, God rest his soul," or "My dearly departed husband George, may he rest in peace," or "My good friend Marsha, who went on to her great reward." And all the while that she reads off a virtual roll call of the deceased, she snips and cuts swatches of fabric with a massive pair of scissors. Twittering and chirping. Chirping and twittering.

It would have been alright if Iris had made his dreams come true. But that was just the problem. She is playing hard to get. He had already opened his door to her, taken her in, and stated his intentions. But she is not satisfied. She wants him to sign on the dotted line and pronto. In the meantime, she has strung her hand-washed 'delicates' in various conspicuous places around the trailer, leaving Big Daddy to fantasize about the day when he could see these items modeled by his bride.

His head warns him against undue haste. His heart feels otherwise. What are the odds, he thinks, that he would end up with another Aurora? This one seems, on the surface at least, to be quite a different animal. His personal experience of the realities of matrimonial bliss causes him to question his powers to decipher the feminine intent. Perhaps it is wise to wait until his daughters have a chance to check her out.

* * *

Iris's move into the trailer park had not gone unnoticed however. Near-by, his friend Eddie's wife has been taking note of Big Daddy's activities for months. She has not always been a nosey meddling busybody. She used to just be superior, plain and simple. She used to just know absolutely everything, as compared to her husband, who is usually the object of her scorn.

She had come to this professional turn in the road following a long career in baked goods, parenting and union organizing. Somewhere along the line Lydia's hearing had started to slip, due to the ceaseless racket of the industrial kitchen in which she toiled. As her ability to hear began to slide, she had placed increasing emphasis on every little detail that had not managed to escape her eagle, presbyopic eye. Over the years, Eddie, her long-suffering husband, had come to appreciate this state of affairs: idle conversation became severely limited. A consequence of this is a marriage that has endured long enough to be acknowledged on the local television news. Eddie has also learned how to supplement Lydia's lip reading skills and relay relevant bits of information via hand signals and notes. She has, despite her infirmity, become the biggest gossip in the RV park. She is a tabloid on two legs. However she relies on Eddie's willingness to cooperate. Eddie is her advance man in a potentially hostile frontier, her spy. She also has a nice set of field glasses.

"Woman moving in next door. Out of the blue."- she remarked one day. "Don't like the look of that."

You just don't like the idea of ol' Big Daddy settling down. Gossip could wind down, shot back Eddie in his arthritic scrawl. They had both enjoyed the vicarious thrill of watching the park's geriatric Romeo from a safe but effective vantage point.

"Still. She looks a little too unreal. A little too flashy. Phony. Kinda crafty. You say she's sixty-two?"

So he says- he wrote back. He took another look out the window. It looked like Iris arrived with only the minimum of luggage. It was his experience that when a woman of that age moved, she needed a lot more than a suitcase or two. Sometimes even an oxygen tank.

"What's she doing with an old guy like him? It's not like he's much to look at...."

Got a nice trailer- he allowed. *Seems she might want to make a change.*

"Oh?" Lydia asked coyly. "What did she do previously? Know anything about her?"

I'm not sure I heard it right. I think he said something about a deceased husband or two. But I could be wrong, Eddie wrote.

"Maybe not. Wonder what the other girls in the park know about her." (Lydia already suspected there would be detractors in that quarter, considering the spurned widows who had previously set their sights on the RV park's only living bachelor in recent memory who didn't need a wheelchair.)

She's from out of state, Eddie scrawled.

"So she says."

* * *

Florida's Gulf Coast had been the answer to Big Daddy's dreams when he had first pulled into Panama City Beach with his home on wheels. After years of a buttoned-down existence, buried many months of the year under a down-filled shroud, choked by neckties and worn out by kissing the behinds of his customers, he had landed in a retirement wonderland, full of seniors on the run from their progeny. Emerald green waters, sugary white sand, all you can eat oyster bars and hot and cold running widows who had shed their dowdy matronly attire and reserved manners for brightly colored muumuus and afternoon Long Island Iced Teas. They were all escaping something and it wasn't just the cold weather. Their bright colors were like a late bloom, caused by the absence of husbands who had died premature deaths due to long commutes and excess cheese curls and gravy on their *poutine*. In the absence of grown children, trying to wheedle free babysitting out of them, they had once again become carefree.

Except when their grown children came to visit, hauling their coterie of whining infants with them. News of the imminent arrival of Big Daddy's demon grandchildren was usually as welcome as a weather service hurricane bulletin. There are only so many water slides, so many outings of miniature golf in which the adult must lose badly, so many marine shows that one can indulge. Eventually, after establishing a first name basis with the dolphins, after being banned for life from two different mini-golf courses, Big Daddy had soured on the whole experience, thrown in the towel and resorted to bringing them to Gulf World, where he had in the past allowed them to run wild, throw sand at each other and run the risk of becoming shark food while he dozed off.

But this time, he doesn't know what he feels. This time he welcomes the opportunity to play doting Grandfather, if it means that he will be able to leave his fiancée in the presence of his eagle-eyed daughters. They understand their own gender. They will be able to determine if Big Daddy is making a big mistake. They might even be able to map out a means of escape if he is indeed headed for disaster. Why Madeline's children alone are enough to scare off all but the most determined potential step-grandmother!

* * *

Meanwhile in another plane headed south, Charles and Diana have broken into a chorus of screaming over the disputed ownership of one Mr. Bunny, which the -Roger's term here- 'nuts and berries' birth coach had encouraged Charles to provide for his new baby sister on the day of her birth. On that occasion, having arrived with great trepidation at the hospital, Charles took one look at his drooling rival, decided that the competition was entirely unfair and ripped the bunny out of the nursery cot, yelling, "Mine."

Ownership of the now soiled and stuffing-depleted rag has been under dispute ever since. Thanks to the new age birthing coach, the harassed parents had never taken the drastic step of tossing it out. She instilled in them a morbid fear of inflicting lasting existential trauma on their newborn. The presumption was that decades later when Diana was undergoing Regression Therapy, this would be one of those crucial events in her early life which would later be used to rationalize a hasty euthanasia bid the very instant her parents were felled by a disease only slightly worse than an ingrown toe nail. After all, it was only after Madeleine's own Regression Therapy that she realized how intensely she wanted to pull her own mother's plug.

Roger and Madeline have grown accustomed to the running battle and no longer hear it. As their children run shrieking up and down the aisles of the plane, the oblivious parents pour gleefully over brochures of Florida's Emerald Coast. For once this big winter getaway is something they could justify as 'family leave', which occasions paid time away from work. Meanwhile, on that same plane, every childless executive en route to a winter holiday is penning the following reminder in his or her PDA: call Doctor. Arrange sterilization immediately.

"Madeline honey," coos Roger, "Do you suppose we could leave the kids overnight with Big Daddy and have a real get-away? Do ya hon?"

"I can't see why not, sweetie. I mean. Who wouldn't want to reconnect with the grandchildren after so much time? I mean...Big Daddy's memory isn't that sharp is it?"

* * *

Arriving at the local airport the same time as her sister is a mixed blessing in Madeline's book. On the one hand, they could trade information about their father and his upcoming wedding before making the trek out to the RV park. On the other hand, there would be no one else to deflect Jillian's criticism of her sister's lack of style. It is relentless. Try as she might, Madeline can never fully prepare herself for the onslaught. This time, she has made what she feels is a special effort, with a crisply ironed shirt devoid of baby upchuck, and pants with a real, (that is, non-elastic waistband). Jillian takes one appraising glance and then reaches out to Madeline's hand, holding it up to her scrutiny.

"Madeline, I'm horrified," she pans.

"What? What could possibly be the problem?"

"Your nails. They're chewed down to the quick."

Madeline hedges. "Well. I've had a few worries."

"I'll say you do! If you don't get to a manicurist's quick and get some artificial nails glued on, people are going to think you're a lesbian." A few feet away Roger smirks and shakes his head. Jillian has a perfect, unbroken record. As they stand there waiting for Jillian to complete her inspection, their father's friend, Eddie emerges from the crowd around the luggage depot.

"I was certain that Big Daddy would be able to make time to collect us at the airport," says Roger as he turns to Eddie, who is set upon immediately by Charles and Diana.

Eddy, giddily explains, "Your Daddy won't be makin' it over to the airport. He hurt his back in a Jell-O-related incident."

Madeline is certain she has not heard him correctly. She slouches in Eddy's back seat and listens to the playful lilt of Eddy's southern accent, and considers the colorful way he had of saying, "Big Daddy slipped on something."

"Have you got the key to his RV?"

Eddie hedges. "Well...I...the thing is your daddy was quite particular. He said I should take you to a motel to get settled and then he'll see you in the morning."

"But we haven't got any reservations!" protests Jillian. "It's Spring Break. We'd be lucky to find space in a tool shed! Room rates will be through the roof!" Matt has a sudden pain in his back pocket. Roger doesn't care where he has to sleep, as long as he can foist his two kids off on his in-law. How could Big Daddy refuse to baby-sit his own flesh and blood?

"We brought moose meat!" wails Roger. "We had to smuggle it past customs. It'd be a shame to let it go to waste. We'll have to leave it in his fridge right away."

"Hummm. Don't think we can let the contraband moose meat go to waste. We'll just have to drop it off at the trailer park and then make a few phone calls."

The passengers of the car sit silently stewing while Eddy drives them through endless miles of trailer parks, and campsites at an excruciating twenty miles an hour, cutting the wheezing Pontiac's engine entirely whenever they hit any kind of downward gradient, and only restarting it when the aged car has ground to a standstill. All around them other drivers blow horns, or shoot them the finger and curse as they pass legally and illegally on either side of the sluggish car. Eddy meanwhile, whistles a happy tune.

"Do you have to drive so slow?" snaps Jillian, who taps her foot in irritation.

"Oh. I like to take it easy. Roads getting pretty dangerous these days. Look at the way these other drivers are behaving! They're always carrying on...Be too dangerous to drive any more aggressive." Eddie muses softly. "Besides, cutting the engine saves gas!" The passengers are left to imagine their own reactions if they were caught behind Eddie's maddeningly slow vehicle. What level of insanity and illegality would they be driven to commit?

"Your Daddy wants me to get you settled...ahem...somewhere and when he gets back from the choir-o-practor he'll be getting in touch."

"And Iris?"

"Oh, she's generally with Big Daddy night and day. Night and day," he says meaningfully, as he opens the RV's door and steps inside, "That relationship took place lightnin' fast. Hmmmm. But just now she's visiting friends out of town. Or something." Suddenly as Big Daddy's grown children are ushered into the Beaver Patriot they are struck with a chilling realization: they have never considered that the occupants might feel acutely the intrusion that their arrival would pose. Big Daddy's children are modern in outlook, meaning they don't expect that they were born under a cabbage leaf. But they also don't have visions of, and here gentle reader I'll put it as delicately as I can, senior citizens doing the wild thing. That would involve way too much sagging, blue-veined flesh and cellulite to make a pretty fantasy. You'll never see it on HBO, for example. Except if it involved Jack Nicholson and Kathy Bates, artfully submerged in a hot tub, with all the nastiest bits cleverly hidden from their viewers.

Suddenly they are confronted with a strange woman's summer-weight nighties and sturdy, structurally sound, but tastefully embroidered bras. A large open case of makeup and a sprawl of large format grooming products transforms the tiny trailer bathroom's counter-top into a distinctly feminine place.

-Damn, thinks Roger, Big Daddy is not going to give up the bedroom to us. Simultaneously the lack of adequate sleeping arrangements is occurring to Jillian, who has not yet informed Matt that she intends to fall in love with him. She certainly doesn't want to jump the gun and sleep with him until that order of business is out of the way. It might appear too forward, and work counter to her plans. And then there are the children to consider. Roger's suggestion of having her play auntie overnight almost made Jillian choke on her take-out order of seafood gumbo.

What is the point of having a parent who has escaped the brutal winter and moved to Florida if you can't mooch off of him?-thinks Jillian. Well, she consoles herself. There's still the inheritance. She casts another steely glance at Iris's industrial-strength bra that is drying over the kitchen curtain rod. Charles and Diana meanwhile are looking at a brochure for the local amusement park. While Diana listens wide-eyed to Charles pretending to read, her brother is explaining that the killer shark in the picture is being fed "... bad children's spankded bottoms."

Matt is not absolutely clueless to the unspoken tug of war that is raging in the Beaver Patriot. But, after his initial fear of contributing money to any endeavor, he's had a change of heart due to his changed circumstances. He can't rouse himself for a fight over a spare coach in a trailer either. After all, for the first time in his entire life he is flush with cash that does not come from a parental source. Never mind that he is living off the avails of his canine. He is in Florida, with a couple grand, and a woman who appears to be hot for him. It also bears mentioning that the fact that Matt hasn't been laid since before Christmas is starting to wear on his nerves. Not that he has enough initiative to do much about that. Suddenly a hot girl has virtually landed in his lap, through no effort of his own. Under the circumstances, he isn't looking forward to staying under a parental roof. If sleeping arrangements would conspire to land him in the same room as Jillian tonight, who is he to complain?

-Besides, thinks Matt- Maybe she might even offer to go Dutch Treat. "I'm sure we can find a motel or cottage near-by that can take us," he allows nervously, "If it's not too expensive on such short notice."

"Well," says the ever-smiling, gap-toothed Eddy, "It might take some flexibility. Like you all said, it is Spring Break."

The truth is, Big Daddy is not even occupying the bedroom that has become such an unspoken bone of contention. But he is the last person to admit to anyone that he has already been relegated to the coach, like a husband doing penance for un-atoned sins. So Eddy tries to play good neighbor and offers to make some inquiries. An hour later, they finally settle on a place called the Roadside Motel. Little Charles starts running around in circles yelling, "Wee, wee! We're going to the 'roadkill motel' Wee Wee!"

By the time they have managed to find this spot, Roger's only request is that it isn't too near a swamp. As he waits, he thinks he'd do his good brother-in-law deed and conduct an interview of his sister-in-law's apparent boyfriend.

"So what do you do, Matt?" he asks as a conversational opener. Matt's usual banter would have included careful stick handling around the career topic as he explained that he did a little of this and a little of that. Alternately, as part of his strategic curriculum avoidance, he would claim to be studying to become something or other. Sometimes he claimed to be consulting on some engrossing topics which he felt were not sufficiently interesting to discuss, (particularly with people gainfully employed and in possession of a healthy bullshit-o-meter). But Matt now has a tidy sum of money in his wallet from the sale of several paintings. He feels, for once in his life as if he has chanced upon the ideal career. No one need ever see him actually produce anything. He will never have to punch a clock. He will never even have to show up for work. And in another thirty-one years, once he hits sixty, he could claim to be 'retired' and that would be that. He clears his throat and tries his flourishing new career on for size.

"I'm an artist." He tries it on, like a shoe. It feels good.

"I heard something about that. What exactly does that entail? Sculpture? Photography? Painting? Film?"

"Abstract art, Roger." Matt is warming to his topic, digging through his database of newspaper art-critic hogwash, hoping to come up with a credible line of discussion. "I make abstractions based on a foundation of reality overlaid with larger human emotion."

"Such as?"

"Well," he continues nervously, "I like to draw my viewer into the dark night of my soul." Roger stares at him blankly, so Matt feels obliged to continue. "...So that my art involves both unconscious as well as conscious processes of the beholder."

"How do you do that?"

Matt coughs. Following up his last burst of codswollop might prove difficult. "This might take a minute to explain. Are you sure you want to go into it here?"

Thankfully at this moment Charles has convinced Diana that the next day she was to be 'feded to a addigato' and his little sister has begun to cry uncontrollably. Matt feels a surging wave of relief rush across him.

By the time they pull into this bargain basement motel, they are all too tired to talk, or even arrange for their morning get together.

* * *

They are awakened the next day by the ear-splitting howl of monster speakers, and a master of ceremonies yelling: "Party! Party! Party! Come on Spring Breakers, let's get wasted!"

Matt and Jillian stumble around their room in a haze. Matt is rubbing his back like a geriatric because the night before Jillian had decided that he would take the coach. Matt, who never bothered to make the first move ever, had obeyed. Jillian is secretly furious with him for not making a pass. She never ever made the first move. Although, the frustration is wearing, it would have violated her unwritten rule that he who makes the first move pays the piper. She decided this morning to bring out the heavy artillery by suggesting a walk to the beach to start the day. "I'll just need a moment to get into my bikini," she says coyly digging out her briefest Brazilian number, jeweled thong sandals and a hat that looks more suited to an outdoor wedding.

Fifteen minutes later, after Jillian's 'natural face' is on, they emerge into blinding sunlight and an additional twenty decibels of noise, coming from the beach.

They walk toward the loud speaker, stumbling through a badly trimmed hedge, until they find an inflated three-story beer can and a crowd of several hundred scantily clad, beer swilling and largely sunburned young adults. A poster boasts that adult film star Ron Bellamy would be guest of honor at some of the proceedings, omitting the word 'adult' from its banner. A white tape stretched across the poster tells a different story in hastily scribbled marker: *Ron delayed due to hot tub incident. Sorry.*

"Ron Bellamy!" enthuses Matt. "He's my hero."

Jillian gives him a puzzled look. "What on earth are you talking about?."

"Only the most successful star in the...in the...ahem...(and here he mumbled inaudibly)... film industry." Matt suspects he has made a mistake in mentioning film. Then again, he is a little surprised that he did have to explain his hero's identity to a woman who appears to vaguely occupy his selfsame demographic.

Jillian gives him a blank stare. What star is he talking about?

Deniro, DiCaprio, Depp?

"You know...Ron...Bellamy."

Still no response. Matt is baffled. Watching the affable Ron's heroic deeds had filled many a bored night during his checkered university career. He is so easy to identify with, thinks Matt. Because of Ron, a seemingly dirty-minded but likeable guy next door, Matt has been able to have a wild, albeit vicarious sex life, without having to expend a single calorie. Jillian still looks puzzled. "Moving right along..." he prompts, as they turn their attention to the beach scene.

Teams of organizers are handing out white, cut-off t-shirts to eager, slightly inebriated young girls, who then try, as discretely as possible, to remove their bikini tops from underneath their white shirts, readying for a wet t-shirt contest. To Matt this is a distinct sign that the day is shaping up nicely. Here he doesn't even have to make the least bit of effort and dozens of virtually topless young women are going to parade around in front of him. Life is good.

Meanwhile, Jillian is aghast at the possibility. How could she conceivably compete for Matt's attentions with the beach crowded with drunken, virtually topless college students? Sure, her sprayed on tan is the very best that Daddy's money can buy, but something tells her a lot of these girls were the sort who could Ma'am her with impunity.

-Screeee...whoomp comes howling from the speakers. Matt's attention is now drawn to the stage where the sound test is causing major feedback. Tapping the microphone is an old guy in a Panama Hat and loud shirt emblazoned with palm trees and Island women carrying fruit baskets on their heads. He is wearing a head brace, consisting of a firm collar, around which are installed four steel posts and a suspended ring, meant obviously to immobilize his injured neck.

Jillian meanwhile is sizing up the female competition in her near vicinity on the beach. She has never felt so nervous before about her little Brazilian number and the flaws she imagined it might be revealing from behind. Her eyes dart from one woman to the next, making a quick inventory of the qualities and deficits of each, as she periodically glances back at Matt to evaluate his behavior and reactions.

"If I could have your attention, please," says the man on stage who again taps the microphone. "Ron will be here as soon as he clears up a small matter about the hotel's hot tub with the management..."

"Ron! Ron! We want Ron!" chants a pack of drunken university students, some of whom are already sporting peeling sunburns. "Give us Ron!" They raise their beer in the air and start a beach-wide chant, "Ron! Ron!"

"So the committee asked me, since I won the Jell-O wrestling contest yesterday if I could start the ball rolling."

-Curious, thinks Jillian. I know that voice. Her eyes are drawn away from a thong-wearing highlighted blonde who is struggling out of her bikini top from under her white t-shirt. She turns to the stage and tries to focus as she shields her eyes from the sun's glare.

"Now I want anybody who wants to compete to form a line up here," the man continues.

Jillian grabs Matt's arm and digs in with her aggressively manicured talons, "Oh good God!" she hisses, through clenched teeth. "That's Big Daddy. We've got to get out of here, before he sees us!"

"Before the contest!" Matt protests, over the shouts of Ron! Ron! that echo across the beach.

"Yes, you moron! We have to get out of here before he sees us."

"Didn't you come here to visit him?"

"What are you, a lawyer?" she snaps. Then in a lower voice, she explains: "Daddy's gone off the deep end! I need to get a hold of Maddy. She'll know what to do. She'll know how to handle Daddy. This is much worse than I thought!" With that, Jillian starts to slouch, shielding her face with her oversized hat, as she skirts the perimeter of revelers on the beach and makes her way back to their own, far humbler living quarters. Once there, Jillian plans to put her sister on high alert over their father's impending incompetency hearing. The one she plans to launch at the earliest opportunity.

When they arrive at the motel, they discover a note on their door from Roger:

Gone to Dad's. Catch you two later. Be good
-Roger
P.S.: could you guys babysit tomorrow?
* * *

⌘ FOURTEEN ⌘

FAME, GLORY AND HARD CASH

Damian is pacing nervously back and forth in his gallery, chewing hard on a hangnail.

Before him, amid the sprawl on his desk lays an article in the *Star*, complete with that slob Matt's picture, extolling his genius as an artist. Since its appearance, the phone has been ringing off the wall. The piece is entitled: *Trolling the soul's dark night*. It had been penned by yet another impressionable and probably love-struck young woman, who painted a portrait of – *"A deeply brooding, soulful abstractionist, whose very existence is an indictment of modern consumer culture."* Immediately after the article's appearance, those selfsame modern consumers tore down to the studio in search of more damning indictments to put on their own walls.

Interested collectors will not be dissuaded by the fact that each of Matt's fabulous works of art has now been spoken for. If Damian can only rush a few more of these works onto the now almost naked walls, he'll make a quick killing for as long as the newspaper article remains uppermost in the minds of Toronto's hyper-materialistic nouveau glitterati and self-anointed intelligentsia. Damian notes with some anger that the article also describes Matt as *"stylishly avant guard and unaffected."*

As Damian paces, his assistant is pacing after him, matching his movements step for step, portable phone in hand. "Call him," he insists, thrusting the phone forward. "He might have someone up here who can let you into his studio."

"I can't let him know how desperate I am!" insists Damian. "He'll want more money. If I'm smart, I won't give him the impression that his work is selling faster than anything else I've got. God knows what kind of concessions he'll try to get out of me."

"Why are you so paranoid?"

"Paranoid? Didn't you notice the female shark that was swimming around him opening night? She's probably a lawyer. Oh sure, she acts ditzy to put you off the scent, but she can smell money like some kind of Basset hound sniffing for truffles." (With this remark, he holds his hands paw-like up to his chest and snorts, more like a groundhog than a hound dog.) "I can tell. She's probably dragging him around Palm

Beach right now, talking up his fame and genius to every shlub with an open piece of wall..."

"Just let him know that you have some more interested buyers, who are happy with the work he's doing and are willing to buy more if the price can be kept to the same level. Call him. Can't you track down a number where he could be reached in Florida?"

"Actually his mother called here yesterday to let me know he was going...I don't know why, and I know you're going to think I'm paranoid, but I had the feeling he was avoiding talking to me."

"Curious. How old did you say he is? Why would he relay messages through his mother? Isn't he close to thirty?" Damian huffs, still miffed by the attention the so-called-arts reporter has paid to Matt's spectacular, boyish good looks.

"One supposes. Anyway, she said something about him heading to the airport on really short notice. Some people just take a little longer to cut the apron strings."

"Well. Use those apron strings and call her. Mothers are scrupulous about maintaining phone contact. Hell, mine could rival the KGB for information gathering!" Damian meekly assents. "You do the talking... And don't tell him anything you don't have to tell him."

* * *

Meanwhile, at the RV park, Jillian and Matt's rental car is disgorging its passengers. Jillian is in a snit because Matt has taken the wheel and driven under the legal speed limit the entire distance, pausing to yawn frequently. She has the impression he drifts through life half asleep. Matt reasons- what is the point of being a tourist if you can't just dawdle along? Although Roger and Madeline had arrived only moments before them at Big Daddy's Beaver Patriot with their two kids, they seem to have already begun staking out some kind of claim.

Much to Madeline's chagrin, Daddy is somehow out, yet again. They decide the only way to catch him, if this is what it is going to take, is to camp out in his living room until he shows up. Letting themselves in with the spare key Eddie has provided, Roger and Madeline have dragged in several cases of toys and related kid equipment, suitable for a long, arduous session of bonding with Grandpa. Opening the toy suitcase is like uncorking a cyclone. While the children warm themselves up for a frenzy of play, Jillian has been working herself into a heart attack. Matt takes Roger aside and tells him about seeing Big Daddy's impromptu role as master of ceremonies at the Spring Break wet t-shirt contest, occasioned by an apparent hot tub imbroglio involving Ron Bellamy.

"Ron Bellamy?" asks Roger, "He's my hero!"

"Oh for God's sake is there anyone here who thinks this is crazy?" wails Jillian, who is feasting on this opportunity for drama in her real life, instead of just on stage. "Daddy's gone off the deep end, for God's sake! And that woman has lead him there! Why can't he act his age, dammit!"

At that moment the phone rings in the trailer. Everyone lunges for it, but Madeline gets to it first. "Hello," stammers a nervous voice on the other end of the line. "Is this where I can reach Matt Elgin?"

"Who?"

"Matt Elgin, the artist..." Damian's assistant prompts.

"Matt? The artist?" It still took a few seconds for this statement to register. It didn't make sense: Jillian has her hooks into an artist of such renown that his gallery pursues him all the way to Florida, while on vacation? How can this be? And here only last night Roger was telling Maddy what an unmitigated phony the guy seemed to be. -It just goes to show how wrong you can be about people, she thinks. She thrusts the phone at Matt, and stands there, enthralled, watching his response.

"Hello Matt?"

"Yes..." he replies cautiously.

"It's your gallery in Toronto calling. I hope you don't mind. I tracked down this number by calling your mother. I told her it was an emergency."

"An emergency?" Matt tries to control his irritation. The less his mother knows about his life, the better. Unless he is the one doing the telling, and the story he tells is one necessary for getting bills paid. In that case, creative truth telling is his specialty.

"I have great news..," begins the assistant. In the background Damian is wincing, drawing a finger across his mouth zipper style. "That is to say, promising news. We have some interested buyers who'd like to see more of your work. Does anyone have a key to your studio? Have you left any work with anyone up here who could give us a bit of a sneak peek?"

"A sneak peek? My studio?" Matt struggles with this request. There isn't anything left to sell. Finnegan is currently in a creative slump. He is also being dog-sat in suburban Toronto. Josh, who is still living with his mother in Etobicoke has probably not even bothered to dig out from under yesterday's thick blanket of snow. Even if he could get into Matt's apartment, all he'd find is an overused drop sheet from

Finnegan's last painting spree. Matt doesn't know a lot about art, but he did know that the trashed drop sheet 'lacked artistic vision'. Matt doubted that it had commercial value. But in the current climate, who could know? "Don't you already have enough to show prospective buyers?"

"Oh no they're all sold." At these words, Damian holds his head as if in pain. "That is, we think they're all sold."

"All sold?" This takes a moment to register. Could he get Josh to set his dog loose on a few paint trays and hope for a good result? Nah. Better to keep all this a secret. If it got out, he'd be exposed as a complete fraud. "I'm sorry," Matt blurts out. "That's just not going to be possible. I need to recharge my batteries creatively. I'll speak to you when I get back."

He hangs up quickly, adrenalin rushing as he thinks of the cash rolling in from the art sales. He feels like such a success. "Jillian! They all sold. Every painting I had in that show!"

A sea change is happening in Big Daddy's RV. From obsessing about a crisis caused by their father's apparent lewd behavior and upcoming marriage, all eyes are suddenly turned on Matt. Jillian's are moist. It is as if she is beholding her savior.

"All sold? Every last one?"

"That last article must have done the trick."

"Really?" She smiles slyly, then adds quickly, "Darling." She looks at him with stars in her eyes.

"Let's celebrate!" She is beaming. "We NEED champagne! I know a place near here where we can get *Veuve Clicquot*!"

They are all so transfixed by this turn of events, by the improbability of Jillian apparently having sunk her claws into a hot one, that they do not even notice the turning of a handle, and the arrival of Big Daddy, neck brace and all, in the RV. His first glance at this trailer's living quarters confirms his worst fears. The grandchildren are camping out. He clears his throat.

"What the hell are all these toys doing in my Beaver?" His eyes dart from one of his offspring to the other. Then he points at the kids. "Aren't those kids staying in a motel?...I told Eddie..."

"Now calm down Daddy," says Jillian, considering strategies. "We're all checked in at a beach side place, kids included. We just thought this would be the easiest way to find you...that is...when you're not on the beach. Not that you were on the beach." She finishes off with a nervous little twitter, eye-roll combination.

"Well I can't entertain you just now...I've wrenched my neck a bit and you're going to have to take your kids back to your motel and meet me later for supper after I've rested a bit." Madeline begins wrestling her children into their shoes, while a crest-fallen Roger starts piling toys back into their satchel.

"Daddy," Jillian asks pointedly, "How did you hurt your neck?"

"Never you mind. We'll talk about it later. At supper."

"When we'll meet Iris?"

"Iris has gone to Miami for the day."

"Is she really?" She can't keep the suspicious tone out of her voice. "Why isn't she here to meet us?"

Daddy is hustling her to the door, and says, distractedly as he shows them out, "She's with her hooking group. Now I'll see you tonight."

This last comment of Daddy's caught Jillian so by surprise that, quite out of character, she has nothing to say. She turned it over and over again in her mind. Did she really hear what she thought she heard? Did he really say what she thought he said? Her group is organizing? Funny they never struck her as the type to unionize.

* * *

As they drive back to the motel, the occupants of Roger's rental car sit dealing with their shock. Big Daddy is the winner of the previous day's Spring Break Jell-O wrestling contest, and cavorting with young women in wet t-shirts. Not only that, he has had some kind of brush with fame, (or notoriety depending on how one looked at it), because of his new acquaintance with Ron Bellamy, the ubiquitous slob-cum-porn star whose chief claim to fame is his indifferent appearance that fans find so non-threatening to their self-esteem. Suffice it to say that response to this last bit of information is sharply divided along gender lines. The men, blinded by hero worship, have a new-found respect for the man, who in Roger's words, had spent the better part of his life as the vassal slave of a lunatic.

The women, on the other hand, are completely baffled. Big Daddy had always struck his daughters as buttoned down and somewhat defeated, a humorless, white-collar suburban work horse. Why isn't he acting his age? -they keep obsessing. How could their father have fit in with a beach full of drunken college students? Won their admiration? Allowed himself to be seen cavorting with young women in vats of Jell-O? And worse yet, ended up acting as a stand-in master of ceremonies at a wet t-shirt contest? Why is he so matter of fact about his new woman's continuing connection to hookers? And who the hell is this Ron Bellamy the guys were so in awe of?

Jillian's attention keeps drifting in and out of this on-going debate. She is mulling over the fabulous news from the gallery, which surely has positive repercussions for her future plans. She rolls this piece of information around in her head as if it were a lozenge. With racing pulse, she goes down through her life's long inventory of inadequate men, punctuated by an ever more frequent number of disappointments. She has always hoped she'd find the perfect man: someone who'd look good in the cute couples pictures she dreams of making, someone who is famous, and someone who can buy her expensive presents. Is that too much to ask? Fame, fortune and good looks? In her case, Jillian thinks not.

Meanwhile Matt is enjoying a new sensation. All his adult life, his biggest achievement has been getting somebody else to carry the responsibilities, to pay the bills. And he has considered this a successful career of sorts. After all, making it all the way to twenty-nine in fine style with no real work history, no goals, no drive or ambition and minimal life skills is some kind of rare accomplishment. Who can blame this slacker for wanting to make the most of his luck? Sadly for Matt, in the next few years, his complete lack of direction will start to take the shine off his image. It may soon make him a marked man, tipping savvy women off that he is a bona fide Peter Pan. His very being will cause ripples of warnings to flow through the pool of available women, older and wiser women who are quick to pick up on the tell-tale signs of extended adolescence and sloth as a career choice. Smart, single, thirty-something women have their radars now permanently attuned to this frequency. Soon they will give him only months, or just weeks to straighten up and fly right, instead of the three years that Lana foolishly wasted on him. The boom is about to be lowered, but is Matt even capable of suspecting it?

Consider Matt. He was a beautiful baby. So beautiful in fact, that every day people would stop his proud mother as she pushed his stroller and congratulate her on her excellent genes. As he grew, the fact that he was born under a lucky star complete with silver spoon in his mouth conspired to make him a most likeable fellow. Easy company with not a care in the world. A relatively clever wit that made him the toast of any party. His natural grace and astonishing good health guaranteed that he'd be picked for the team. Any team. Every team. (Even though he played in an off-handed, lackadaisical way, his teammates barely resented him.) He never developed the habit of competition and therefore had no malice toward anyone. What was not to like? His door and refrigerator were always open to people in the mood to party. Until recently, his access to Dad's money was never in dispute. Over the years he became so accustomed to the privilege of his birth that he was blissfully unaware, on a conscious level, of how much he traded on that privilege. The Beauty Dividend made sure that he had always lived a charmed existence, even though he never realized he was making steady withdrawals from that bank account. And hence, Matt has never once in his life had to work for anything. He is a bum, but a likeable one who is able to make other people feel happy that they can be of assistance to him.

Who can then blame this former golden boy for becoming a spoiled, lazy, worthless slob, and a moocher of the highest order? The kind that sensible mothers everywhere would caution their daughters to avoid, if only they themselves hadn't been charmed by his astonishing good looks and pleasant demeanor, during their first and probably only encounter? After a decade or two of the red carpet treatment, who is to say that they wouldn't start to feel entitled to the best for free? (Britney Spears being a case in point). Who among us wouldn't grow docile in the face of other people's relentlessly scrambling to please and coddle us? If you want ambition, first create hunger.

But here is a new and thrilling sensation. Despite himself, Matt is a success in his own right. Well, almost. True his dog is the real artist. But Matt is at least instrumental in getting his dog to make these apparently inspired paintings. He is the dog's Svenghali, if you will. That is almost like being a self-made man, isn't it? Suddenly Matt feels a rush of pride. Of having, in his pocket, money that he doesn't have to wheedle out of Dad or Mom or some other relative. And while it is true that it is earned by Finnegan, as long as he keeps the *Jerky Treats* and the trips to the dog park coming, it can't be considered exploitation. Can it?

* * *

Walter makes a minute adjustment to his ball cap, cramming it down once again over his troublesome head of hair. He is beginning now to understand why Sonia had advised him to lose the springy top knot. Her contention was that it lost him as many followers as he gained. And, since it also made it harder for him to pass unnoticed through customs, with their bothersome questions anyway - "aren't you a little tall to be a Sumo wrestler?"- they had asked more than once, he is considering giving in to her on this point. He is a bit put out by Sonia from time to time. Since she had infiltrated his organization, she had made herself alarmingly indispensable, so much so that she is now angling to get rid of some of his favorite minions. Harold was a particular target for her wrath.

Whatever did she expect? -Walter asks himself. His followers to a man were all dim bulbs looking for pat answers. But this is the best following he had ever assembled, and he certainly needs a fall back position after the disappointing non-doom of Y2K. Why can't Sonia understand that? Perhaps because she is not forced to travel under an assortment of aliases and living in fear and dread of revenue officials, all over his failed survivalists' food supplies empire.

All these thoughts are racing through his head as he makes his way along the line at the Kennedy Space Center. Drifting around, trying to look as unworthy of notice as possible, (considering his six-foot-eight frame and hulking body), he has managed to get an appreciation of space flight that comic books had never given him. The absolute best is the Air Force Space Museum's parking lot, containing over four dozen rockets! Walter falls in with a group of people who have freshly disembarked from a blue tour bus. He pulls a small camera from the pocket of his caftan and begins snapping shots of a Firebee Drone Rocket, imagining as he fires away, the excitement that these pictures will create among his people. They worry every day about how they are going to get their frozen undead pre-remains shot into some intergalactic medical center. This should certainly whip up fresh interest for his proposals.

In this post-9-11 universe, his picture-taking enthusiasm is his undoing.

"Hey buddy! What do you think you're doing?" shouts a retiree in Bermuda shorts and Argyle socks, that partially cover a pair of starkly white and undeveloped legs. Walter feels a 'disturbance in the force'. He starts to hyperventilate. "Are you some kind of spy?" The man shouts. "Look! It's a terrorist!"

More people start to cluster around him. A glance over the shoulder of one man, in the direction of a small whirring motor, draws Walter's eyes to a tiny surveillance camera. In a security room somewhere on the compound, two space museum personnel begin speculating about the stir that is developing around a man who looks like a massive loaf of white bread, freshly removed from a top-loading bread making machine, and wrapped in a linen tablecloth.

"We'd better send somebody down there," one of them remarks, as he reaches for the telephone on the desk.

Walter, meanwhile is seized with panic. From the corner of his eye he can see a pair of commissionaires advancing toward the burgeoning mob. He reaches into his pocket for the key of his rental car and starts backing toward the vehicle as quickly as he can without cause for alarm. Finally, he throws caution to the wind, turns and bounds like a medicine ball towards the car, leaping inside with impressive vigor, considering his girth. The engine starts without trouble and Walter races off, narrowly missing a woman on a walker, who hurls a stream of impressive curses after the disappearing car. He doesn't start driving under the speed limit until he reaches the Bee Line Expressway.

His only worry is that Sonia might be upset. He has come to expect her tantrums when ever he messes up. She had even once remarked that they ought to find a new 'face man' for the organization, so that Walter can fade from the public eye and they can manage their empire/religion from safely behind the curtain. Just like the Wizard of Oz.

But where could such a man be found? And besides, Walter loves being the face man. It is his *raison d'être*. All his life all he's ever wanted is to be some kind of savior. All he really needs is a trouble free passport and a new identity. But where could such an item be found?

* * *

✧ FIFTEEN ✧

A MAN FOR ALL REASONS

Back at the Roadkill Motel, as little Charles likes to call it, Jillian makes a hasty retreat to her own room before Madeline and Roger can suggest that she take the kids somewhere for the afternoon. Matt suddenly finds himself standing alone in the entranceway under the scrutiny of Madeline and Roger while their children race around full throttle overturning chairs and making car noises, complete with collisions.

"So, Matt. Your show was a big success!" says Madeline as she watches Matt look on in horror at the mess her children are making of the motel lobby. She has reached that threshold of parenthood where she now regards the child-created chaos with complete indifference, and actually finds the reaction of childless individuals a point of amusement. Madeline is big on public diapering. Madeline doesn't mind food fights in the least. Besides, her new age birth coach assured her that if her children were 'high needs', they were therefore more intelligent. And children in possession of superior intelligence would be emotionally scarred by limits. Parents of such children were to allow the life force to flow freely from their little bodies, however destructive a turn it takes, lest they decide in early adulthood that it's high time to pack their parents off to an assisted living complex located in the middle of nowhere and run by cruel fascists. Madeline sits calmly rotating her foot, exercising her ankle as she scrutinizes Matt's distress and guesses at his willingness to reproduce.

"According to the gallery it was."

"Interesting. How many shows does this make?" She tries to catch his eyes, but they have begun darting around the lobby distractedly. Given the circumstances, she can't pinpoint a reason for this.

"What's that?" He watched as several potted rubber trees are set spinning by the shrieking children. Roger slouches drowsily into a lobby chair, fanning himself with a brochure. He exhales deeply, as if preparing to sleep.

"How many shows have you had?"

"Oh. A few," he hedges, not too effectively. He shifts his weight from one foot to the other. It is mid-afternoon and time for a rest. He wonders idly what games are on the room's satellite television.

"Well, how many?" Madeline persists in her interrogation.

"Not too many." He dodges.

"So a couple?"

"Well..." he coughs. His eyes dart from side to side. Although he certainly practiced his share of the seven deadly sins, (sloth being his personal favorite), Matt is always a poor liar. He thinks quickly for a partial truth that would allow him to finesse his way out of this line of questioning. "This is the best reception my work has had."

"Humm." By this time the kids are practicing their Indian whooping cries. 'Interesting name you have. You wouldn't be descended from the famous Lord Elgin, would you?"

"Who?"

"Lord Elgin," she prompts. "You know. Arguably the biggest thief of antiquities of all time. He made off with a king's ransom in Greek marble, most notably big chunks of the Parthenon's sculptures. He was quite the lad. A real art lover."

"Now, now," interjects Roger, still fanning himself. "You play nice Madeline. I'm sorry, Matt, you have to excuse Madeline. She has a hard time leaving work behind. Antiquities specialist and all that."

Roger nervously gathers up the kids and hustles them into the motel room, for once grateful for the excuse that children provided for getting out of a tight conversational corner. "Coming Madeline?"

When Matt enters the room he is sharing with Jillian, it is like entering a mirror image of her apartment back home. Clothing, shoes and makeup kits are scattered throughout the room. Jillian, standing amid the rubble, is engaged in a frenzy of buffing, scrubbing, moisturizing, moussing, tweezing, teasing and squeezing. Several dresses were laid out on the bed, complete with coordinating shoes, pashmina and jewelry.

"Good grief Jillian, did the maid throw a tantrum?"

"Don't be silly. Hurry up and get ready. We're meeting Daddy at *Billy's Oyster Bar and Crab House* at five o'clock."

"That's two hours from now."

"I know," Jillian replies, with one of her characteristic eye rolls. "That doesn't leave much time does it?" Curiously, this did not come across as a joke.

Matt surveys the room, looking for the remote control. Has she buried it under one of her heaps of rejected potential outfits? He starts shifting things around, gently at first because he suspects she didn't really want him tossing her clothes all over the place. Finally, he starts moving whole piles....He keeps trying to conjure up a list of today's games and events. Would different games be broadcast here than at home? Are there any spring training baseball camps near-by? ...As time wears on, with still no remote, he begins to grow more anxious. He is a little nervous about this trip as it is unfolding. Why is Jillian so hell-bent on getting them photographed together?....Isn't there a men's Giant Slalom going on?... He worries about Finnegan and his creative block. He worries that Josh might not take him to the dog park, or that his dog might be lonely without him. And he wonders about the reception he is getting from Jillian's relatives. He is under the impression that he was just hanging out with her, avoiding the snow and passing the time until the roads are clear enough back home and Josh and he could drive out to the ski hill...But Jillian's family! They are acting like he is her knight on a white charge card, here to show Jillian a fat cat's version of a good time. It isn't like they had any kind of thing going on, is it? It's true he's a bit slow on the uptake, but wouldn't he have noticed? Matt has just drifted into this pseudo-relationship, without giving it a thought. It is not unlike one of those airport conveyor belts, that people use to get from one terminal to another. The belt just hums gently as it moves its confused and jet lagged passengers along, from one end of the terminal to the other. And then, there they are: at a destination they hadn't made one actual step towards, and not the least amount of conscious thought. Is he on a relationship conveyor belt? Has he just stepped into Jillian's alternate universe and come out on the other end of the terminal as some kind of live-action Ken doll?

"Come on," Jillian prompts. "There'll be pictures!"

How has this happened? Is this what is happening? He has managed to escape any real commitment for twenty-nine years by simply doing nothing that would ever move a relationship forward in any tangible way. And now here he is with Jillian, who he barely knows, and her family is acting like they have registered for china patterns and are picking out invitation stationary. He can feel beads of sweat trickling down his neck and his pulse is starting to quicken. He has no idea how to get himself out of this situation. After all, he has done absolutely nothing to get into this bind in the first place. He isn't even sure what the situation is. Finally his hand wraps around the remote, which is buried under a shoe box beside the mussed up bed. Matt gives a huge sigh of relief and collapses in front of the motel TV.

* * *

In Madeline and Roger's room, across the hall, the kids have decided, in the absence of an audience, to quietly draw some pictures with the crayons brought from home. Roger cracks open the room's small, noisy bar fridge and pours themselves each a beer.

"God it's hot." Roger mops the back of his neck with a hotel towel.

"And getting hotter. Did you get a load of that line of manure Jillian's latest is slinging?"

"Yup." Roger closes his eyes. Sips slowly on his beer.

"Don't you have any thoughts?"

"You're the antiquities specialist. You should be able to tell if he's the genuine article or not. Frankly, I don't get a sense that they have any relationship at all."

"Hummm." Madeline has the same suspicion. "I'll tell you. On the one hand, I find it hard to believe that a bona fide artist would not know about the Elgin marbles. On the other hand, he has apparently made a splash with some paintings, enough to tweak Jillian's radar at least."

"That's true, Maddy. She wouldn't be bothered with him if he didn't look promising. Poor sap looks like a freshly hooked fish that is stunned by what's happening, but hasn't had his head slammed on the dock just yet. He just seems to be swept up in the whole thing."

"Jillian is a force of nature," allows Maddy. "There's no doubt about that."

"Force of nature? Jillian is a tsunami."

"Hummm." Madeline considers this last statement. Jillian is her mother's daughter, no doubt about that. But part of her wants to believe that this time Jillian has actually connected with a suitable man. After all, Matt is roughly her (nominal) age, and not decades older. He does not appear to have a wife stashed somewhere. And apart from the 'deer in the headlights' aura about him, he does not seem to be as utterly clueless as some of Jillian's earlier conquests. The litmus test is how he could cope with intense contact with Jillian for the duration of this Florida excursion. Especially if the girls try to confront their father about his goings-on. "How on earth are we going to bring up Daddy's spring break nonsense over dinner?"

"I'm not going to do it." Roger is even more slumped down in his chair. He is rolling a cold beer can across his forehead, letting the condensation leave little droplets across his furrowed brow. As little rivulets make their way down his face, he has a look of profound ecstasy.

"Roger! That's so unfair. I have to field all his crazy, 'Oh Maddy I think I'm having the big one' calls all the time. It's your turn."

"Maybe Jillian will do it. She almost let the cat out of the bag this afternoon."

"That's true. She seems to have a special gift for putting her foot in her mouth and backpedaling at the same time."

* * *

Back in the Beaver Patriot Big Daddy's head is spinning with the possibilities. Jillian has brought a man down with her. Obviously they are involved, although they are acting pretty coy. Could this be it? Could he finally experience the joy Big Daddy has hoped for ever since Jillian had been a young girl clutching her very first store credit card in her hot little adolescent hands? Now he understood why men, walking their daughters down the aisle, had been known to cry like a baby with profound joy. He practically danced a jig. He hummed a happy little ditty as he shaved the coarse grey stubble from his sun-damaged face.

Yes, he thinks. Free at last. Free at last. Jillian is off the payroll.

But peace of mind is never something to take for granted. Just as Big Daddy is practically orbiting the moon with joy, the phone rings.

"Father," says a pompous voice on the other end of the line.

Big Daddy feels like he is in an elevator in which the cable has snapped. His heart catches in his throat. "Walter?"

"Precisely."

"Where are you?"

"I'm driving a car. I'll be at your place within the hour."

"Jesus! You're in Florida?"

"Yes. I haven't changed my name to Jesus yet, father. You should still call me Walter."

Big Daddy feels himself getting dizzy. Where was his blood pressure kit? Did he take his Lipitor today? Why the hell did he keep up a satellite phone anyway? "I won't be here!" he blurts out. "The girls are taking me out to supper."

"Oh? Where would that be?"

And before Big Daddy can think of a possible maneuver to avoid answering, it slips out. "Billy's. The oyster bar. You know the place," he adds dejectedly. "Five o'clock."

What else could he do? The boy is his flesh and blood. He possesses the same burley, bouncer's build. The same full eyebrows and turquoise eyes. No need for a blood test. No question about it. He is family, after all. Well, he thinks crestfallen. He has been deliriously happy, if only momentarily. -No wonder they call it Happy Hour.

SIXTEEN

WHEN THE WORLD IS YOUR OYSTER BAR

Jillian is angling for a compliment from Matt, to no avail. They have arrived first at Billy's Oyster Bar to scope out the restaurant for a good table: not directly under any harsh, unflattering overhead lights, and with a good view of the coast in the background so that, (with a fill-in flash, of course), pictures would include a lovely sunset reflected off the water.

She really needs something, anything from Matt, in the way of positive stroking. She is already feeling a little vulnerable because the waiter had initially tried to lead them to an out of the way corner, where she would not have been noticed.

This could only mean one thing: the recent influx of university students has bumped her out of top place in the restaurant's notable hotties factor. How would she have been noticed back there by the kitchen? Being noticed is one of life's biggest pleasures, a reward for all that grooming and expense. It may be true that once one reaches the top rung of the acting profession, dark glasses and a hat are often worn to provide a disguise and a break from celebrity. But when you are a second-stringer like Jillian, a legend only in your own imagination, getting noticed is the sole reassurance that you are in the game at all.

And then, to top things off, Matt doesn't even comment on her outfit after she had struggled with three complete wardrobe changes before she got everything right, (Gucci, Dolce & Gabbana with just a soupçon of Hermès). Only for a split second does he look away from the menu and at her, even as she is trying to press every button, with long, lingering glances, lightly touching his wrist as she points out the cosy oyster bar's casual charm, and leaning deeply forward over his menu so that he could, with little prompting, get a spectacular view of her expensively augmented cleavage. The only reaction she has prompted from this man is a quick scratch at his leg and a mumbled comment about the size of Florida cockroaches, after she had gingerly brushed her freshly pedicured big toe up against his ankle. What the hell is wrong with this man?

But wait, while she is sitting considering whether or not it is advantageous strategically to pitch a fit, she catches a disturbing glimpse of a hulking man being led to their table by the selfsame waiter who had initially tried to sequester her in the land of invisible women over near the kitchen. His hair is tied up with a topknot on his head, like the foliage topping a bunch of carrots. He is wearing some kind of...what is it linen?...or sackcloth?...caftan that looks like a nightie for a rhino. The face is a younger version of her father's right down to the piercing, turquoise eyes. "Walter! You made it!"

Matt wheels around. He doesn't know anything about her brother, Jillian and Madeline both having kept strict silence about him. But something about the knowing glances whenever Walter's name came up has caused Matt to be nervous. Good God! The man is a giant! At least in terms of girth. Maybe height too, but for that, Matt would have to take a few steps back to take him all in. He is wearing a soft, clumsily hand-crafted leather kit bag, strung across his considerable chest, and the biggest pair of Birkenstocks that Matt has ever seen. He looks like an intergalactic apostle with his finger in an electrical socket.

Jillian and Walter seem to have a special bond. After several loud, dramatic hugs, they simultaneously start rooting around in their respective bags for packets of photographic self-portraits to show each other. Matt stands back in amazement as they both recount, in turns, and with strikingly similar enthusiasm and expression: "And this is me with ...(fill in the blank here)...and another of me during an appearance at...(another item is tossed in willy nilly), and here I am with some of my associates." Many of Walter's associates are dressed in the same goofy caftan.

While Jillian seems to be a minor celebrity in Toronto, Walter has achieved some other mysterious kind of cult status, which includes followers, book signings in obscure locations and robed attendants. And most significantly, fully-catered and highly profitable Armageddon Conferences, with titles like: *Making Total Annihilation Pay*.

But before Matt can gather his wits about him, Roger, Madeline and their children are brought to their table, followed closely by Big Daddy.

The family patriarch cuts right to the chase: "What?" he barks at Walter, "There must have been some small blip in the Final Judgment Cash Cow."

"Now that you mention it, the Final Judgment agenda has been put on hold for a while." Walter smiles weakly.

"Gosh I'm hungry," interjects Roger purposefully, as he rubs his hands together. "Let's order." And he proceeds to park his two noisy kids between his father-in-law and Walter. Because Matt finds himself trapped between Jillian and her brother, he has a choice of conversations: he could deal with Jillian's constant fishing for compliments or he could try to get to the bottom of Walter's strange get-up and bizarre behavior. He decides to launch into some small talk with Walter while they wait for their jumbo orders of blue crabs and crawfish to arrive.

"So Walter, I hear you've been at some kind of conference."

"Yes. I've been on a speaking tour throughout Europe and North America." He nods significantly and sighs. "Everyone's searching for answers. And what do you do?"

Matt clears his throat nervously. "I'm an artist."

"Hummm," Walter's bushy eyebrows twitch and he fixes his bright blue eyes at him in an unwavering stare until Matt feels his palms grow sweaty and the hair on the back of his neck tingles. "And how do you feel about the insane amounts of money that are now being paid for the work of somebody like a Van Gogh or a Munch?"

This line of questioning puts Matt instantaneously on edge. Apart from the fact that he knew that Van Gogh was the dude who cut his ear off, he is completely lost. He is definitely going to have to Google some art sites tonight back at the motel so he won't be caught saying something that is total bullshit. Well, in Matt's case it would be total bullshit but as long as he is the only one who knows that, he supposes it would be O.K. "Just what do you mean by insane amounts of money?"

"Millions and millions."

"Well yeah. But I certainly wouldn't mind it if I got millions for my paintings."

"But that's just the point Matt. If I may say so, you are unfortunately in a profession where you are worth more dead than alive."

Matt takes this in slowly. His father has always told him he is next to worthless. Having just dropped into the art world by some extreme accident of fate, he has not yet had the time to consider his self worth from a *post mortem* perspective.

Walter continues: "Have you ever considered how profitable it would be to die?"

"I've never really thought of dying as a good career move."

"But if you could die, temporarily, wouldn't you like to inherit your own assets?"

At precisely this point in the conversation, Matt and Walter are interrupted by a frenzied Jillian demanding that Matt pose for several dozen photographs with her. "It must happen now!" she commands, with absolute conviction. "The sun is setting at just the right angle and the clouds are just darling. They'll make the perfect backdrop!"

Every adult at the table, save Roger, pulls out a digital camera from a holster, and brandishes it like a Smith and Wesson in a spaghetti western. The instant everyone's cameras are pointed in their direction, Jillian strikes a well-practiced pose and smiles ear to ear, her head turns expertly toward the light source at just the perfect angle so that every possible shadow that could have been thrown on her face miraculously disappears. She wraps Matt's arm around her shoulders, clutching his hand in a death grip, and holds her perfect frozen smile until every camera at the table has been fired a half dozen times. To top things off they start firing pictures at each other's cameras.

"Cheese!" she gushes. "Come on Matt. Say cheese!" she commands pointing him in six directions in rapid succession, as he becomes progressively more blinded by multiple flashes. "Come on!"

"You were saying?" Matt tries to continue his conversation with Walter. "I've always thought of death as a kind of one-off proposition."

"Not necessarily..." continues Walter. Jillian and Madeline give each other wary looks and engage in synchronized eye rolling. Roger nudges Jillian under the table. Before they can intervene, Walter has handed Matt a business card, emblazoned with an ice cube, and bearing in a Gothic typeface, the words: *Cryonic Future Life Center, (patent pending) The Reverend Walter Yarwood President.*

"Say cheese, Matt!" commands Jillian. Flash goes another camera.

"Oh look!" enthuses Roger. "There's our waiter. Let's ask him for bread while we're waiting."

"Look over this way Matt. Whooho! Say cheese!" Matt is blinded by yet another flash.

"Enough already," he snaps.

"O.K. O.K. I didn't know you were so camera shy," Jillian pouts. Matt considers the wonder of modern digital photography when it falls into the wrong hands, namely the Yarwoods'. He imagines that they are fascinated with these devices because they enable them to take many more bad photographs than ever before. And then, they could get the instant gratification of seeing how bad the pictures are at the press of a button. Surprisingly, neither Jillian nor Walter care about the competency of the photographer or the artistic quality of the picture taken. All they care about is the sheer number of images and how good they look, on a relative scale, compared to every other picture. The rest of the wait for the seafood is spent in a frantic evaluation of each photograph to determine how the two of them look together.

Jillian's anxiety fades as she concludes that the pictures are adequate and she and Matt "look perfect together."

Madeline and Roger shoot devious smiles at each other.

Jillian announces, in a petulant tone normally used by a toilet-training toddler, "I need to visit the little girls' room. Madeline, I need you to come with me right now!"

This is new, thinks Matt. He didn't realize that Jillian had a fear of strange toilets.

Jillian squeals as she drags Madeline off to the toilet. "Isn't he just so perfect? Don't we look ideal together? And he's the darling of the arts writers back home. It's like he's everybody's favorite dessert all of a sudden. I can't figure out how I didn't notice him sooner."

"Well," Madeline allows. "I suppose he is cute."

"Cute? Why did you see that chiseled jaw? That smile? Those broad shoulders! I can't get over how photogenic he is."

"And you two are getting along well?" Maddy asks gingerly. She never likes to delve too deeply, lest Jillian horrify her with bizarre sexual details that no self-respecting WASP would entertain. These are usually followed by tales of woe about ex or current wives, insider trading, or purloined designer goods.

"Fabulously. I think he's the one."

"Really."

"Yes Maddy, I think I've found my first husband."

"Jillie, sweetie. Are you going to bring up Daddy's attendance at Spring Break?"

"I don't know if this would be a good idea in front of Matt."

"Oh?"

"If we get into a big blow out here in the restaurant, he might think we're crazy! I wouldn't want to scare him off."

"Hummm."

They return to the tables, with Jillian's heart beating an eager little tap dance. Something wonderful is definitely coming her way if only she plays her cards right. Ever since Jillian became a redhead her fortunes had begun to change. Hair color was so much more effective for bringing about personal transformation than *Feng Shui*. Here she had rearranged all her furniture twice last year, and all she had to show for it was bruised shins. The remainder of the evening is a blur as more photographs are taken of Jillian with the children, Jillian with her father, Jillian with Walter and Jillian with her sister and her husband.

These are slightly less successful. As they stroll back to their rental car, Jillian confides to Matt that, "If Madeline shows up again tomorrow in that dowdy sweatshirt and God help me, those Scholls sandals, I will burst into flames!"

* * *

That night, in the face of Matt's continued reticence; Jillian decides to take the bull by the horns. Gentle reader, this is a PG rated book, so she doesn't really take a bull, and it isn't really the horns she grabs.

But you get the picture. Suffice it to say that she brings all her enthusiasm to the endeavor, wears a see-through designer peignoir, and hops on top of a startled Matt while he is still watching the recap of the Men's Slalom on satellite television.

She remains decidedly on top. This position is a personal favorite of Matt's, since it allows him to just lay back and let the woman engage in full throttle lust while he barely breaks a sweat. Sometimes, when one of his lovers is too preoccupied to notice that he has left the television on, he is able to catch the occasional glimpse of the Sports Network or some other coded message from Man Land, while his excited inamorata is bobbing up and down.

Later, in the subtle blue-green glow cast by the thirty-inch television screen, as Jillian curls up and pulls her new lover's left arm around her in the proscribed manner, with her head resting on his downy chest, feeling his refreshingly sweat-free warmth, she tells him: "I can't believe how fate has thrown us together."

"I was thinking the same thing," he replies nervously, as his other arm hangs over the side of the bed, gingerly poking around in search of the remote.

SEVENTEEN

DUE TO CIRCUMSTANCES BEYOND OUR CONTROL

When Matt emerges from the subway station, his olfactory sensors are hit immediately with the aroma of authentic Greek souvlaki being lovingly char broiled. Bouzouki music filters through the other sounds of Danforth Avenue's late evening scene. Matt looks up at the full moon: soft, pale yellow on a night so crisp and clear you could see the man in the moon winking back. He breathes the cool night air in deeply and moves towards the smell of expertly seasoned lamb roasting on a spit. Off in the distance a dog howls. Then another. Then a third. Then the dogs howl in unison, their canine voices combining eerily. Wait! Matt can distinguish the howls. They are doing a rendition of *New York, New York*.

"No!" Matt shouts. He bolts upright in bed in a cold sweat. Feels around in the sheets. His hand zeroes in on a firm, perhaps too-firm-to-be-real breast. Jesus. It is a corpse-like Jillian sleeping peacefully under her thick layer of cream and chilled antifreeze-filled sleep mask, her gloved hands clasped across her bosom. Matt is still disoriented, but less so. He goes to the window. Palm trees are outside. No snow. He must still be in Florida.

Oh Christ. He has made love with Jillian. Or rather, she has made love to him. What could he have been thinking? He has become a piece of lost luggage thrown haphazardly onto a conveyor belt leading to Commitment City. Before he even realized what was happening he had unwittingly become the lover of a woman who is already talking wedding cake. Is he being shoe-horned into an engagement?

He slips out of the bed and pulls on a pair of blue jeans he finds on the floor. As he fastens the buttons of his shirt, he slips barefoot out of the room and pads across the asphalt driveway to the motel's office. The night manager spots him at the door, reaches into his drawer to finger a weapon.

"Can I come in?"

"Is there a problem?" the night manager asks nervously, before he recognizes Matt as one of his guests.

"Could be. I was wondering if you had a computer I could use?"

"I shouldn't really let you in at this hour," the night manager says. "But you look harmless enough." He swings the door wide.

Matt stations himself at the office computer, fires it up and Googles his favorite travel site, *Expedia* to start. He searches every airline that flies remotely in the direction of Toronto. There is nothing, absolutely nothing that is going to get him to Toronto any sooner than the ticket he has booked with Jillian. Damn Spring Breakers. He is sunk. There is nothing better to do except play along and wait until, like his previous girlfriends, she gets fed up enough with him to throw him out.

He thinks of his hero, Ron Bellamy. What would Ron do? He puzzles over this last question but an answer does not come. Jillian seems to have too much zeal to be easily dissuaded by Matt's usual technique of ignoring all commitment-related signals, coupled with his aggravating cheapskate ways. Still too wakeful to return to Jillian's bed, he drifts idly into Google, his curiosity piqued. First he types in his own name. He wants to confirm that his career as an artist still exists. A recently archived article in the *Globe* assures him that he won't be forced back into dog walking, in particular walking singing dogs. How many more sleepless nights will he have because of Diva's tuneless howling of *New York, New York*, he wonders?

Then he Googles Jillian. Just how much acting has she done, really? he asks himself. Apparently she has done some. There is an assortment of lukewarm reviews from which to choose. A mention of a small stage role in Stratford. A talent agent's site has some more information, including the fact that she was featured on a calendar for an auto parts manufacturer in Ajax, thumbnail sized pictures of which are featured on their web site. He isn't sure, but in the dim light of the motel office, he thinks the picture shows her hair as a different color.

But Matt can't stop with Jillian. He wants to know about Walter. That's not quite correct. He is driven by a compulsion to know about Walter. In particular, how is this guy on the loose? Does insanity run in the family, and if so, how come they haven't noticed? Eagerly he types in his full name. Hundreds of citations came up. He has hit the mother lode. Or so he thinks.

Here is something strange. His name continuously appears in relation to a pseudo religious group called End Times Incorporated. Prior to the new millennium, it had turned a tidy profit in extended-time-frame canned goods which were supposed to outlast a Y2K meltdown of epic proportions. Many of the web sites went back to a couple of years before Y2K. But as for postings after the year 2000, the End Times Inc. citations petered off. There are scattered references to the disappointment that the world had not experienced the kind of near-total annihilation that would have made End Times Inc.'s canned goods enterprise a really sweet idea. And quite obviously, since the sales revenue was deposited in Swiss bank accounts, End Times Inc. considered Switzerland above any Final Judgment cataclysm ordained by a higher power. Now that's what you call stable currency. And of course, among the web postings, there are numerous condemnations of Walter. But when Matt double clicks on many of the sites' URLs, he finds only a 'page not found' message.

By 2002, the internet trail of Walter's survivalist canned good enterprise/religion had grown cold. The last End Times Inc. story had made references to a federal audit, and then that was it. No fresh End Times Inc. corporate blog. No appeal for donations to spread the good word of Final Judgment for everyone but card carrying, dues paying, tin can buying members. It was as if they had disappeared without a trace, taking their tin can empire with them.

But what has Walter been up to since then at the Cryonic Future Life Center?

Matt wants to Google some more, but the motel employee is staring at the back of his head and yawning audibly. Matt supposes that this is the time of the night when the man must generally have grabbed a bit of shut eye. Matt understands. When you're paid minimum wage, sleeping on the job is one of life's pleasurable compensations. He says his good nights and pads back out into the still night. Matt is just curious enough that he decides to give up on escape routes. He slinks back to bed, and passes out, certain that the morning will reveal more of Jillian's relatives' high jinks.

* * *

Across the parking lot, in the stillness of the night, Roger is whispering to his wife. "I never cease to be amazed by the Yarwoods and their cool as an English cucumber approach to reality."

"They are WASPs Roger. What did you expect?"

"Even so. There are limits. But where your family is concerned, it wouldn't matter how crazy one of your own acts. It's as if a white elephant were sitting in the living room reading the paper. Nobody will remark on its existence."

"That's not quite true. You have to look for the subtle signs of distress. They aren't really so out of touch that they wouldn't notice the elephant reading the Globe," contends Madeline. "There'd be that flicker of acknowledgment, that single twitching eyebrow, that minute lapse in *sang froid* that reveals that something could possibly be amiss in their carefully ordered universe."

"Who is going to look for an eyebrow twitch when Walter is acting completely off his rocker?"

"I can assure you it's there. Watch Daddy next time that Walter says something absurd. Suddenly his attention will flash elsewhere, he'll execute a ninety degree turn, and then it will be as if there were no white elephant at all."

"But how do they manage that? Where did they learn to live in such deep denial?" asks Roger, who is still adapting to the Yarwoods after more than half a decade.

"You have much to learn grasshopper," Madeline kids. Then more seriously, she continues, "You didn't really get to know Mother. You see, Roger, we learned at her feet how to pretend that everything was normal in the face of solid evidence that this was not the case. And now the same little one act play is being staged for the benefit of Walter. Why else do you think I changed my name? Tradition? Don't be daft! Of course he's insane, but as long as no one acknowledges it, then the men in the white coats might never be called. The exposé on *60 Minutes* might never happen. No one need ever know. The thing is to play along, not draw attention to the white elephant in the living room, and leave it to finish reading the paper in peace. Then it will go away."

"You don't fit in with them, you know."

"That's a relief."

"How is that?" puzzles Roger.

"I think I'm adopted. In fact I just know it," says Madeline. "I just know, from the deepest recesses of my heart that I am not a blood relation of Walter and Jillian."

"Very funny. You can't deny them. You have the identical coloring." With that, Roger rolls over and goes to sleep, leaving Madeline to her ruminations. It is true that she doesn't fit in. Why, Jillian and Walter positively channelled Aurora from beyond the grave. Although dead, her manic narcissism still directs their every move.

But why had they not told her? Why hadn't they come clean? Didn't they realize how much knowing she was adopted would put her mind at ease? Sure she looks a lot like her siblings, albeit without the obsessive and high end grooming in which a woman like Jillian indulges. Her hair is a low-key russet brown, instead of Jillian's current brilliant red. Her nose is not quite so bobbed, her breasts less pert and rounded, (after the kids especially). Still while the particulars differed, the generalities are alike. But that could be just a coincidence, couldn't it? I mean- Madeline thinks as she lays next to the gently snoring Roger -how can I possibly be a blood relation of these two, when I do not possess their streak of insanity? Could it have skipped a generation? Could that explain the extreme aggravation of her children Charles and

Diana? Aren't all kids irritating as hell?

Madeline sighs. Maybe she was switched at birth, and that's why her genetic disconnection was not detected. That was another possibility. After all, a busy hospital nursery could be jam-packed with little WASP babies, especially ten months after the last game of the Stanley Cup Playoffs. Just how do you distinguish one screaming orange-headed ball from another? Sigh. There is still the strength of the undeniable family resemblance, on the outside, minus the peroxide, rhinoplasty, implants and capped teeth. At least Jillian is threatening to settle down. Her latest pigeon, Matt, seems like the type that could be easily lead down the garden path by a woman like Jillian. She never let male reticence stand in the way of a relationship. Maddy glances over at her children, now blissfully asleep and astonishingly beautiful on their motel cots. Would Jillian get to experience the mixed blessing that is parenthood? She is thirty-six. Still had a few good eggs left. It isn't exactly Jillian's good eggs that intrigue Maddy. It's the bad ones. Could Jillian turn this rumpled artist into a family man? If she does, Madeline takes perverse pleasure in the certainty that Jillian's children would be at least as much hell as her own.

God makes toddlers beautiful so we won't strangle them, thinks Madeline. It's only when you get older that the luster wears off. Speaking of decaying luster, what kind of nonsense is Daddy up to? Tomorrow morning, she and Roger are just going to have to get to the bottom of his partying. After all, his last escapade left him in a neck brace. What could be next? And where the hell was the famous Iris?

* * *

In a Seminole casino further down the coast, a hyper Iris is feeding tokens into a one armed bandit. She had won a short while ago. At least she thinks it was a short while ago, but a quick glance at her watch tells her that her big win was three hours back. She had brushed all the coins the slot machine had paid out into a big noisy tin bucket. All around her she could hear the tantalizing racket of other machines, but not hers, paying out.

She is now down to her last buck. She itches to just draw some more cash out with her bank card and start piling more money into the slot machines. After all, she has to make up for her losses yesterday. That last win was supposed to do it. But sadly, she hasn't been able to turn that lucky streak over into another little nest egg. She supposes it is time to be getting back to her new fiancé, Big Daddy.

He is perfect husband material, she thinks with satisfaction. Settled. Owns his own top of the line RV. No other pesky relatives anywhere in the state. Solvent, hypertensive and close to eighty. You couldn't ask for more than that.

* * *

But while the rest of Florida sleeps, the trailer park is a hot bed of activity. More or less. Overactive bladder syndrome could take the blame for some of it. It is also partially due to the fact that many seniors sleep for only a few hours a night, and the RV park is chock a block full of geriatric nighthawks. Eddie is among them. Big Daddy joins him this night, not because of a touchy bladder or nocturnal habits. Rather, he is troubled by his fate in much the same way that a condemned man considers the lethal injection that awaits him in the morning.

"This neck brace is a pain in the ass, Eddie."

"Maybe you ought not to have gone into that Jell-O contest."

"Are you nuts? And miss a chance, at my age to wrestle with college girls? An opportunity like that will never come again."

"Point taken." Eddie nods his head, which is covered in a cat's cradle of carefully combed over white hair, of which he is extremely proud. "But what you gonna do if Iris finds out?"

"That's just the point. I was married and well-behaved for forty-two years. If Iris is going to be the kind of woman that expects me to behave again, well, I'd just as soon not get married again."

"Plenty o' men think that way, to be sure." Eddie is married, but it is a mixed blessing. She is a formidable cook who is now so hard of hearing that he is no longer required to really converse with her. After fifty-two years of fighting tooth and nail, it has come as a great relief to be able to eat his meals in peace. He is enjoying the kind of bliss that he had dreamt of since he had first put the ring on her finger. His stomach rumbles. "Is Iris a good cook?"

"Nah. Mostly she just makes those little rugs of hers. Sweet though. She brings me rum and raisin ice cream every night just before bed. Even spoons it into me like I'm her little kid. Oh hell, I don't know. Maybe she'll understand about the Jell-O. Maybe I don't have to tell her."

"How'd it come about in the first place?"

"Well. I heard this God awful racket coming from the beach. I like to go down to Harpoon Harry's for coffee. So I was just walking around minding my own business when this guy comes up to me and says, which way's the party?"

"He didn't just follow the racket?"

"This guy was from out of town and was coming in just for the occasion, as it were. And I thought, do I know you?"

"You recognized him?"

"Course I recognized him. He was Ron Bellamy! You claim you don't recognize Ron Bellamy and I'll tell you, you're a liar."

"Point taken." Eddie certainly does know who he is. Many nights when he couldn't bring himself to climb into bed next to his irate wife, he had stayed up watching videos on the television and vicariously enjoying the exploits of this particular star. He was a kind of superman of the small screen. He could leap tall women in a single bound! Eddie is eager for details. "Did you get an autograph?"

"To hell with autographs! He asked me if I wanted to come to the party and the next thing I knew it I was in! I was in the orbit of a superstar! And all these college kids were partying with me. Next thing I knew I was in a big tub of Jell-O and the rest is on the medical chart."

"Maybe you can just tell Iris you fell in the tub."

"Hummm. That's clever. I mean, it was a tub." Big Daddy starts to feel hopeful.

"Muhumm. And it's not really lying. It's just the annotated version of otherwise true events."

"Now I know why we're friends, Eddie." Leave it to Eddie, thinks Big Daddy, to know exactly how to get around the sticky problems that would be unleashed by absolute truth telling. A lie is a tricky thing to tell effectively. But a partial truth, if sufficient to allay suspicion and explain the neck brace, isn't a lie at all. It's just the truth without full disclosure. The trick is to say as little as possible. The sin of omission isn't exactly the sin of deceit, is it?

"Where is Iris, anyway?"

"She said something about visiting an old friend after she went to her hooking workshop."

"She still doing workshops, is she?"

"Sure, why not?"

Eddie sputters, "Well, I thought she was retired." This was the most delicate response he could think of, without twisting himself into a pretzel. He isn't quite as liberal as his northern friend, here. But he isn't from any Red State either, so he tries to keep an open mind. Even if he did think Iris was a little too 'blue-rinse' and gravity-challenged for the trade. And since when did they organize into groups?

"She still likes to keep a hand in."

"That's an interesting way of putting it." Eddie sits back in his chair and considers what he would do if he suddenly found himself in a vat of Jell-O with a bunch of college girls. Would he incur the wrath of his silent but still formidable wife? Or would he throw caution to the wind? Eddie asks himself: What would Ron do?

At the entrance to the RV park, as the residents settle down for the night, Charlie, the good-for-nothing son of Big Daddy's next door neighbor is keeping watch. Rather, he should have been keeping watch if only his Game Boy had run out of power. Instead, he is boosting his attention deficit disorder while frantically pushing the buttons on his toy. Charlie had arrived several months before at the door of his parent's mobile home, with a greasy thrift shop suitcase and a garbage bag to carry the overflow luggage. He had driven from Wisconsin in a rusted, phlegmatic bucket of bolts that breathed its last just outside Tallahassee. He took a bus to cover the remaining distance.

It was obvious that he intended to stay, having been evicted from his previous apartment following his personal bankruptcy and subsequent second divorce. His mother, who had 'an in with the management', got her slovenly offspring a security job with the RV park. Now settled into a job where he is paid to do little more than doze off or sit in a chair, he has descended into a digital universe. All the while that his calloused thumbs push on the buttons of his Game Boy, the Florida night is sizzling with untamed energy. People are plotting deception. Some are gambling on life and love. A few are mulling the dubious joys of parenthood. And a game warden is frantically on the lookout for a love-lorn eleven foot alligator that has broken out of his theme park home and is making for the coast, heeding the urgent call of mating season.

He has just finished a hearty supper of stray cat. And still, Charlie plays on, unaware.

* * *

When Iris enters the compartment of the bus, she notices that an older man with dark, salt and pepper hair topped by a felt cowboy-style hat is seated alone. He has the same kind of deep brown, almond eyes that many of the casino workers had. A Seminole. He is wearing a short sleeved golf shirt, which draws even more attention to his wrists and hands: one hand is missing several fingers, the other is nicely set off by a flashy Rolex watch. He wears no ring.

"Are you saving this seat for your wife?" Iris asks in her most gracious tone of voice.

"Oh no, not at all," the man replies, as he removes his shopping bag from the seat next to him. "I'm not married."

"Handsome man like yourself?" she asks incredulous, as she sizes him up.

"I'm a widower."

"You don't say!. I'm a widow myself." Iris plunks herself down next to him, begins playing with her platinum, almost but not quite white hair. "Here on holiday with some friends, but they had to go back."

"So you're not from here?" the man asks, making idle, polite conversation. How many tourists had he met who held forth on exactly the same topics, he wondered?

"I'm from Omaha. Retired, though. Thinking about moving down here." Iris gives a little smile as she turns toward him and bats her eyelashes.

"I'm retired as well. Actually, I'm sort of disabled," he offers, proudly holding his truncated hand up for her to view the stumps where fingers were once attached. "Gator wrangling accident."

"Gracious!" Iris holds her hand to her chest. "Does that happen often?"

"Only if you're lucky!" How he loved showing off his battle scars for the tourists.

"Oh don't be silly. I've always wondered, though. You do see a lot of gator farms around here, and everglade tours and those parks where alligators are in evidence. If they're dangerous, why do people wrestle them?"

"That's just the point. It keeps the tourists coming."

"Don't they kill people, though?" Iris is still acting, and feeling vulnerable and awestruck by this man's mangled hand, and its cause.

"Oh that's a bit of an exaggeration. There have only been...oh I'd say...less than two dozen people killed and eaten clean up by gators in the last fifty years. Course, that's not counting the occasional loss of a limb. That's the beauty part."

"How so?"

"It's a damn good job! Tourist trade, you know. Why I wrangled gators for decades. And my daddy did too. It certainly did put food on the table. And not just grapefruit either. But my sons, you can't talk them into the family line of work."

"Why's that?"

"Casinos are a soft touch. I just come from visiting one of 'em down here where he's pursuing his pantywaist career." This last comment is delivered with an aggravated sneer. "I can't even interest them in trying gator wrangling. I have no one to pass my skills on to anymore!" he concedes. "The art will die with me."

"Is it hard to get started?" says Iris, who is making an effort to not look at his hand. She can see that he wants to be drawn out, would be flattered by her interest in his story. She leans in a bit to show her enthusiasm.

"Well. It's a good idea to start small. Practice say with something like a family dog, a big one, mind you, and then you can graduate to a gator once you get the hang of grabbing them from behind and flinging them into the water. Course, most dogs don't have the kind of tail that you could swing them in the air with, so you'd have to grab their hind legs. But you get the picture."

"How fascinating!"

"Course, once you swing a gator around enough and you tire it out, then you have to climb on its back. You can't really climb on your dog's back, so you just have to wing that part. Anyhow, with a gator, that's when you are supposed to yank its head backwards, like."

"Wow!" Iris is genuinely impressed.

"Exactly! That's when everybody cheers," he says with a satisfied smile, as he is obviously reliving past glories.

"That must be the tricky part."

"Can be. Of course, once you got the gator's jaw shut you can hold it shut. But if you slip up, and they get to clamp their teeth down, look out! Whoooo! That's where the health and accident insurance comes in handy."

"So what you're saying is that if you do get hurt, you're insured."

"That's right." He holds his fist up again for closer inspection. The second and third fingers are missing below the knuckle. "I had a beauty of a policy. Set me up for life. But my kids, they're just chickenshit, sorry ma'am, pardon my language. They can't see the good points of gator wrestling."

"That you can get set for life?"

"That's right," he enthuses.

"Well, thank you so much to telling me about this fascinating career. I'll have to tell my friends back home, when I go back. Maybe we'll practice on their house cat," Iris adds coyly.

"Oh you can come see me and I'll give you a demonstration. I still wrassle little gators from time to time, just to keep a hand in, so to speak," he chuckles a little at his cleverness, and as he does she notices a missing incisor and several substantial gold fillings. "Here let me give you my address."

"Well thank you very much. I just might do that."

"It's no use telling me that there are bad aunts and good aunts. At the core, they are all alike. Sooner or later, out pops the cloven hoof." - P.G. Wodehouse

⊱ EIGHTEEN ⊰

BACHELORS ON THE RUN

Matt is lounging in his bed, hovering between wakefulness and a marginal dream state. Somewhere close to the start of business hours at the coffee shop across the asphalt parking lot of the motel, he had heard a garbage truck load and chew up the establishment's trash. The drone of the truck's gears had been enough to destroy his reverie: he had just climbed the gentle slopes of a low foothill, (not a full-fledged and challenging mountain), and at the top had crossed paths unexpectedly with supermodel Heidi Klum. They were standing together in a verdant meadow dotted with edelweiss and daisies, about to kiss, when the garbage truck began its steady drone. Matt had buried his head in his pillows and hid under the blanket, like a turtle retreating into his shell, trying as he 'turtled' to recapture his lost dream. But to no avail.

He had allowed himself to drift off again, hoping that it would be some kind of Freudian moment, the type where dreams supposedly repeated themselves over and over again until the patient reaches some resolution. He should have another shot at kissing Heidi. But no. All he can remember from this second episode of 'turtling' was the rustling of sheets on the other side of the bed and then the muffled sounds of Jillian's ablution and grooming rituals. He was still 'turtling' when he heard Jillian slip out the door and close it with deliberate gentleness. But still no Heidi returned.

Eventually, after more tossing and turning, Matt sits up, reaches for the remote and starts flipping through the channels. Nothing of interest pops out at him.

Suddenly he misses Finnegan. How is he doing back home? Matt doubts that Josh is taking him for walks. Even though Finnegan is not troubled overmuch by a few feet of snow on the ground, Josh would probably hold out about getting outside until there is a good likelihood of his mother's car being repaired.

In the meantime, leaving the house might involve the pointless digging out of the family driveway. And with no car to drive to the slopes, Matt is guessing that Josh is not up for that odious task. Still, he is hoping that Finnegan is getting his quota of love and attention. And Matt wants to share with his friend the tremendous success he is now apparently enjoying over his, (albeit Finnegan's) paintings. Not to mention mull over the recent events with Jillian.

Good God. He had slept with Jillian. He shakes his head in disbelief. It's not that he is particularly happy about this turn of events. Terror is a more accurate description of his feelings. But he knows that his best buddies would certainly be impressed, as long as he is short on details about the situation in which he now finds himself stranded. They are not above bed hopping as a competitive sport. He is pretty sure he'd get a few five point nines and a five point seven or two, less certain about scoring perfect sixes. But still, a pretty impressive showing, all things considered.

It's funny how that event actually feels after the fact. Before yesterday, he had found her wildly exciting, exotic and interesting. If he hadn't been so nonchalant by nature, he might have actually gone out of his way to pursue her. Plenty of men would. But suddenly last night, as she laid her flamboyant head of red hair on his chest and, more or less informed him of the fact that they were in love, he had felt panic stricken.

This isn't really supposed to happen in the new millennium. People are supposed to troll around looking for lovers, like jackals scouring the South African veldt looking for fresh kill. They are supposed to present the very best of themselves in an artfully packaged format, with close attention to their best selling points. They are then supposed to engage in some casual, technically adequate but largely non-committal sex. And then they are supposed to decide, by more or less mutual consent, that they were horribly misled about the possibility of a relationship actually being a good idea. This would free them up to start the whole merry-go-round over again.

It is just a question of getting the timing right.

Matt has generally been pretty good with his timing. He has usually grown tired of his girlfriends at just about the same time that their initial infatuation with him has blossomed into murderous rage. Usually his typical young adult male reticence ran totally counter to the twenty-something female desire to get life's plans in order. This served to create a handy little unresolvable conflict at just about the time that he began yearning for his freedom in earnest. But this is different. He had wanted to be free of Jillian even as she was frantically shoe-horning him into one 'cute couples' photo after another. And her family! Is her brother from Mars? Matt casts his mind back to the evening before: Walter pressing his cryogenics religion/business card into his hand and advising him to "Die for a while to boost your artwork's value". While Madeline and Roger seemed relatively normal, they looked like they were ready to foist their perpetually combative children off on any unsuspecting quasi-relative or cult member that crossed their path. Any minute he expected to see the kids' heads rotating and the exorcist to be called. The only light in the whole scenario was Big Daddy, who had managed by sheer coincidence, to land in the orbit of famed dirty boy next door, Ron Bellamy. Jillian's dad is probably going to drop dead of his antics, but it certainly beats a lingering drama of decay and bed sores on life support.

Yes, Big Daddy has his priorities sorted out. But what about Matt? What is he to do about Jillian? What would Ron do?

Matt reaches for the telephone and calls Josh's number in Etobicoke.

"Jeez Eh, how's it goin'?" Josh yawns and scratches the hair trimming his navel as he asks this. What is Matt doing calling before noon? Why isn't he still in bed? Perhaps he awakened early because he has no work to avoid.

"How's the weather?" Matt asks cautiously.

"Snowy. Chris St. Clair says we're getting more. Yesterday Mom made me dig out the driveway in case we can't find where it begins and ends after the next storm."

"Yesterday? Did she get the car back already?"

"No. Can you imagine? She didn't have a hope of getting it back yesterday and yet she refused to sort my laundry unless I dug out the driveway. She's some kind of maniac, man. She couldn't have waited to see if the second storm really hit, or not. God."

"So when will she get the car?"

"Any minute now she should be pulling back in with it. Roads are pretty slippery. She probably should have just given up going to get it until tomorrow." Josh yawns.

"Great. Do you think you can make it over to my place to get my mail and check my messages and water my plants and stuff?"

"Your plants? What plants? I don't remember any plants."

"The ones in the hall closet," Matt hints conspiratorially.

A dawning realization comes over Josh. "...Right... Those plants..." Matt can hear the himming and hawing starting deep in Josh's throat. Finally the exasperated exhale through his nose. "It's not a really great day to drive Matt."

"Come on. Take care of my plants and I'll give you a couple buds.

You can stay at my place even, if you take Finnegan with you. I've got satellite television, all sports all the time. A fridge full of beer. It's right downtown. You can go out partying and you only have to crawl back home. No drunk driving charges to worry about."

"Well," Josh allows, pausing to scratch his three-day old beard. "Mom has been giving me a hard time. She says I'm not looking hard enough for a full-time job. Says I have to get -(and this last word is delivered with a mocking whine)- motivated. Wants me to do my own laundry! If she keeps it up, I might just get motivated right out of the house."

"And start paying rent? Are you crazy? Take my advice man and avoid those rent paying situations at all cost."

"You're right about that, eh. First thing that happens once a guy gets a place of his own, his girlfriend starts thinking about moving to the next level. Starts thinking he's a going concern. Tries to turn him into the sperminator before her biological alarm clock goes off. Hell, I'm only twenty-eight!"

"Can't have that happen. Whooo! Tell you what, though. You stay in my place till I get back and that'll give your Mom a chance to cool off. She'll come around. They always do."

"Oh all right. I suppose hiding out in Man Land might be a good idea for a while. I'll head out as soon as she comes back with the car."

"By the way Josh, is Finnegan perking up?"

"What do you mean, perking up?" Josh casts his memory back to the last time he let Finnegan out for a pee. Did his mother let him out this morning? Would there be a puddle greeting him in the back porch?

"You know, enjoying the change of surroundings, getting into his walks, chasing some birds, coming out of his creative slump."

"What the hell are you talking about? Creative slump! Sheesh. He's a dog, for crissake."

"Yeah, you're right. What was I thinking? Anyhow. I'm wondering if you could check my messages too. The guy from the gallery tracked me down to Jillian's dad's trailer, but there might be more messages."

"The guy from the gallery, huh?"

"Oh yeah. I'm like some kind of success. All my paintings sold out. I've even got my own money. I mean, money I didn't have to nag Dad for!"

"Go figure."

"So if anybody calls, tell them my number here at the motel where I'm staying with Jillian. Seems I'll probably be hanging out around here more than Jillian's dads. She went there on her own this morning."

"I can't believe you're going out with an actress."

"Me neither," Matt replies nervously.

"Way to go, buddy. Wait till the other guys hear."

* * *

Jillian had decided to leave the rental car and Matt back in the motel and proceed to Big Daddy's in Roger and Madeline's rented Toyota Echo. They have wedged her in between the two kids, turning her into a human demilitarized zone between two hostile entities. She sits there nervously squeezed between them, worrying the entire time about their runny noses, sticky fingers and other potentially threatening body fluids that kids simply oozed or even gushed without warning. They are little mucus geysers, for God's sakes! Roger and Madeline are trying to prompt the kids into opening up a dialogue about amusement parks and how much they'd like to visit one with their favorite aunt.

"I wants to see a addigator eat chickens all upded just like in the pictures," enthuses Charles.

"Me too." chirps Diana.

"You can't!" Charles asserts.

"Why not?"

"Mommy says it's too yucky. You're too liddle," he taunts. "Not like me!"

Diana bursts into loud, seemingly inconsolable crying. Roger turns back toward them. "Stop it you two. You'll upset your aunt. You don't want to upset your aunt, do you?"

Madeline looks at Roger significantly. "Daddy's right. You shouldn't upset Auntie Jillian or she won't want to take you anywhere."

-Jillian receives this piece of news with horror. Take them somewhere? Who? Where? When was this decided? While she struggles to find an escape route, she listens to the ongoing prattle in the front seats.

"Roger, you're going to have to say something to him."

"Why do I have to say something to him? He's your father, for crissakes."

In the back seat, the children begin chanting, "Not in front of the children!" even before Madeline does.

"You have to speak to him man to man. Daddy's just having some kind of delayed mid-life crisis. Maybe he's panicked that he's engaged. There must be some reason why he got involved in a Jell-O wrestling match with a pair of college girls, for heaven's sake."

"I can think of at least four."

"Funny. I don't think sarcasm is appropriate at this time."

Jillian chirps up in the back seat. "What four reasons could that be Roger? Tell me why our father has decided to besmirch the memory of our sainted mother."

Roger hoots. Madeline muffles a snort.

"O.K. I take that back," says Jillian. "But he's still too old to be carrying on like that. And what's with the supposed fiancée? Where is she? What do you suppose she's up to? After all, and don't take this the wrong way, Daddy is not exactly Pierce Brosnan."

"That's an understatement." Roger agrees. Madeline pokes him in the ribs, just as they are pulling into the RV park.

At just that moment a solicitous driver is unloading from his cab a disheveled woman with obviously fake platinum blonde hair. She looks a little frenzied and unsteady, like she has had a long night. She is carrying a large patchwork tote bag, and wearing the sort of flamboyant beribboned sun hat that, had it been red and not made of cheap straw, would have been used to terrorize women who had newly turned fifty and didn't want to be found out by the likes of the Red Hat Society.

"Well, that must be our new step-mother," Jillian spits out. "Apart from the hat, she's managed to avoid the fashion crime of wearing a muumuu among the non-visually impaired."

"Meow," chimes Madeline, then adding, with nary a shred of personal guilt. "Either she has cerebral palsy or she's been drinking."

Big Daddy has spied Iris's shaky arrival through the kitchen window of his Beaver. He nervously assesses the situation, realizes its gravity and rushes out to meet her. His attempt to hustle her off before his children could intercept fails. Just as he emerges from his home on wheels, Jillian comes bounding out of the Echo's back seat. "You must be Iris!" she gushes, hand thrust forward, ready to shake Iris's own blue veined and liver spotted appendage.

"Ever so charmed, I'm sure," Iris responds as she holds her shaky hand out. Jillian catches a slight whiff of rum on her future step-mother's breath and then it drifts away as Iris finds herself surrounded by Roger, Madeline and the two kids. Walter thumps out of the trailer in a wrinkled caftan, pads across the small grassy patch between the Beaver Patriot and the dazed woman, and envelopes her entirely in a bear hug which leaves only her scrawny legs visible. One of his meaty paws is grasping a sandwich made out of a Kaiser roll which drops some of its contents at Iris's feet. "Welcome to the family, Mommy!" he says in his thunderous voice.

Madeline and Roger give each other significant looks, and drift away from the crowd surrounding Iris. "Walter spent the night here? How did he manage to get his foot in the door when Daddy wouldn't put us up?" Madeline hisses.

"Walter doesn't have kids, honey, maybe it's as simple as that." Roger struggles to say this quietly between clenched teeth.

"What are you saying Roger, that Daddy doesn't want our kids under his roof?"

"No! No! Not that honey. It's just that there's only so much space. And I guess normally he and Iris want to be alone. He probably just put him up because he arrived too late to find a room and Iris was out of town anyway."

"And where was she? I might ask."

"Honey, don't be like that. Look on the bright side. Maybe she'll like kids."

Jillian meanwhile is sticking close to Iris, assessing her the way a sniper checks out a target. Iris casts a sly glance around herself with her glassy blood-shot eyes, checking out the make and year of the rental car, casting a quick assessing glance at Jillian's hands and jewelry, alighting on the stunning pink diamond, glancing up to meet Jillian's eyes sizing her up.

* * *

By mid-afternoon, Matt is still drifting in and out of consciousness when the phone rings in his motel room.

"You bastard!" bellows a curiously familiar voice from the other end of the line.

"Excuse me?" he mumbles as he shakes off his blanket. "Do I know you?"

"You're damn right you do. I'm going to sue you. I'm going to sue your dog. I'm even going to sue whatever the hell dog is responsible for this mess."

"In the first place, you can't sue a dog. In the second place, I don't know what the hell you're talking about." Matt struggles unsuccessfully to place the voice.

"My darling Cleopatra has just given birth. It's a disaster. And you're responsible."

Suddenly he places her. One of his clients. "Look Lady. My father may have accused me of doing nothing but 'fucking the dog' but I assure you it was just a metaphor. I had nothing to do with that dog getting pregnant!"

"Oh? And you know nothing about the fuzzy all black progeny that look decidedly like their half-Pomeranian father? Do you know how much Cleo's pedigree puppies were supposed to sell for?"

"Oh, Oh."

"Oh, Oh Is right. Admit it. I'll do DNA testing if I have to. Cleo was knocked up by that mongrel Bartender. All this time I trusted you with my darling and you were letting her cross paths with that mutt and his disgusting owner. I'm suing you. And I am definitely suing that bastard Randal. How much did he pay you?"

"Nothing. He didn't pay me anything. It just happened."

"Tell it to the judge, buster. When I'm finished, you'll never walk dogs in this town again!" With that, the enraged pet owner slams down the receiver, leaving Matt in a terrible state of agitation. He has a hard time getting back to sleep. When he finally does, he has the dream again. This time however, Cleo is foremost among the singing dogs, and is trailed by a pack of small, fuzzy black puppies. When they sing *New York, New York,* they sound like Alvin and the Chipmunks and their tiny, fluffy tails wave in time to the music.

* * *

Meanwhile, back in the Beaver Patriot, conversation is heating up among the siblings. Iris however, has stumbled off to bed, blaming a bad headache.

"What do you mean, I don't know enough about this woman. She's from Omaha. She's sixty-two. What's the big deal?"

"She doesn't look sixty-two to me. She's had work done," interjects Jillian. "Did you know that?"

"You mean like dentures?"

"No. Not dentures. Work. She's had a face lift."

"How can you possibly know that?"

"Daddy," says Jillian in a pedantic, almost scolding voice. "I practically have a degree in plastic surgery. I've been preparing for my own face lift since I was twenty-two. I can tell. If they tighten her up any more, they may as well put a corkscrew behind her ears."

"Come on. How can you tell, just like that?"

"Just look at the skin on her hands and compare it to the skin on her face. She's more likely eighty-two than sixty-two."

Big Daddy sputters, then barks. "Oh who cares what she's had done. She's a nice woman and I have every right to do whatever I want in my golden years."

"He's right Jillie," said Madeline. "Even if she is, in your opinion, a geriatric gold digger."

"How can you possibly know that?" demands Big Daddy.

"I have my ways." How is Jillian to explain how she has deduced all the subtle signals that as a now-experienced private eye, she has been able to detect just by looking at her? Sure Iris is a bit old for this game. But even when drinking Iris had betrayed a certain animal cunning common to the species. The innate ability to size up a diamond at three paces and arrive at a good rough estimate as to carat, color, cut and clarity. Jillian knows this because she too possesses this uncanny skill. "Besides. You yourself said she was a retired hooker, Daddy. Do you want to marry someone whose past will haunt you?"

Roger and Madeline gasp. Walter whistles through his teeth sending a small spray of saliva and food particles flying. Jillian has said the unsayable. It is hard not to cheer. All eyes turn on Jillian, waiting for one of her famous back peddling maneuvers. It would take a pirouette to get out of this one. None comes. The others fall silent. From outside the trailer comes the sound of Charles and Diana fighting over a discarded plastic ice cream container.

"A hooker? I said that?"

"The first time you mentioned her. You said you were shooting up with a retired hooker from Omaha."

"I was doing whisky shooters with a bunch of retirees from Omaha. They hook rugs."

"Oh." Jillian blinks. Feels her face heating up and knows that, for the first time in many years, she is blushing. "Never mind."

"Well Daddy," Madeline interrupts, deflated and embarrassed. "If it's what you want, we'll give our blessing. Won't we Roger?"

"Huh?" Roger's attention has turned to watching his children who are now engaged in a fierce wrestling match. Secretly he hopes Charles will win, since Diana often resorts to underhanded tactics and works the younger sister angle to advantage too often.

"Our blessing." Madeline pokes him in the ribs.

"Oh yeah. Yeah. Say, Dad," (and this name he uses with an annoyingly syrupy tone that makes the others cringe), "Could you take the kids tomorrow?"

"Not on your life," says Daddy, without a second thought. "I just might be headed to Vegas for a short but sweet wedding and honeymoon."

"Not so fast Daddy. Have you asked her to sign a pre-nup?" says Jillian, seemingly out of the blue.

"A pre-nup? What do you mean a pre-nup?" Big Daddy responds with scarcely concealed outrage. At these words, Iris stirs in the bed and creeps over to the bedroom door, pressing her ears against a slight gap between the door and its threshold. "When a couple gets married it should be based on a sentiment of absolute trust! Marriage is based on complete honesty and integrity."

"Hah! Don't crack me up." Jillian shoots back. "If you believe that, I've got some hot property in the Everglades I want to sell you."

"Jillian! I'm shocked," interjects Madeline. "How could you have become so cynical?"

"Because of how I make a living."

"How do you make a living, Jillian?" growls Daddy. "I thought it was by putting the touch on your father."

"That too. But you're not paying all the bills. I make some handy cash spying on errant spouses, so I know what I'm talking about. It just so happens that my next to last fiancé gave me a copy of a pre-nuptial agreement to sign just before we broke up. I've got it right here." With that she thrusts her bejeweled and taloned hand into her Gucci bag and drags out a neatly folded document, trimmed with a blue cardboard corner protector and embossed with a legal seal. She waves it in the air, like a weapon. "Have a look. It's iron-clad."

"Then why didn't you sign it, Jillian?" interjects Walter.

"What do you take me for? Like I said. It's iron-clad. If I'm going to marry an old geezer, I'm going to want to know it's worth it." She places the document on the Beaver's kitchen table.

"Jillian, I'm shocked," says Walter, indignantly, but with a visible lack of sincerity.

"I'm not," says Madeline, who has always suspected a shrewd mind lurked behind those Christian Dior-rimmed eyes. She is proud. Jillian is so much more than a witless fashionista.

"I'm impressed," says Roger.

"That's it. Get out," Big Daddy bellows. "All of you. I've been your patsy for long enough. I've been a good boy. I've mowed the lawns and dug out the driveways and changed the diapers and cleaned up the kiddie puke and paid the bills. It's my time now. It's time you all grew up. You just want her signing this pre-nup because all you care about is the money. Isn't it?"

"Not at all, Dad," says Walter. "No one's worrying about the inheritance at all."

"Isn't it? Well you're on your own." Big Daddy grasps the handles on Walter's satchel and starts stuffing his spare rumpled sackcloth caftan and dirty socks into it, before making for the door. A trail of cookie crumbs follow the satchel.

"But...but...but. I was going to offer you discount cryogenics! We could freeze your assets indefinitely!"

"That's it. You are not putting my assets or my ass on ice! Get the hell out of my Beaver!" He is waving an accusing finger at them all.

"But Daddy!" shouts several offspring at once.

"You are all off the payroll!"

With that Daddy opens the door and ushers them out. A small crowd of seniors are outside, ostensibly trying to separate the now muddy children. A few are fiddling with the controls on their hearing aids, which they hastily reinsert when Big Daddy's family emerges, followed by Walter's bedraggled satchel.

"You don't need a lift, do you?" asks a terrified Roger.

"Not at all," says Walter, indicating a small red vehicle. "I've driven here from the space center in a rental car."

"Is that where you parked your space ship?" Roger asks, while trying to maintain a humorous tone of voice.

"Funny, Roger. Very funny. I was just looking into a possible business venture."

Madeline jabs Roger in the ribs and hisses under her breath, through clenched teeth, "Don't ask. Don't ask. Don't ask. If you don't notice, it's not really happening."

Roger continues, cheerfully: "I guess you're O.K. then."

"Well..." Walter looks from Roger to Madeline to Jillian. "I couldn't find a room last night. And Daddy's definitely not letting me stay here tonight." He looks forlornly at the steps of his father's trailer, where several mis-shaped and discolored socks had fallen from his satchel. "Do you suppose some of the Spring Breakers will be headed back? Where am I going to get a room?"

Eddie is among the seniors snooping around the RV. "Not many free rooms in this town this week. You should bunk with one of your sisters, till your old man cools off."

Madeline and Roger cast panicky glances at Jillian. Would her new supposed romance trump a married couple in need of a break from their exhausting offspring? If the hotel has no rooms, who is going to be saddled with Walter? "There's no room in our suite, ah, room...Walter. What with the kids and their mess...heh heh heh."

Jillian rolls her eyes. Why hadn't she spoken sooner? "I suppose you forgot Walter that I'm down here with my new fiancé?"

Roger receives another poke in the ribs from Madeline. "Ow. If you keep it up Madeline, I'm going to get a restraining order."

They climb into the front seat of the Echo and wait while Jillian climbs into the back with the two kids in tow. Roger flips on the air conditioning, and rolls up his window. Walter is left standing outside, digging through his satchel for his rental car's keys. Madeline takes advantage of the 'cone of silence' provided by the air conditioned car to turn around and confront her sister. "Fiancé?" she asks, incredulous. "When did this happen?"

"Well..." Jillian hedges. "I just have a feeling that he's about to ask. That's all."

"That's not the same thing as being engaged."

"I can get engaged whenever I want!" Jillian shoots back. "I've been engaged dozens of times."

"Oh?"

"And I am most definitely engaged if it means Walter is trying to crash in my room," she snaps. "And I don't want to hear another thing about it."

The rest of the drive is conducted in stony silence. Even Charles and Diana, exhausted from their previous battle, manage to stay quiet.

* * *

Back in the RV park, uniformed men from the Florida Fish and Wildlife Conservation Commission, and a few helpful local cops, are combing among the bushes following an alligator sighting. A neighboring trailer park has reported another missing cat. Seems that cat meat is a favorite snack of the escaped gator, which the amusement park has taken to calling Houdini. A bad precedent has been set with the eleven foot Houdini. It seems that gators by their nature are shy of humankind. If you don't feed them, if they don't sense that you have food available to them, they won't start to think of you as food. There are laws against feeding the alligators for this very reason. But Houdini's big role in the gator show is eating a whole chicken for the pleasure of the throng of blood thirsty tourists. It is like a gladiator show in a Roman forum. A real crowd pleaser. One day Houdini took one look at his human handlers and thought, "Owwhee. Tastes like chicken!"

This can't be good.

Big Daddy, always the dutiful resident, has joined the search and is rustling the bushes with a broom. The racket, and her fiancé's absence from the trailer is enough to stir the hungover Iris from her rest on Big Daddy's lamented queen sized bed, which she has requisitioned for her sole use. From the bedroom window, she catches a glimpse of several uniformed men. Iris tip toes out to the kitchen of the Beaver, for a better look. Her mind is racing. These kids, these future step-children, added a new complication to her plans. She spots the neatly assembled pre-nup on the kitchenette counter, with its telltale legal seal and sky blue corner enclosure. Her heart is racing. Would Walter Senior really make Iris sign a pre-nup? Even though they've had a whirlwind courtship, Iris has already seen just how cantankerous and irrational he can get. Wouldn't spite alone compel him to just want to rush off to Vegas and tell his kids to go to hell? Just how trusting is the guy, after all?

Her eyes keep wandering back to the document on the table. That bitch Jillian has left it to drive a wedge between Iris and her father. Iris glances at the first page. As she is looking, a patrolman glances in the window and catches her eye. Iris drops the paper.

She walks calmly to the trailer bathroom where her makeup is sprawled across the counter. Iris refreshes her makeup a bit, adding more lipstick, wiping away any eye shadow smears that had crept into her crow's feet. Then she pulls off her blonde wig, shovels the scattered makeup items off the counter and into their case and snaps it shut. She takes the industrial strength bra off the bathroom hook and retrieves the drying panties that have been strewn around the trailer on any available knob. These she stuffs into her tapestry bag. Then she reaches in to one pocket of the bag and pulls out the kind of turban that 1950s movie starlets and chemotherapy patients favor, assesses the effect in the mirror, dons her oversized sun glasses and steps outside. She hopes she looks as *incognito* as the mistress at a married man's funeral. As she walks toward the RV park gates, Eddie pulls up alongside. "Where you goin' Iris? Need a lift?"

"No I just need to get a little fresh air. Ah. Tell Big Daddy I'll be back soon."

"Will do," says Eddie as he pulls away in his Pontiac, followed by a puff of blue smoke. He isn't fooled. He sees the tapestry suitcase in her hand, and judging from the earlier Yarwood family conference which echoed through the trailer park, he guesses at the lay of the land with some accuracy.

Hours later Iris has not returned.

* * *

"I'll tell you Eddie, I'm getting worried," Big Daddy confides over his late afternoon beer and barbeque. He's found a reliable local source for Moosehead and he and Eddie are polishing off some cold ones. This despite the fact that the RV management explicitly forbade the outdoor consumption of liquor by their residents. Big Daddy has such a stockpile of Canadian Beer that half the RV park's snowbirds are in the habit of restocking from him if they run short during a party. Does the fact that he adds a slight mark-up for cartage and storage count as bootlegging, he wonders? Perhaps, but why quit when the small profit offsets the cost of supplying himself?

"How's that?"

"The kids. They really put off Iris, maybe." Daddy sounds uncertain. "Maybe she's left me."

"What makes you think that?" Eddy sucks back the last of his beer, reaches into the cooler for another. He has kept his council, telling only his wife of Iris's hasty retreat. The consequences of not confiding this tasty bit of advance gossip would have been calamitous to marital harmony.

"Her stuff's gone out of the trailer," Big Daddy explains as he pokes some of Roger's contraband moose meat on the barbeque.

"It's an R.V," Eddie corrects. He knows he can't fake being shocked about Iris taking off, so he doesn't even bother. He simply pulls his Dolphins cap further over his forehead, shielding his eyes from scrutiny.

"You know what I mean. I looked all over and everything is gone. Even her Andy Warhol kitty cat rug."

"Boy. That's harsh." Eddy tries to strike a sympathetic tone.

"Thing is, I was starting to think that I was rushing the whole marriage thing. That the reason that I was in such a hurry to marry Iris was her reluctance to take things to the next level."

"You mean, she didn't even..."

"That's right. Silly isn't it? She was put right out when I reminded her that it wasn't like she could get pregnant."

"Sheesh."

"On and off, I was already thinking of ways I could back out of the whole thing. Then the kids came along and suddenly I was ready to head to Vegas."

"That so?" Eddie whistles through his dentures.

"Yup. I mean it's not all that bad being a bachelor at 78."

"That's a big ten-four," says Eddie, who casts a nervous glance at his own trailer. Lydia is being curiously reticent about hunting Eddie down this afternoon. Probably because she is hoping he'll bring back an additional load of good gossip that he could convey to her via a combination of hand signals and Post-it notes. The trailer is full of Post-it notes.

"Good evening gentlemen," says a patrolman. "Can I have a word with you?"

Eddy's and Big Daddy's eyes dart from the patrolman, to the grill full of illegal moose meat, to the cooler of bootleg Moosehead and back again. "We can explain about the beer."

"Strange to say what delight we married people have to see these poor fools decoyed into our condition." -Samuel Pepys

⊗ NINETEEN ⊗

BUNDLES OF JOY

Back at the motel, Roger and Madeline fall into an excited huddle. Is Jillian about to reel in a live one? Could she really have this guy on the hook? is there any way they could push events further towards their own devious purpose of seeing a plumped-up, and dressed-down Jillian irreversibly saddled with some unmanageable toddlers of her own? Hopelessly trying to cram herself into an oversized pair of sweat pants while she mops a screaming infant's drool from her shoulders? Roger has a plan. It just so happens that he has brought some home movies, (DVDs actually) to show Big Daddy. In the absence of their intended audience, it seems only fitting that they be viewed by some other family member and her intended. Roger rushes into his room to retrieve the DVD from his suitcase.

"Matt," gushes an excited Roger when he arrives in Jillian's room. "Have we got something to show you. The day little Diana was born!"

Jillian's eyes roll in a full three-sixty motion, (she has already partaken of this treat), and she makes for the bathroom where she begins running a bubble bath and applying a cucumber masque on her face. She needs time to think, time to plan. Daddy has cut them off the payroll. This could only mean one thing. She is broke. Either she is going to have to do a lot more private investigation, her acting career is going to have to make a miraculous assent, or she is going to have to get married. It's a good thing, thinks Jillian, that her new lover Matt is succeeding as an artist.

Matt was still lounging around in bed with nothing on but a pair of Toronto Maple Leaf boxer shorts when Jillian had returned from the RV park. Since then he has remained frozen in his bed. He can foresee no path of escape from Roger, not wishing to streak down the motel parking lot in his jock shorts. For all he knows, Roger could be a Ducks fan, after all. On top of that, he has just received a pizza from a delivery guy, and he is hardly going to let it go to waste. Resignedly he sits back in bed, covered up to his neck in blankets, gnawing on a slice of triple cheese pizza while an excited Roger loads the DVD and starts extolling the virtues of family life.

Through the bathroom door Jillian can hear Madeline's groans, and sometimes ear-splitting screams, interrupted by cries of "You bastard! You had to stop for batteries!" and "Where the hell is that goddamned anesthetist?" while an earnest Roger keeps commanding his wife to breathe.

This is pure B-movie material, and a transfixed Matt watches in horror as a sweaty, red-faced and Johnny-shirted Madeline grabs a nurse and threatens violence if she doesn't give her morphine immediately. Roger's camera angles jostle so much that Matt feels his stomach lurch.

"It's too late for the drugs, honey. The baby's coming! It's coming!" cries an excited Roger, who is zooming in for a close up between Madeline's fleshy pink thighs. -Oh good God, thinks Matt, is that Madeline's crotch he is looking at, at five times its natural size? What would Freud have to say about the trauma inflicted by birth movies -he wondered?

Baby Diana's head is now bursting through the enlarged birth canal, looking like a small greasy alien. The screaming and threats continue. It sounds like Madeline has a touch of Tourette's Syndrome. The camera jostles some more as Madeline's left foot shoots out from the stirrup where it had been planted by staff. Has she kicked her husband/cameraman?

"Breathe honey," comes a pained and shaky voice off-camera.

"I'll tell you to breathe, you bastard!" Madeline swings at the camera, but her husband is just out of striking range.

"Here it comes! I can see a shoulder."

Matt can not turn his eyes away from the shaky image. He is overwhelmed. It is as compelling as a war film, a natural disaster, or a burning car wreck on the side of the highway.

Madeline screams one last time. "Ahhhhhhhhhhh!"

"She's out!" screams Roger, still a detached off-camera voice.

"Wait! Here comes the placenta!" The camera rapidly pans back and forth from the slime-covered baby to Madeline's crotch. A huge bloody mass bearing a gooey resemblance to the triple cheese pizza comes gushing out of Madeline's super-sized vagina. Matt leans forward, alarmed. His eyes dart around the room, alight on a waste basket next to the bed. He empties his entire stomach into it.

An elated Roger looks back at Matt as he is wiping his mouth with a corner of the bed sheet. "Wasn't that something?"

"I think I need to shut the DVD off now."

"Don't you want to see me cut the cord?" Roger's eyes are glowing, maniacally.

"Nah. I think I'll give it a pass." Matt reaches for the remote and shuts off the DVD player. The television switches to a spot news broadcast. A newsman is standing in front of a muddy pond explaining to the viewers that fish and game authorities had just apprehended the errant alligator. A few articles of clothing and a pair of pink flip-flops complete the tableau. The announcer is standing next to a uniformed man who is holding what appears to be either a pale blond hairpiece, or a scrap of cat fur.

"Hey! Isn't that your father's trailer park?" asks a dazed and shaky Matt.

"It certainly looks like his RV park," says Roger. "Look Honey, they're broadcasting from Big Daddy's RV park. Seems that they caught that runaway alligator." Madeline, is across the corridor in her own room with the door ajar, trying to engage the children in some quiet play. She has been listening to Roger and Matt's interaction through her open door. She strides across the hall to see what is going on.

"Could you explain for our viewers what the investigation will now entail?" continues the announcer, who is striking an authoritative pose.

"We can't be certain that there is a problem. But if there is a....ahem...problem our first indication of a problem generally is a report of a missing person. If there was a problem. Which of course we have no way of knowing there is. And I'm not saying there is. Mind you."

"And how often does that sort of ...problem happen?"

"Oh. Not too often."

"How often is not too often?"

"Oh. Often enough."

"What exactly are they looking for?"

"Of course, we can't be certain that anyone has come to a bad end just yet. We unfortunately have had a report of a missing person, however. It seems she recently got engaged to one of the residents here. Usually we confirm a...problem is really a problem if we cut the gator open and find an arm or a leg or something."

"An arm or leg?" says the announcer, now affecting an anxious, alarmed tone. Ratings are going to soar tonight! Why hadn't he worn the navy blue Hugo Boss? He might get the attention of network brass!

This is definitely going to picked up by the cable news networks. He could hardly suppress his excitement so that he could achieve the appropriate look of respectful concern. Frowning dramatically however is out of the question. Damn that Botox!

"That's it!" shouts Matt, shutting off the television. "I can't take it anymore. First the birth movie and now this. I'm going for a walk to settle my stomach." Jillian lurches in the tub, sending a tidal wave of bubbles over the side. What if Matt takes off before she gets him to pop the question? This movie of Roger's has made a real mess of her budding romance.

"Wait for me!" she shouts from inside the bathroom. "I'll come with you!"

Jillian tears out of the bath with such haste that she barely has time to scrape the sticky cucumber mash off her face and pull her clothes back on. Matt is waiting distractedly in the hallway, a good distance away from the television. Inside his and Jillian's room Roger continues to discuss the finer points of film making with Walter, who feels that he should learn to wield a camera so that he can add little movie and sound bite clips to his cryonic business/religion web page.

Matt is struck by the transformation in Jillian. Without makeup and wearing an outfit hastily retrieved from the damp bathroom floor, she suddenly resembles his kind of girl. They pick their way to the beach, which in this early evening hour is littered with university students in various states of inebriation and partial dress. After several days of hard partying, they come off as far less competition for Jillian than they had when they first arrived. But how can she turn Matt's attention to romance when all that ever seems to be on his mind is pizza, beer and hockey?

"So I imagine your father is quite eager to tie the knot?" he asks.

"Well," Jillian replies nervously. "I suppose. But I'm not so sure about Iris."

"Why's that?"

"A small legal matter might be hanging between them," she says vaguely. "Can we just forget about it and go dancing?"

"You'll go dancing dressed like that?"

Jillian acts surprised by his suggestion. "Sure. Why not? Do I strike you as the kind of girl who can only enjoy herself when she's dressed to the nines?"

"Oh no! Not at all," backpedals Matt.

"Good. We really have so much more in common than you think.

To quote Bogart, 'this could be the beginning of a long friendship.' At least I hope." She looks up at him with her mesmerizing aqua eyes, so identical in color to those of her father and brother. Her hair looks like she has just crawled out of bed and she has a faint musky smell. Matt feels his knees weaken, but struggles to keep his head clear. Is this girl, this woman seriously interested or just out for fun? If she is out for fun, well, he supposes that is all right. But if she is serious, he had better start planning his escape. Doesn't he already have enough on his mind with a doggie paternity suit awaiting him in Toronto, and his own canine refusing to paint?

Both career options are in shambles. He doesn't want to be in trouble with his next door neighbor, on top of all his other disasters.

When they arrive back at the motel hours later, Madeline and Roger are spellbound by the news coverage of the alligator's capture and the mysterious disappearance of a woman named Iris, from Daddy's RV park. The media doesn't exactly link the two events. That would be sensationalizing. They merely imply it any way they can, without appearing to be clamoring after ratings. They are merely saying that, "Police are now searching for a reportedly sixty-two year old blonde woman named Iris Toklas, who was last seen at..." and then, in the following news story they recap the alligator's capture. Charles is quick to offer an explanation, in plodding, sincere tones:

"Daddy says that our new grandma got eated up by a addigator before she gotted to clean grandpa out. What did she have to clean out, Mommy? Will we have to clean Grandpa out now, Mommy? Will Auntie Jillian?"

Madeline titters nervously.

* * *

Much to Jillian's horror, the following day is spent with her niece and nephew. It couldn't have been helped. She is in this position because she reasoned that Matt could surely detect any lack of maternal instinct on Jillian's part if she refused. She has found it to be a deal breaker before. She couldn't risk making that kind of a bad impression on a man she has decided is her lifesaver. Her 'contingency man'. Her ace in the hole, now that Daddy has cut her off. For, without Daddy's continued support what are the chances of her staying in the acting game long enough for her to strike it big? The more she thinks about it, the more she decides that falling in love with a famous painter might be a very good plan of action.

In any case, Walter has decided to camp out in her room, sprawled flat on his back on the floor, snoring. The presence of this rumbling heap of hair and burlap is making further inroads in the sack impossible. If she isn't going to be able to work her magic on Matt by playing on his male weakness, she is going to have to get through to him with her -(and here I ask you not to laugh)- sweet, considerate and self-effacing side. Luckily for Jillian, losing at mini-golf is not that difficult.

Besides, she is completely preoccupied. If Iris wasn't eaten by the alligator, the aging tart could possibly come back to claim Big Daddy's heart and wallet. Jillian is cheering for the alligator. But, remembering some lines from a brief part she had played in a medical drama, she is only cautiously optimistic. (In truth, these lines belonged to another actor, and were uttered over Jillian as she lay prone and supposedly semi-conscious on a gurney.)

The first part of the day is spent feeding the children ice cream until they complain of stomach ache. Then she discovers how easy it is to cajole them into not fighting by stuffing them with hot dogs, chocolate bars and Coke. These are three items which Madeline has strictly forbidden because their high sugar content triggers frenetic whining. When that starts to wear thin, she resorts to outright bribery. Matt seems suitably impressed with her parenting skills. By noon hour, the whole charade has started to grow old, however, so the afternoon is spent by the pool of a resort. They have crept into it like a pack of thieves when the desk clerk was inattentive. Jillian parks the tots in the resort's wading pool, where an expatriate Cuban attendant is already keeping several other young charges from drowning.

"This parenting thing is a breeze," she remarks glibly to Matt. "I don't know why Madeline and Roger are so done in."

"Me neither." Matt answers, as he feeds another chocolate bar to the already sugar-charged kids.

"Maybe they're just not cut out for it." Auntie Jillian stretches out on a deck chair to work on her tan, while Matt finds a spot of shade and snoozes.

The children spend the rest of the afternoon throwing water in the attendant's face, shrieking next to sleeping parents, tossing toys over the resort's play area fence, and chasing away the occasional sea gull.

* * *

While Jillian is busy making herself as appealing as possible to the alluringly indifferent Matt, her brother is combing through their personal belongings. (Jillian has been hostile for the past two days, Walter thinks, only slightly resentfully. Could she really have wanted to be alone with Matt that much, when she has so much catching up to do with her beloved brother?) Walter is growing used to hostility, inured to it. He isn't going to let a personal set back like getting disowned stand in the way of his empire building. And when he thinks of it, being in close contact with his father for the next little while might prove inconvenient anyway. What if his father gave away his location to federal authorities? He has already found himself in the uncomfortable position of having to crash at Jillian's for the simple reason that he didn't want to have to produce a passport to motel staff and check into a room of his own. Maybe Sonia is right. Maybe they do need a new face man, one who doesn't have the law after him.

On the surface, Matt seems like a good option. A fill-in. After all, he's harmless enough and in Jillian's words, her contingency man. Why can't he be a bit of a life-saver for Walter as well? But Matt is unfortunately the type to overlook the profit that one could make of death. In Walter's opinion, he lacks dynamism with regards to his own demise. Matt always seems to be either drifting off to sleep, or reluctantly awakening from a nap. How could he rouse an audience? Besides, Walter just loves that spotlight.

He is after all Aurora's flesh and blood. Four simple melodies play out in Walter's brain: -Is this all about me? -Why isn't this all about me? -Are they all looking at me? and, -Why aren't they all looking at me? From these simple tunes Walter has managed to create a symphony that provides the *leitmotif* of his life.

No, the next best thing, the smart thing to do, is just to help himself to Matt's birth certificate. It's a simple document, just a small paper rectangle. No doubt worn and almost illegible, if Matt's general state of grooming is any indication. Walter is certain that Matt must have left such a document in the room safe, rather than take it to the beach.

After a bit of searching through the chaos of her luggage, he finds Jillian's magnetized card-key and opens the safe. Sure enough, Matt's passport and wallet, complete with birth certificate, are there, crammed into a tattered brown wallet emblazoned with an NHL logo. Walter looks at the two documents. There is no way on earth he could pass himself off as the insouciant Adonis who even for a passport picture looks drop dead gorgeous. But the birth certificate is another story, since it features no picture at all. And coming from the same northern clime, they both have similar, indeterminately bland mid-Atlantic accents. Who would question that the hulk before them is not a Canadian named Matthew Elgin? For that matter, why would they bother, as long as he pays for his plane tickets and hotel rooms with cash?

* * *

Early the next day, having taken their leave of Jillian, Roger and Madeline settle their children into their airplane seats and commence bribing them to behave with toys and food. As the cabin signs alert them to an impending take-off, they sink into their seats and look languidly out of the plane window. "That's the end of the good weather," she sighs. "We should have stayed longer."

"Yeah. Even so, I feel like a new man."

"That's funny. I feel like a new woman."

"That was great getting Jillian to take the kids yesterday," says Roger. Then a pause. "We should have gone out."

"Yeah...Did we do anything?"

"You mean apart from getting a good look at the motel room ceiling all day? Just snuggle honey bunch." Roger sits quietly congratulating himself on his virtuoso sexual performance, most marked by its rarity.

"Mmmm. Maybe the worst part of parenthood is over," sighs Madeline, hopefully. "I mean, Charles and Diana seemed to be pretty played out by this morning."

"After the insulin rush and then crash, you mean." Roger nods his head.

"That too."

"I mean," says Roger, hopefully, "Maybe now that they're getting older, maybe they won't fight so much. I'm so glad we're out of that stage."

"Perhaps this isn't the best moment to bring this up, Roger. But I can't think of a better moment."

"What is it Madeline?"

"I'm pregnant."

"You're right. There is no good moment to bring this up."

* * *

Jillian is curiously subdued in the departure lounge. (Matt has given up trying to draw her out of her shell and has started in on a small carton of Milk Duds.) Walter has finally left for parts, (or planets unknown), after spending the past two nights stretched out on her floor like a beached whale. His snoring had rocked the walls, and left her frantic and finally resigned to the lack of sleep. It had thrown a wrench into her romantic designs for the rest of the long weekend. Now how is she going to move things along? She gently places her hand in Matt's, and turns on the vulnerability, like adjusting a tap to just the right temperature.

The headlines of several Florida tabloids jump out at Jillian: TRAILER PARK GATOR DRAMA says one. FOOD FOR THOUGHT MAKES FOR BAD ENGAGEMENT says another. Jillian reaches out to buy one, then stops. "I suppose it's yesterday's news, isn't it?"

"Probably. You're more likely to know what's going on than the reporter. After all you were there."

"Matt, darling, you don't think poor sweet Iris was eaten by that alligator, do you?"

"That is probably just Roger's sense of humor. I'm sure there's a logical explanation. Maybe the family was just too much for her to cope with."

Jillian flips her flaming red hair seductively, squeezes his hand. "Do *you* think my family is too much to cope with?" She eyes him intently, her eyeballs popping out of their sockets in her best imitation of innocence. -Would he do? she thinks. She considers what a serious involvement with Matt would say about her, how it would be perceived, whether it really is a good career move, or career suicide.

"Well," he hedges, trying to strike the right tone, somewhere between a well-varnished truth and an outright lie. "Lots of other families are...interesting too. I don't think that should stand in the way of two people getting married."

"Oh Matt, darling, are you asking?" Suddenly she wraps her arms around him and presses her astonishingly firm, silicone-enhanced breasts to his chest. How had he just walked right into that one? Jillian congratulates herself on being alert enough to pounce when the opportunity presented itself. She is thrilled at having scored the game-winning goal. "I accept! We'll have to call the papers as soon as we unpack!" She has visions of being profiled as half of a new, trendy power couple, like Posh and that soccer-playing husband of hers, what's-his-name.

Matt almost chokes on his Milk Duds. -Had he just said what he thought he said? How the hell did he say that? Now what? It is bad enough that he had found himself roped into playing the role of suitor the entire long weekend. Suddenly, inexplicably, she seems to be set on him becoming the real thing. It can't have been their one lackluster roll in the hay, could it? Why would a woman feel that going to bed with a man once is something like staking out territory, a kind of rent-to-own relationship maneuver, a down-payment? The exact opposite notion seems to factor in Matt's entirely masculine mind. Often, once he'd sampled the delights between the sheets, such as they were, and a woman finally felt free to let her hair down psychologically, he was just as likely to want to run for the hills as he was to settle into a relationship. Even so. As a general rule in the world of love, Matt is happily recyclable, content to be left curbside on a regular basis. Happy to be dumped, but generally too feckless to do the dumping unless he feels genuinely in danger of getting roped in by a real looney chick. In this case, he is already looking for an opportunity to bolt.

Previously Matt owed his continued freedom to a well honed strategy of blissful non-compliance. He seems to draw the sort of women who are so panicked by the specter of spoiling ovum and overflowing with domesticating energy that they don't notice initially that the relationship is entirely one sided, and that he is a man with no substance whatsoever. He will simply sleep walk down this one-way street, accepting whatever crumbs of attention, affection and home-cooking that come his way, without feeling anything is due from his end except his handsome and jovial company. His *joie de vivre*.

Now how is he going to get turfed out? Won't a woman feel a higher level of commitment to a man, once he had, however unwittingly, popped the question? He's never been engaged before, so this presents a whole new level of irritation that he had to arouse in this woman, if he intends to be set free.

By force of habit, Matt feigns indifference to Jillian during the entire flight home. It backfires. There is nothing that seems to stir up her juices more effectively than rejection. She snoozes on the plane with her head pressed against his shoulder and a proprietary arm stretched across his chest. As they make their way through customs, as they declare their Jack Daniels and collect their baggage, as they hail a cab and pack their bags in the back, and all the way back to their apartment building a panic-stricken Matt considers his predicament. Jillian hangs off his arm and lurks around him like a cat in heat.

"I'm going to have to check my messages," she gushes. "And then I'll be right back, once I get into something more comfortable."

"Gosh Jillian. I'm pretty beat. Let's call it a night and then I'll drop in on you in the morning."

"Oh," she says, somewhat perplexed. "Don't you want me to stay over?"

Matt panics. "Oh. Ah. My pal Josh is there with Finnegan. He'll be pretty excited to see me."

"Your pal Josh will be excited? I didn't realize you played for that team."

Matt considers making this claim for a moment. Would that get him off the hook? Nah. He doesn't think he could pull it off. He is just too uncouth. "I'm talking about Finnegan."

Back safely inside the apartment, after a lengthy kiss outside her door, Matt bounds for the fridge and pops open his first can of cheap but curiously addictive Bulgarian beer in five days. The room is suffused with the smell of damp towels, old socks and stale beer. The television is blasting. In front of it, his friend Josh is sprawled on the coach with a bowl of Cheetos in his lap. He doesn't bother to get up. He is watching basketball, surrounded by empties, and crumpled chip bags. "Jeeze. This all sports all the time is pretty great stuff. Do you need a roommate?"

"Can you pay rent?" He feels uncomfortable asking the question, but to be fair, rent paying is practically a new experience to Matt himself.

"Well... No...Is that a problem?" Josh looks confused.

"It is now that the dog walking business is probably wrecked. And my painting career has...humm run into a few problems."

"Well, you got a couple messages on your machine," Josh mumbles as he turns back to the television.

Matt reaches for the answering machine, as his mind races with the possibilities. It is probably nothing but the crazed ranting of Cleopatra's owner, an assortment of bill collectors, and quite likely some high pressured pleas from his gallery owner. Creative pressure is something new to Matt. He isn't sure he likes it. "I'll check them later," he thinks.

Matt looks over at Finnegan, who has hardly raised his head to acknowledge his master's return. Why is his dog so down in the dumps? Maybe he needs a trip to the dog park.

Could he get out the door of the apartment building without Jillian catching him? He decides to make a break for it, grabs Finnegan's leash and his coat and starts for the door.

"If anyone calls, any woman, can you just say you don't know where I'm going or when I'll be back?"

"You mean like that crazy dog owner?"

"With the puppies?"

"Yeah, man," says Josh, who suppresses a snort. "She is some bent out of shape."

"Tell me about it...No I'm talking about something else."

"Are you in some kind of trouble?" Josh is mildly interested. It's a vicarious thrill to hear about the various messes his buds often got themselves into.

"Worse. I'm engaged."

"Bummer." A horn sounds. Josh's eyes revert to the cool blue light of the television screen. Half time is over. Josh pulls the tab off another can of beer, which hisses seductively.

Matt leaves Josh to consider the terror of being hog-tied and proceeds to the dog park. It is a bleak scene. Most owners are hardly venturing from their own apartments. Matt doesn't have any little companions along with Finnegan to keep him company in the mud and slush-filled park, with its land mines of clandestinely uncollected dog poop. Over the winter, these had sunk through the sporadically evaporating snow like heat-seeking missiles. And his old pal, Sommersby had obviously stayed home to nurse his bottle by the fire.

He sits sullenly on the frosty park bench and considers his current state of mind. It is a shame really. Until now, he's managed to get through life without ever having to give any thought to his, or anyone else's frame of mind. Thinking only ever ran as deep as fears that the NHL would never get its act together. Or that there would be a province-wide liquor strike. Now he is faced with the possibility of failure. Which when you think of it, is a quantum leap for Matt, since he has never tried to succeed at anything. He had been briefly dazzled by the thought that others would consider him a genuine artist. He had actually started to believe in himself. That he had played a vital role, albeit Svengali-like, in getting Finnegan's paintings off the ground. It was like being a stage mother. His dog's triumph had been his triumph. Now he is wracked with the fear that he might actually be a fake.

I know what you're thinking. He is a fake. A bona fide, dyed in the wool fake, as opposed to someone who merely fears he is a fake. But even so...for a time at least he had started to believe otherwise. He had read of this 'Imposter Syndrome' before. He is worried that, being an authentic fake, that he might have a touch of the old Imposter Syndrome himself. He fears that it might put him off his game. Matt wants to strengthen his resolve. He really does, just this once. The thing is to get over being an authentic imposter and actually become something real, to live up to the hype, however misplaced or erroneous. There is nothing for it but to get back into the swing of things. To restock his dog's supply of squeaky toys and tartar bones and get cracking.

After a brief throw of the Frisbee, they make their way back to the apartment.

*　*　*

It's worth noting that Jillian entered her own apartment in an uneasy state of mind. She has lead the proverbial horse to water, but it is proving hard to make Matt drink it. She had hoped that she could at least retire from her 'serious acting career' into a nice cozy role as arm-piece to somebody whose success would reflect well on her. But Matt seems to be too clueless by far to even realize the direction she is prodding him towards. What's his story? He couldn't really be that superficial? Could he?

If there's anyone who understands superficial, it's Jillian. It doesn't seem to be fair to have a man who has even less depth that she does. (In truth there are more synapses in Jillian's brain than many are lead to believe. They just take a meandering, labyrinthine path). Where is she to go from here, if Daddy is determined to cut her off the money tree? She begins running a bubble bath, so she can strategize. (Her brain always works better when she is immersed in superheated phytoplankton and aromatic oils). As she roams about the apartment, scattering the contents of her suitcases, she spots the flashing indicator light of her answering machine. She lunges toward it.

Could Daddy have changed his mind? Has he regained his senses and thrown Iris out, in favor of his ever-attentive and dutiful heirs, especially her? Have the alligator's stomach contents revealed pieces of her father's missing fiancée? She could only hope.

It's her agent. "Jillian. You need to call me back. I have a part for you. It's perfect. Bye."

For some time now she has been weary of speaking with her agent. The parts he had been offering her lately were more and more minor. Commercials for deodorant soap. A terminal patient in a television medical drama who dies on the stretcher after a brief spell of coughing. An infomercial for a new kind of mop. The cattle calls and auditions are growing more aggravating, more scarce. Increasingly, when she is forced to look at the other women who attend these cattle calls, she is driven to ask herself: are these sad sacks my peers? Her agent keeps assuring her that this or that script calls for a woman of her type, but when she looks over a room crammed full of her supposed 'type', these presumed clones spawned out of the scriptwriter's imagination, she is often aghast at what she sees. Their glossy eight-by-ten call shots must occupy the same pile as her own in her agent's file cabinet. Her fate depends on his split-second shuffling of these glossy photos, and she has ended up in the same heap as them! The spectacle of all these hopeful, thirty-something fake redheads staring back at her is often terrifying. Sometimes, when she speaks to her agent, she can hear despair creeping into her voice and she has to struggle to contain it. She has to remain perky at all costs. Bubbly. Appealing. And above all youthful. (After all, if a barely pubescent Olsen twin has to neck on-screen with a man old enough to be her great-grand-dad, who is she kidding? She knows how it works.) Now here is her agent, once again sounding excited. Dare she hope? She dials his number, takes a deep breath and prepares to sound self-assured.

* * *

When Matt reenters the apartment, Josh is prone in the same spot, mesmerized still by his basketball game. He looks away from the television, briefly. "A woman called."

"Christ." Matt has briefly managed to forget about the crazed dog owner who is pursuing him. "Did she say who?"

"Your fiancée. Said she had news."

"Did it involve an alligator?"

"Can't say..." Josh's attention drifts off. Nash is making a foul shot. Matt plunks down on the sofa next to him and starts flipping through a stack of menus from local restaurants that offer free delivery. No need to go out again tonight. He'd be a fool to chance the hallway again. Jillian might be laying in wait. She can keep till the morning when he has a strategy in place.

✿ TWENTY ✿

MATT'S BEST FRIEND

Matt can wait no longer. Finnegan has been whining and pawing at the apartment door for so long that he fears a clean up will soon be in order. He decides to pluck up his courage and make a break for it. He grabs his down jacket, takes Finnegan by the leash and heads off to Tim Horton's for his breakfast doughnut and a 'medium double, double' coffee. This is one of Finnegan's favorite outings, because they always gave him a Timbit.

He runs into Jillian in the hall. She looks startled, nervous even. What is the protocol when running into one's fiancée before the morning's first cup of coffee? There is a lot to consider. Should he invite her along? Will that land him deeper in trouble? Will she pay for the coffee? It has often been said that the true test of a relationship is waking up together in the morning. He can only hope that the sight of him, unshaven for days, un-showered and pre-caffeine will be enough to make her second guess her feelings for him. Such as they are.

No sooner have they settled into their trays of coffee and baked goods does she begin to squirm nervously. "I have something to say, Matt. And I don't want you to get upset."

Matt gulps. The bad news is starting already. Had the condom leaked? Is that it? Is he condemned to become the parent of another little Jillian? Cut down in his prime for one mediocre roll in the hay? But wait...could it be news from Florida? "It's Iris, isn't it?"

"No, I have no word about Iris."

"Then what?"

"Oh Matt. This is so much more than I've ever dreamed of. I've got a part. In a television drama/sitcom/nighttime soap opera."

"That covers a lot of bases."

"They want me. They really, really want me. And get this, they don't want some girlie type who hasn't even hit her twenties yet. They want someone to play a housewife!"

"A housewife! You? I thought that was the kind of stereotype you were battling against, Jillian."

"That's just the thing. Red is the new black. Big butts are the new fashion must-have. And housewives are the new sex objects. Isn't it rich? I've waited all these years to be cast as the young lead. And now that housewives are in, I can actually be me! Or at least a reasonable facsimile."

"Wow."

"So the thing is," she says, now picking her words gingerly. "I can't marry you. A career move like this is just so demanding. Playing a housewife is going to be hugely engrossing. While they're filming I won't have time for anything, especially a relationship And then of course, there'll be product endorsements, and promotional tours, and daytime talk shows when they're not filming. I can't imagine fitting in a marriage in the middle of all that."

"What are you saying Jillian?" says Matt, who is trying hard not to sound excited or relieved. Tears of joy are welling up in his eyes. Getting engaged to Jillian has been like a near-death experience! He's been dumped plenty of times before, but this is the first engagement he's had broken off. Is this the right way to play it?

Matt is a gentleman, after all. He likes to take his rejections in such a way that the woman doing the dumping can feel that casting him off is the best for both of them. Noble even. He is careful to act hurt because of his supposed genuine feelings for her, but not so much that the dumper feels excess guilt, and backs out. You have to play it just right to satisfy her need to feel that your heart had once been fully involved, and that it hasn't just been a trashy and meaningless liaison. He is amazed though, at how quickly the turnaround has occurred this time. Usually it takes weeks, months, and in the case of Lana, three years even for his lovers to tire of him. This time his engagement lasted for fewer hours than Britney Spears's first marriage. He is so overwhelmed with relief, he is afraid it will show on his face. "I feel stunned," he says, finally.

"Oh Matt. I'm so sorry. I had no idea you would take it this hard." Jillian is touched. Even Finnegan looks at her with downcast eyes. She had no idea she had this effect on Matt. She feels flattered. If only this feeling could last! "We'll stay the best of friends, won't we?"

"Jeez, Jillian. I guess so. I'm just going to have to sit here and have another coffee and maybe a cruller and think about things." He searches in his pockets in an off-hand sort of way. "Hey, I'm out of cash. Can you get me another coffee?"

"Yeah. Sure." She feels she ought to throw a little kindness his way. It's not that he isn't a nice guy and all that. But, truth be told the only difference between Matt and his mutt is that he doesn't circle his bed three times before lying down.

"And a cruller?"

"O.K. Matt. Whatever makes you feel better."

"And some of those peanut butter cookies...I really like those peanut butter cookies..."

As Jillian gets up to buy Matt another 'double, double', she notices that Finnegan is lying prone with a barely touched Timbit by his nose, amid a small pool of something gooey. "Hey boy, don't you feel good?"

Finnegan rouses himself and gives his master and Jillian soulful looks. Jillian looks at the dog vomit with a mixture of distaste and alarm. "I think your dog is sick Matt. You better get him to the vet." She looks at him guiltily. Here she has just dumped him and now his dog is puking up all over Tim Horton's. She better get out of here before poor heart-broken Matt starts begging her to take him back. After all, he has a smile that could double sales of Colgate. It runs against the grain to give up a man so good looking.

"But Finnegan was fine just a while ago."

"I don't know anything about dogs. But not eating his treat has to be a bad sign. I've got to go to a fitting. Look. I'll lend you cab fare. Let me know how it goes tonight."

Let's be perfectly honest here. Jillian doesn't really have any pressing business today, or for the rest of the week. But once she decides to cut a lover loose, it's like she's rooting out a malignancy. She wants to make sure she doesn't leave any undetected Matt cells that might metastasize in her life. Who knows what could happen if she started to actually feel something for a man whose career could definitely not outstrip her own prospects for fame and fortune? As soon as Jillian is in the clear, she makes for home. She has to get some crucial wardrobe issues sorted out. She is due for a facial. She has nails that need filing. She needs to get her roots touched up. At all costs, she needs to avoid Matt, and his devilish smile and washboard stomach. For the next while, before filming begins, she wants peace. This should be her time to regroup. A time of beauty, grooming and rest. Maybe a little *Veuve Clicquot*.

* * *

Several days later, Jillian is awakened by a phone call.

"Jillian, it's Walter!"

"Oh Jesus." moans Jillian as she carefully removes her antifreeze sleep mask.

"Why do people keep saying that? Are you trying to tell me something? Do I exude signs of divinity?"

"Funny Walter, funny. What do you want?" Jillian is not in the mood to indulge Walter, after several nights of his snoring the week before. Especially when she was trying to seduce Matt at the time. As always, Walter has a gift for throwing a wrench in her plans.

"It's about performance, public speaking. You know a lot about relating to an audience."

"You're going to have an audience?" Jillian asks, ineffectively hiding the alarm in her voice. "I would find that a terrifying prospect if I were you."

"You're not telling me you have stage fright Jillian."

"Well no..." she tries to find a way out of this line of conversation. "Just tell me where you are."

"You'll never guess!"

"You're probably right."

"I'm in an airport departure lounge, headed to Colorado for the Frozen Dead Guy Days."

"Oh Jesus. What are you going on about now?"

"Surely you know about the world's first Cryonic Mardi Gras?"

"Do they throw beads at you for exposing frozen body parts?"

"Cute...no they are actually celebrating the town's most famous citizen. He died back in 1989."

"What did he do?"

"He died, Jillian."

"Apart from that. What made him famous?"

"Nothing much apart from dying and then getting frozen on a block of dry ice. He's in an aluminum coffin in a storage shed."

"And people throw him a party?"

"You ought to come. It's going to be a blast. There'll be a frozen pizza toss, a brain freeze contest, a frozen t-shirt contest, and a pub crawl in honor of the old guy. They're even going to have a Frozen Dead Guy Look Alike Contest. People will have so much fun, it'll raise the dead."

"Funny Walter. Very funny. I'm not going to grace this Popsicle Pete guy with my presence, so I'd like to know why you called."

"I'm going to have a chance to give a keynote address!"

"Oh good God."

"That might be a good title, Jillian. I should hire you to do my public relations. Anyway the talk is going to launch my new immortality website."

"Are you serious?"

"Absolutely."

"Are you telling me this with a straight face, Walter?"

"Why not, Jillian? It's a serious subject."

"Then, Walter, I have no advice to give you. If you can tell this to anybody without laughing, then you're a better actor than I am."

* * *

"Well," says the vet, who for several days has been running tests, poking and prodding the beleaguered animal. "I'm afraid Finnegan is in for a hard time."

"He is?" asks Matt, who clutches his pal tightly to his chest, as the whimpering dog crouches nervously on the stainless steel examination table.

"I'm sorry, Matt. Finnegan has a tumor...And it's not benign."

"Oh Finnegan no!" Matt feels crushed, panicked. If something happens to Finnegan, he'd be all alone in the world. "Is there any hope?"

"We can't know that until we operate. Then there should be at least one or two rounds of chemo. I'm afraid it's expensive."

Matt gulps. The trip to Florida had cost him quite a bit more than he had anticipated, even though it was mostly Dutch Treat. Then there is the fact that Finnegan had stopped painting and Matt's dog walking business had gone bust. There isn't much cash left, and with no paintings left to sell, that could be the last of his cash for the foreseeable future. "How much?" he asks nervously.

"It can add up," the vet whistles between his teeth. This is the most objectionable part of his job. It is his experience that people often part with relatives easier than they give up on their pets. (Especially his relatives.) He pulls out a pen and begins tallying up the cost on a scratch pad suitable for ransom notes, "You still have the tests to pay for. We'd have to operate right away. First there's the anesthetic, the overnight boarding, the X-rays, the antibiotics, more blood tests, then the chemo..."

Matt gulps. He looks down at the page. "That's about three month's rent."

"Afraid so." The vet's eyes go from dog to master and back again.

"I don't have much more than that in the bank. In total."

"Well...if you can't handle the costs, we could try to make his last days comfortable, give him a nice exit when it comes right down to it..."

"Finnegan!" Matt clutches his beloved dog to his chest. His pal! His dog who loved him no matter how slovenly or undirected or superficial or drunk or smelly. Who loved him even if he snored or lied or told bad jokes. "I'll pay it," Matt says. He might have to move home with Mom. And that moocher Josh is going to have to go. Matt gives his dog one last hug and hands him over. Finnegan looks back with plaintive eyes.

"You're sure now?" the vet asks. "There are no guarantees."

"I know. But you'd do it for your best friend, wouldn't you?"

Gentle reader, I know what you're thinking. Here I promised you a romance and instead all you've read about is broken engagements, superficial people and a dog puking up in the Tim Horton's. What's with that?- you are probably thinking. I paid for a love story and instead I get this? You're thinking right now of angling for a refund. Admit it!

But consider. Shakespeare once said, *'the course of true love never did run smooth.'* If that's the case, how can phony love fare any better? In love, there are no guarantees. And let's cut to the chase here, that lazy, aimless layabout Matt, (not matter how good they looked together in the pictures), would have driven Jillian crazy in the end. She is a woman of burning ambition. And as for Jillian, you'll have to admit that good old Matt managed to dodge a bullet. Jillian is best off sending herself Valentine's bouquets. As for Iris and Big Daddy, well. That course would have lead straight to the morgue.

But let's not forget.

It's about the love. And Matt, despite his many faults, known only too well to you by now, truly loves his dog. He is man's best friend, after all. Didn't this pure, unselfish love repay some of Matt's Karmic debt, accumulated over almost three decades of an Entitlement Syndrome? Can't you, the reader, spare a kind thought for this lovable good-for-nothing? (After all, he is very good looking.) As Finnegan's best friend trudges home all alone from the animal hospital, he goes over all the events that had happened in the last few months. So many ups and downs! Success, however undeserved, for the first time in Matt's life. His very first failed engagement. A roll in the hay with a self-proclaimed up and coming actress. A potential future mother-in-law fed to the alligators. (And don't some of us just wish that would happen in our own lives!) A brush with a failed doomsday prophet and cryogenics entrepreneur who claimed to have achieved space travel.

It is all too much. All he wants now is for Finnegan to pull through.

To be cancer free, back in the park playing Frisbee with him. He would give anything for the true object of his pure, unselfish love. He puts his key in the lock of his apartment door and steadies himself to tell his pal and free-loader, Josh, that he is broke, that they are both going to have to give up their satellite television, their all-sports-all-the-time lifestyle and move back home with their mothers. As soon as they harvest the plants in the closet, that is.

"Mr. Elgin," comes an official sounding voice.

-Oh shit, thinks Matt. A cop. I gotta get in there and get rid of those plants fast. Unless, he asks himself in panic, do you suppose they could be considered medicinal plants for Finnegan? Matt looks nervously at the man in the perfectly fitted and freshly pressed suit. Asks coyly, "Can I help you?"

"Matt Elgin?"

"Yes..."

"I represent the estate of one Mister Randal Sommersby the third, now deceased."

"Randal? Randal Sommersby died? God! I was only out of the country for a few days. When did this happen?"

"This Sunday."

"What did he die of?"

"Liver failure." The man gives this information in reverential tones.

Matt feigns an expression of surprise. Poor Sommersby. Matt has never been gainfully employed before his dog walking gig. So his deceased dog park pal is as close as Matt's ever been to a workmate. But why is this guy here? "Can I help you?"

"Mr. Sommersby left a considerable estate to one Bartender Sommersby. Since he has no other living relatives in the country, except one ex-wife who he specifically wrote out of his will, everything goes to Bartender to be enjoyed until his death."

"Great news for Bartender. Couldn't have happened to a nicer dog."

"There is one catch."

"Yes?"

"Since Bartender is a dog, he can't manage his own affairs. You've been named as his guardian and Bartender's eventual heir. You get to immediately take over the Sommersby building where Mr. Sommersby lived..."

"The Sommersby building! That explains why the landlord never kicked him out for having a dog."

"Mr. Elgin, there's more. There is a sizeable inheritance that you will receive as long as you take care of Bartender until he has a natural death. There is only one stipulation."

"Just name it." Matt's head is spinning. He can hardly take it all in. Bartender an heir to a sizeable fortune. And he gets to step in as Bartender's new daddy! Out there in the universe, Matt has reaped some Karmic reward for his one instance of pure, unconditional love. Even though it's for his mutt.

"Bartender must never be neutered. Mr. Sommersby was very particular about that. He said something about the fruit of Bartender's loins bringing him great joy in the last days of his life."

"You can count on me."

* * *

-Nederland is just the kind of place for a man of my vision, concludes Walter, as he steps out of his rental vehicle, (a fully-loaded SUV, rented using Matt's ID.) -Population of only fifteen hundred and still an eclectic range of restaurants and lots of things to do. Not only that, but the populace seems to have really embraced the undead.

It is true that on the outside, the population of this little Colorado town appears pro-zombie. The most visible occupants, at least this week, consist of a collection of oddballs euphemistically called 'socially reforming transients' and glittering exiles from Lotus Land who are enjoying life in a comic Dawn of the Dead wonderland. In the bracing winds of March, while the state is still in its last days of its seasonal deep freeze, a raucous party is brewing for its oldest resident, known affectionately as the Grandpopsicle. This revered patriarch is a Norwegian man named Bredo Morstoel who would have found himself pushing up daisies at the ripe old age of eighty-nine, had his now fugitive grandson not decided to have him cryogenically frozen. For a while, the wild-eyed young man roamed the continent searching for a suitable, albeit temporary resting place, until such time as Grandpa could be thawed, or reborn. (Take your pick). Finally, he came to Nederland, and decided that the appropriate place to keep Grandpa was on a slab of dry ice in a tool shed behind his house. That is, until the grandson was deported, leaving Grandpa to cool his jets on his own in the Tuff shed out back.

All over town Walter can see promotional literature for the upcoming Cryogenic Parade and coffin races.

Such are the misconceptions that can arise when one plans one's life around information gleaned indiscriminately from the Internet.

Walter is entranced. -This may be the perfect place to attract followers, he thinks. Maybe even establish this as the central location for my church. Hummm- I wonder what the caliber of baked goods is here...

Everywhere he turns, his first impression is confirmed. As he checks into his room at the Nederhaus, he is thrilled to receive a handbill inviting him to the Blue Ball. The young woman who hands it to him is dressed in a traditional French Maid uniform, and such is her dedication to her profession that wearing it in the brisk sub-zero weather has given her a pronounced blue pallor, and the look of being near, if not through death's door. Her hair is done in a classic, Bride of Frankenstein up-do.

Walter isn't sure if he is going to go out for something so frivolous as a dance. There is the possibility of drumming up some local support for his cause, (and financing a full scale immortality operation is no small feat). But, he reasons, it can't have been that serious minded, since they had thrown in an Ice Queen and Dead Guy Look Alike Contest. Beauty contests, however minor, seem to render any gathering into a trivial social occasion beneath his dignity.

While he is intrigued by the French Maid vixen, (despite her ghastly pallor), he decides to sequester himself in his quaint old-fashioned room and produce the final draft of his speech.

* * *

As the next day's festivities begin, Walter shuffles out to the podium that has been erected before the crowd of curious on-lookers. A number of floats are being readied with Tuff sheds and blocks of hardened snow have been made to look like dry ice. A few of the audience members have brought some levity to the gathering by wearing Frankenstein masks. No doubt, thinks Walter, this is a sign of solidarity with the frozen patriarch.

"Friends, frozen and otherwise, we've come here not just to celebrate the continuing life of Nederland's oldest resident."

"You've got that right!" yells someone in the audience. "We've come to party."

Walter ignores the comment, which appears to come from a toothless, plaid-jacketed yokel, who is holding a beer can rather early in the morning for Walter's dignified tastes. He clears his throat, fixes his audience with his iridescent blue eyes and continues: "We've come to consider what will happen to us after we breathe our last. Will our bodies decay and return to the ecology? Or will we make a wise choice and have ourselves properly tended to, so that one day, we can rejoin the living?"

"This guy is great," enthuses one man in the crowd, who is sporting a zombie costume. Others are less impressed, and they start jovially pitching snow balls at him and booing.

Walter continues, despite the heckling. "Have you given any thought to how you're going to feel after you're dead?"

"Cold, I expect," shouts another, closer to the desk which serves as command central for the organizers. The apparent core personnel of this group are frantically shuffling through papers, checking and then double checking the list of speakers and entertainers who are slated to appear. They huddle together trying to ascertain if one among their number recognizes the near-seven foot behemoth in the burlap toga that now stands at the podium. For all they know, he could be a Yeti with a shave.

"Ask yourself," prompts Walter. "How are you going to feel after you're dead? Let's hear you say it!"

"How are we going to feel after we're dead?" some members of the crowd begin chanting, amid muffled giggles, "Damn cold."

"Do you know this guy?" hisses one of the Nederland officials, who peers at this top-knotted creature in a gigantic sackcloth nightie with a mixture of shock and amusement. "He looks kinda nuts to me."

"Don't we all?" muses another official.

"You might have a point there," replies the first official.

"What did you say his name was?" asks a third visibly drunk man who is holding the coffin race and parade agenda in his shaky hands. In the midst of the crowd the giggles continue, but the general atmosphere of frivolity is not universal. Sad to say, but in the 'Post Nine Eleven Days', no stone could be left unturned by a government that once has been caught asleep at the switch. Especially since official invitations to Frozen Dead Guy Days had been extended to Norway's King Harald and his lovely bride, Queen Sonja. To add to the festival's troubles, the Norwegian-born progeny of the late, lamented Grandpopsicle are both fugitives from justice, having violated the terms of their visas and garnered a drunk driving conviction. Two FBI agents who had been standing amid the crowd tried, (as discretely as possible considering they are almost as large as Shaquille O'Neal), to edge their way up to the podium. Suddenly two outsize hands clamp down on Walter's shoulders.

Walter senses a disturbance in the force. His pulse begins to race. "Come on buddy. We want to talk to you," says a sonorous voice next to his left ear.

"There must be some mistake. I'm just here for the festival."

"Tell that to our boss," says one of the grim-faced pair. Walter is marched reluctantly off to their unmarked vehicle, in the driver's seat of which is another menacing looking man. Walter is then whisked off to a makeshift FBI office in a nearby hotel. The three hapless officers who have been sent on this low level duty are a trio who have so aggravated their boss that he can think of nothing better to do than to send them to an obscure hamlet's oddball festivity to supposedly ensure the safety of some foreign hoity toity about whom he cares nothing. Royalty sheesh. Not that anybody expects them to show up. But if his men did screw up in some way or other, and given these three morons that is a distinct possibility, the boss would have the perfect excuse to kick them out of the force.

Walter decides to play it cool, knowing that inside his satchel he carries his *'get out of jail free'* card. He is lead into a small, bland hotel suite and sits in front of a colonial dining table.

"O.K. buddy. Tell us who sent you!"

"Nobody. I'm telling you I came on my own."

"None of the organizing committee recognized you. Are you telling me that was an oversight?"

"Well no...I...I just decided that this would be a good place to bring up the possibility of making the most of dying..."

"Just like I thought. A terrorist. Let's see some ID."

Walter proffers Matt's dog-eared and marginally legible birth certificate. Thank heavens he had stolen it. Otherwise, they'd be after him over the tin can revenue from his ill-fated apocalypse business venture. The investigating officer looks at it, reads the birth date to himself. Then says, "What's your star sign?"

Walter sputters, looks from one officer to another in panic. He has one chance in twelve of getting this right. "Sagittarius?"

"Wrong. Matt Elgin here is a Pieces. Now do you mind telling us who really sent you?"

"No one."

"Do you have any intention of harming King Harald? Or Queen Sonja?"

"I don't even know them." Unfortunately at the mention of these esteemed personages, Walter twitches, since among his underlings is a harmless but witless man named Harold, and a woman named Sonia who had recently undertaken the management of Walter's numerous ventures.

The facial tic is unfortunate.

"That's how it works isn't it? Sending someone unknown. You can't fool us. We've met your type before, bombs in the sneakers and all that. Agent Cole, call up head office and tell them we have someone we want to put into nice discrete custody. We'll drop you right off the face of the earth. Find out if they have a free cell, a roomy one in Guantanamo Bay. Unless of course, you feel like talking. We'll leave you alone to think about what you're going to say next."

Walter sits in a trance-like state of panic, his blood racing through his adipose tissue at an alarming rate. From the other side of the door he can hear the officers speculating about the real identity of this supposed Matt Elgin. "Let's just Google him and see what comes up," he hears one say, rather loudly. That would be disastrous. Walter knows from Jillian that Matt's latest show had received considerable press back in Toronto and among the articles are several which are still lingering about cyberspace complete with photograph. There is no way he can explain the disparity in appearance. Walter looks out the window of the room. What he sees gives him pause. The room appears to open right over a steep slope, and no fire escape of any kind. A wrought iron railing covers the bottom half of the patio door, so that the room, theoretically at least, offers its guests some semblance of a balcony in the summertime. At this time of year, there is nothing but an expanse of snow.

Through the door that leads to the suite's bedroom, he continues to hear the officers bandying about the words: Guantanamo Bay, third-party interrogation, and Syria. He takes a deep breath, removes the tacky plastic table cloth and opens the patio door. He can barely squeeze himself through it and onto the iron railing, on which he stands like some hopeful superhero of gigantic proportions. He holds the plastic table cloth aloft and jumps into the drift of snow fifteen feet below. He sinks in up to his shoulders and has to free himself with a swimmer's backstroke. Then he grabs his plastic tablecloth which had fluttered down a short distance away. He lays on top of it, and shoots himself down the mountain slope like an Olympic luge sled, sackcloth nightie flapping in the breeze.

-With any luck, Walter tells himself, Daddy will still have that spare coach available in the trailer park. After all, what parent could turn his only son out in the cold? His own flesh and blood?

* * *

"So that's it," says Eddie. They are once again sitting in their fold-out lawn chairs, enjoying a cold one. It is early evening. Lydia had been so excited about the last report that she has sent Eddie back out there to pump his pal for more information. Meanwhile she is posted in front of her closed caption news report with a big bowl of homemade popcorn and a bootleg bottle of Moosehead beer, courtesy of Big Daddy.

"You going to tell the kids?"

"Nope. I think I'll let them stew in their own juices for a while. It's time they were cut loose anyway."

"The whole thing comes as a bit of a shock."

"Indeed," Big Daddy sucks back some more beer. "But I realize now that I was never really in love with her. So I'm kind of relieved."

"Can't say I don't agree with you. Good riddance, huh? I guess it was bound to catch up with that crafty gal of yours anyway."

"Still though. It'd be kind of fun to just leave the kids wondering. Up north they won't even hear when the gator autopsy is announced. What do you think the chances are of that piece of local news making it all the way to Canada?"

"Nil. I have to admit though," says Eddie. "It came as a bit of a shock."

"You're telling me!" says Big Daddy. "She had eight husbands."

"Eight, huh?" From the corner of his eye, Eddie is looking to see if Lydia is watching from their trailer. He leans forward toward his friend, prompting more revelations.

"Five of them dead, amid mysterious circumstances. Three others parked in some old folks home with their savings accounts cleaned out before they knew what happened."

"A black widow! " Eddie whistles between his dentures. "You sure know how to pick 'em."

"Imagine! Feeding them all that sedative in their Rum and Raisin ice cream. Getting them to sign all those forms. Might just turn me off romance altogether."

"That's something", says Eddie. Wait till he tells Lydia. "How'd the cop know?"

"Recognized her from some photograph posted in the station, I guess," says Big Daddy. "Lucky thing he went back and checked. She had a whole whack of aliases."

"How come she wasn't charged before?"

Big Daddy is philosophical. "Who's going to bother doing an autopsy on an eighty-nine year old guy with a bad heart? She had most of them cremated anyway. No evidence to exhume. Nothing to go on. One old guy's kids finally started an investigation, when she tried to have him buried at sea. On their honeymoon."

"And you aren't telling the kids?" Eddie laughs. "You aren't going to let Jillian know that she scared a Black Widow off just before it was too late?"

"Now why would I do that? Now that I finally got to cut her loose. Think about it Eddie. After all those years of being a family man, I'm free at last. All of my kids are off the payroll!"

They click their bottles together. Eddie concurs. "Free at last!"

"That's right. Free at last. Free at last. Halleluiah! I'm free at last. A toast," says Big Daddy. "To the golden years."

"To the golden years."

-end-

AFTERWORD

I would like to thank Kevin Deagle and Greg Fong for their technical expertise. Although all characters and situations in this story are fictional, Frozen Dead Guys Days is a real festival in Colorado. There really are men as gorgeous and as lazy as Matt. Women still fall for them. A canine is still man's best friend.

Cover design by Kevin Deagle

ALSO BY TRUDY FONG

Maritime Provinces Off the Beaten Path, Now in its 6th edition (Off the Beaten Path Series) (Paperback).

- Globe Pequot; Sixth edition (May 1, 2007)
- **ISBN-10:** 0762744170 7
- **ISBN-13:** 978-0762744176